Praise for

Northern Lights

by Raymond Strom

"Good news for readers who love coming-of-age stories and don't mind their fiction soaked in drugs: *Northern Lights*, a debut novel by Hibbing, Minn., native Raymond Strom, might be described as a cross between two of the greats in those categories: *The Outsiders* by S. E. Hinton, and *Jesus' Son* by Denis Johnson."

—*Star Tribune* (Minneapolis)

"A powerful depiction of the currency of intolerance and addiction in one small town. Strom's debut novel follows Shane Stephenson, who's trying to find his mother following the sudden death of his father. Shane's mother abandoned them a long time ago, leaving her son a $100 bill and sending him a Christmas card with a return address in Holm, Minnesota. Shane has long hair and an androgynous appearance, and he clearly doesn't fit into the small town of Holm. Strom paints a portrait of small-town life that is sure to make readers shiver, giving us death, alcohol, addiction, drugs, sex, bigotry, all wrapped up in the neat package that makes up Holm. Shane is heartbreaking, and readers will have a hard time parting with him after the book is over."

—*Kirkus Reviews*

"Strom's challenging debut follows recent high school graduate Shane's roundabout search for his mother. Strom's insightful navigation of family trauma, sexual identity, and small-town despair blends with his chilling depictions of drug abuse. [Will] resonate with readers who like gritty coming-of-age tales."

—*Publishers Weekly*

"One of the first lines in Strom's powerful first novel is 'Are you a boy or a girl?' And from the moment we meet Shane Stephenson, we feel his confusion. Shane must come to terms with his past and his identity as a queer, androgynous teen living in a hostile environment. Though set in the pre-Trump Midwest, the characters and dead-end towns Strom portrays could easily be found now, and he has a sure hand as he addresses such timely issues as identity, sexism, prejudice, drug abuse, conformity, and community from a queer perspective."

—*Booklist*

"[An] incredibly well-crafted debut novel. Strom strikes a painful chord as he takes a hard look at the meth epidemic in the upper Midwest. He also offers a heartwarming glimpse at the goodness of humanity.... You come away from this novel feeling as though you've met real people and engaged with them in their lives."

—*Faribault Daily News*

"Raymond Strom was born in Hibbing, and lived in small towns across Minnesota, North Dakota, South Dakota, and Wisconsin. So it's not surprising his depiction of young people in the fictional town of Holm, Minn., rings so true in his debut novel, *Northern Lights*.... The reader roots for Shane, who is grieving his father's death and grieves another when he returns to Holm after searching in another city for his mother."

—*St. Paul Pioneer Press*

"His novel features captivating characters and a plot that could have been mundane in lesser hands, but which never falters in Strom's. And his prose packs punches in stark and arresting passages. . . . A blend of pain and promise, *Northern Lights* also offers, in Strom, a fresh and gifted voice from which much can be expected."

—*Free Lance-Star*

"The search for identity, both familial and sexual, is at the core of this outstanding debut. Shane Stephenson and his friends inhabit a harsh world where drugs and violence are omnipresent, hope of a better life too often thwarted. Strom renders their lives with sympathy but not sentimentality, and we come to care deeply for Shane and his friends as the novel moves toward its powerful conclusion."

—Ron Rash, *New York Times*
bestselling author of *Serena*
and *Above the Waterfall*

"Written with a mesmerizing voice as crystalline and startling as the title suggests, *Northern Lights* is a beautiful, drug-fueled coming-of-age set in the strung-out, debt-crushed American upper midwest. Strom's cool, sharp-eyed clarity and tender pathos calls Denis Johnson to mind—the ghost of *Jesus' Son* shimmers in these pages."

—Brendan Kiely, *New York Times*
bestselling author of *All American Boys* and *Tradition*

"Raymond Strom's lovely and unflinching coming-of-age novel tracks a non-binary youth looking for acceptance and discovering self-worth among friends in a struggling midwestern town the summer before college. The powerful bonds of at-risk youth are vividly portrayed and movingly rendered. I found myself rooting for this crew of troubled, resourceful kids. A stirring debut."

—Emily Raboteau, author of *The Professor's Daughter* and *Searching for Zion*, winner of the American Book Award

"Sweet and sneaky, *Northern Lights* is a novel to savor, a sad and heartfelt exploration of the families that fail us and the ones we construct after. This is a book to read, and Raymond Strom is a writer to remember."

—Greg Downs, author of *Spit Baths*, winner of the Flannery O'Connor Award for Short Fiction

"In Raymond Strom's haunting, propulsive, and beautifully rendered debut, a group of misfits chase transcendence in a dying town. Cut with both violence and tenderness, *Northern Lights* deftly captures the knife-edge of addiction, the electricity of first love, and the insatiable search for belonging."

—Jessie Chaffee, author of *Florence in Ecstasy*

"With echoes of Richard Ford and early Hemingway, Raymond Strom's *Northern Lights* shows us a cold landscape, a heartland that has never had a more frightening hold on the nightmares of this country, illuminating an American sadness that needs to be understood before it overwhelms us all."

—Mark Mirsky, author of *The Red Adam* and *Blue Hill Avenue*

Northern Lights

A Novel

Raymond Strom

Simon & Schuster Paperbacks

New York   London   Toronto   Sydney   New Delhi

Simon & Schuster Paperbacks
An Imprint of Simon & Schuster, Inc.
1230 Avenue of the Americas
New York, NY 10020

Grateful acknowledgment is made to Georges Borchardt, Inc., for permission to reprint
a poem from *Hotel Lautréamont* by John Ashbery. Copyright © 1992, 2007 by John Ashbery.
Reprinted by permission of Georges Borchardt, Inc., on behalf of the author. All rights reserved.

First Simon & Schuster trade paperback edition February 2020

SIMON & SCHUSTER PAPERBACKS and colophon are registered trademarks of
Simon & Schuster, Inc.

For information about special discounts for bulk purchases, please contact Simon & Schuster
Special Sales at 1-866-506-1949 or business@simonandschuster.com.

The Simon & Schuster Speakers Bureau can bring authors to your live event. For more
information or to book an event, contact the Simon & Schuster Speakers Bureau at
1-866-248-3049 or visit our website at www.simonspeakers.com.

Interior design by Alexis Minieri

Manufactured in the United States of America

1   3   5   7   9   10   8   6   4   2

The Library of Congress has cataloged the hardcover edition as follows:

Names: Strom, Raymond, author.
Title: Northern lights / Raymond Strom.
Description: First Simon & Schuster hardcover edition. | New York : Simon & Schuster, February 2019.
Identifiers: LCCN 2018032240 | ISBN 9781501190292 (hardback) | ISBN 9781501190315
(trade paper). Subjects: | BISAC: FICTION / Literary. | FICTION / Coming of Age. |
FICTION / Gay. Classification: LCC PS3619.T774 N67 2019 | DDC 813/.6—dc23 LC record
available at https://urldefense.proofpoint.com/v2/url?u=https-3A__lccn.loc.gov_2018032240&
d=DwIFAg&c=jGUuvAdBXp_VqQ6t0yah2g&r=4pGeBDxULaxT2wXULFKqzz0AK5Eqfq
FLl-R98w8RarqkuD-ninvvCG0t1kE36ZhM&m=62fvpJCtRfUAfUvXx6MsAOfV2dhJU463x6j
mhFixj2w&s=00_GHrGYpluRSmbADN7uX4oAEbk3t56z0yMMi_7J_eE&e=.

ISBN 978-1-5011-9029-2
ISBN 978-1-5011-9031-5 (pbk)
ISBN 978-1-5011-9030-8 (ebook)

For Ria

And now I cannot remember how I would have had it. It is not a conduit (confluence?) but a place. The place, of movement and an order. The place of old order. But the tail end of the movement is new. Driving us to say what we are thinking. It is so much like a beach after all, where you stand and think of going no further. And it is good when you get to no further. It is like a reason that picks you up and places you where you always wanted to be. This far, it is fair to be crossing, to have crossed. Then there is no promise in the other. Here it is. Steel and air, a mottled presence, small panacea and lucky for us. And then it got very cool.

—JOHN ASHBERY

Northern Lights

I

One

Day was breaking when I rang the buzzer. Birds chirping, morning traffic sighing eastward, the sky lightening. When I was sure that my mother wasn't home I rang the super and he showed up red-eyed and angry, wearing boxer shorts and an old T-shirt, the long white hair that circled his dome standing up in an odd comb-over. I stuttered a hello and began to tell him why I had come.

"Wait," he interrupted. "Are you a boy or a girl?"

"A boy," I said, then finished my story. I had come to Holm to find my mother, to spend some time with her for the first time in years, before I made my way to Minneapolis to begin college in September. My backpack held all that I owned: three changes of clothes, an old video-game system, and a Christmas card with the return address One Center Street East, Apartment 3D. Everything but nothing.

"She was your mother, eh?" he said, rubbing an eye with a fist. "Yeah, I remember her. Whyn't you head into the Arlington there and I'll meet you with some clothes on."

The building where my mother lived was once known as the Arlington Hotel and Restaurant, though by the time I arrived the restaurant was merely a diner, a few booths, a line of Formica tables, and a long lunch counter with round, padded stools mounted on steel pillars, and there hadn't been a hotel for decades, the rooms converted long ago into rentals, the dusty first homes of the newly divorced and others down on their luck. A bell sounded as I pushed through the glass door and two bearded men in red baseball caps spun on their stools, watched me with matching slack-jawed expressions that I didn't like as I crossed the dining room and took a booth near the window. A waitress came over with a "Good morning, darling" and a menu and the two men turned back to their toast.

The smell of bacon started my stomach growling like a wild animal and I realized I hadn't eaten anything warm for twenty-four hours. I had fried an egg the previous morning, before I had gone to my high school commencement, but returning home in my cap and gown I found a note from my uncle next to my empty backpack. *You can fill this up, but that's it. Be gone before I return. Bus at Cooper's at 2:30.* The house closed in on me then, the arched doorways narrowed, the walls moved toward one another, squeezing me out as I scrambled to fill my sack. My uncle and I hadn't gotten along since my father's death. The six months since the funeral were proof we had never been close, but I didn't think it would come to this. *Be gone before I return* played as a refrain in my thoughts and I grew afraid of what he'd do if he found me there. My hurry was so great that I had no lunch and at the transfer station in Duluth, where I had waited until one in the morning, the vending machines only contained cookies and chips.

Looking over the menu and taking in the dining room, the aproned waitresses, the symphony of jangling silverware and glasses, I was glad to see that my mother had a good place to eat while she lived here—I often wondered about her after she left, hoped she was looked after, well taken care of. Like my uncle, and my father before he died, I hadn't

4

ever had anything nice to say about my mother, but when I turned seventeen, the age she was when she had me, I could no longer say what I'd have done in her place. She had been trapped from the inside into a life she didn't want. Until then I had blamed myself, but it became clear on my birthday that she hadn't run from me but rather the situation, and I planned to tell her before I went on with my life that I understood her decision and had forgiven her. My uncle had done me a favor by kicking me out this early in the summer because I wouldn't have had the time to stay and look for her if I had found her missing in August—I'd have had to get right back on the bus to school.

The next time the bell on the door sounded, it was the super in paint-splashed blue jeans and a gingham vest. He turned to the waitress with a finger in the air and answered her question of "The usual?" with a nod and a smile, then I blotted my eyes with a napkin and ordered what I thought my mother might have gotten: bacon, chocolate chip pancakes, and coffee. The super took a seat across from me and said a soft "Thank you" when the waitress brought our drinks.

"Karen," he said, "do you remember this boy's mother? She used to live upstairs."

Her face betrayed her when he went on to say my mother's name. Karen had known her and, though she said nice things, I could tell she wasn't a fan. I wasn't offended. My mother did what she pleased—I knew that better than anyone.

"You don't happen to know where she went?" I asked, but only got a "Sorry, darling" in return.

We sat there in silence for a moment preparing our drinks, my spoon tinkling softly on the ceramic as I stirred in my sugar while the super squeezed the last drops out of his tea bag before setting it aside.

"I checked my records and saw that your mother left just over a year ago," he said. "Her place is still open if you want to take a look or whatever. Shit, you could even stay a week. No charge." He dug down into his pocket, then threw a key ring on the table. THE ARLINGTON HOTCL, it said on the plastic fob, the thin crossbar of the lowercase *e* scratched away so it looked like a *c*. I picked it up, this object my mother had held, and my hand trembled.

"No one's going to need that room and even if they did, I got six other rooms open now anyways. Maybe you could poke around town and see if you can find out where she got off to. Who knows—you may know where she went before the week is up. Let's hope."

"That's very generous," I said, happy for the first time since I had left Grand Marais, and my face must have lit up because the super's eyes widened at my reaction. "I'd love that."

The super gave me a price for the remainder of the month, nearly all the money I had, and said we could talk about it on Thursday. He stuck his hand out across the table and I shook it, then Karen brought our breakfast. I ate like the howling wolf that my stomach had become while the super forked cut fruit into his mouth. His meal was small and he finished quickly, throwing a ten on the table as he stood to leave.

"Boy, I wish I could still eat like you do," he said. "Chocolate and bacon in the morning. What, you gonna have the peanut butter burger for lunch?"

"That sounds delicious," I said, pushing my bacon toward him. "One won't hurt."

"There'll come a time in your life when you too will need to make decisions that go against your desires. It hasn't come for you yet so you better enjoy it while it lasts. I'll see you on Thursday."

I didn't watch him leave, too concerned with the final smears of chocolate on my plate, and when the bell that sounded his exit evened off into silence I signaled Karen for a refill and turned to the warm summer morning outside. A red light hung over the intersection, blink-

ing, swaying on a cord in the wind. How many times had my mother
stared out at these streets over her morning coffee? The handwritten
letter inside the card that led me to Holm described a simple life: her
job at the plastics factory, her long walks around town, and her inability
to save any money. It looked like a lonely crossroads but, given life as it
had been lived in my father's house, it must have seemed to my mother
a world of opportunity, as even this small town was five times larger
than where we had lived according to the sign posted at the city limits.

I waved Karen away when she came by with the change. The super
had left enough for both of our breakfasts plus a two-dollar tip, and as
I watched her walk back to the kitchen my attention was drawn to the
bearded men still sitting at the counter, now harassing the girl working
the coffee machine who was at least ten years their junior.

"Just a date," the guy sitting on the left said. "I don't see why you
won't let me buy you dinner. I'm a gentleman."

"It's true," the other guy said. "And he's got a huge cock."

"I do have a huge cock," the first guy said. They laughed loudly
and slapped a high five before the girl blushed and ran off toward the
kitchen.

I wanted to say something to these men, to show them this wasn't
right—no one deserved to be treated like that, especially a woman so
young—but the impulse sent quakes of fear through my body, driving
my heart to pound like a trip-hammer. Unable to confront them, I lifted
the last of my coffee to my mouth and then stood, took up my backpack,
and made my way to the door, spinning the unoccupied seats at the
lunch counter like prayer wheels as I passed, leaving the grown men to
continue acting like children, uncorrected. The same bell that sounded
my entrance now marked my exit and then I was in the street, free from
all but guilt and the resonance of my pounding heart, my pulse so loud
in my ears I was deaf to the world, the blood vessels behind my eyes

RAYMOND STROM

throbbing so that colors appeared before me. Lightheaded, I stepped to
the curb, turned on pointe, and looked up at my new home.

Four stories of dark brick, the Arlington was the tallest building in
Holm. Nearby, many of the downtown storefronts were empty, windows papered over, names still legible on the signs above the doors.
Kristina's Pet World, Karl the Kobbler, and The Bible & More were all
closed. The dime store and the rodeo supplier were still open, for now.
The barber shop. The Spirit River Theater two blocks down. Beyond a
string of chain restaurants—tacos, pizza, and burgers—a Tweed's Discount and a More-4-You stood at opposite ends of the Old Rail Terminal Mall, a long brick building that housed the army recruiting station
and a dozen other empty storefronts. Holm wasn't quite a ghost town,
but given half the stores were now abandoned it was clear something
was eating away at it.

After fumbling with the keys for a minute I was inside the door
where I had met the super, creaking up the stairs in the near dark, each
flight turning back on itself once between floors. The other key opened
the door marked 3D, my mother's square room with windows in two
adjacent walls looking out on the intersection. I stepped in and took a
deep breath. Nothing. The passing year had erased her smell, leaving
that of an old closed room. A beat-up mattress on an iron frame took
up most of the space and an old desk stood near the sink and mirror in
the corner, all covered in dust. The door I assumed was the bathroom
turned out to be a closet, as the shower and toilet were down the hall
past the pay phone.

I opened the windows and stripped the bed—I would need to
do laundry—then took a pillowcase and wiped all the dust from the
windowsills, bedside table, the chair, the desk. Opening each drawer, I
hoped to find some lost thing that had belonged to my mother, an old
picture or a note, but I found only more dust. I had to turn the pillow-

case inside out to get the last of it. Once that was finished, I sat on the corner of the bed and tried to take it all in, this room where my mother lived, realizing finally that I might not find her, that this might be as close as I would get. Who was I kidding anyway? I was no detective, but I had nowhere else to go. I'd put in some time looking for her, but it was only a summer after all, then I'd make my way south for my first day of college. If I didn't find her I could still see what she saw, do what she did. Work and wander the streets. Spend all the money I could find.

As I considered my mother's life in Holm, a flash of red played across the wall among the shadows, catching my eye. The traffic signal at the intersection, blinking outside the window, battled the rising sun so that the hairline cracks in the plaster took on alternating hues of light and dark to the beat of a pulse. The slow encroachment of the white light held me captivated, the flickering shadows on the wall growing into images familiar yet unnameable, until finally the red light was overpowered by the day.

I asked the man at the laundromat if he had known my mother while he changed my five for quarters but he said he'd need a picture.

"Don't get to know too many names here," he said. "People like the anonymity of it, I think. You got dirty clothes and cash? I won't judge."

I told him that was fair then walked over to a washer near the Pac-Man game and threw in my dirties. As I prepared the wash I noticed a couple in the corner arguing in hushed tones as a young girl danced around their legs, oblivious to the conflict. The woman had half her head shaved and the other half's hair hung long and straight, down to her waist, fire-engine red. Her partner had done something wrong, his shoulders slumped, eyes on the floor.

"I can't believe we have to wash everything we own and use this cream because of your stupid ass," the woman said. "Have you seen your daughter's arms? Rashes up and down. Are you a fucking idiot?"

At this question, the man slammed a fist down on a washer, then walked out the door and the woman picked up her daughter and ran out after him, hair trailing behind her, like a superhero with a long red cape. I wanted to step out behind them and find out what they were talking about, what this guy had done, but instead I turned back to my washing.

Once I got the machine running, I set all my money out on the nearby folding table. After taking out what I'd owe for the remainder of the month and setting aside money for food I had eleven dollars leftover, enough for laundry and toiletries. Certainly no money for cigarettes—I wasn't old enough to buy them anyway—but I had alternatives. The wash cycle still had at least thirty minutes on it so I stuffed all my money back in my pocket and went outside, stood on the sidewalk, and looked both ways down Center. That was when I heard the catcalls.

"Hey pretty lady, look over here. Yeah you, blondie."

I didn't think they were yelling at me until they got more specific:

"Hey, you in the flannel!"

An old, beat-down pickup truck slowed as it rolled by, young men leaning out the windows, leering. Another whistle stopped in the middle, then came the yelling: "Get a haircut, faggot, you look like a woman."

A bewhiskered young man in a cowboy hat snorted like a pig and spit at me. The loogie slapped the ground near my feet, an unsettling green in the mid-morning light, then the engine roared as the truck hurdled the train tracks and the boys disappeared around the corner.

I did look like a woman from behind, I'm sure, though more like a tomboyish girl. My hair hung past my shoulders and I wore jeans and flannel shirts no matter the season. There is something about seeing a thin figure with long hair on the side of the road that makes a guy want to be heard, I guess.

The crossing arms came down, red lights flashed, and steam whistles sounded in the distance: two long, one short, one long. A minute later a train engine chugged out from behind a grove of leafy trees, pulling a hundred and fifty boxcars, creaking and groaning as the weight shifted, railroad ties keeping rhythm with odd clicks and snaps as the wheels passed. Graffiti covered the sides of many cars: thin-lined scribbles, illegible tags, and squared-off pieces that must have been done with a paint roller, but only one artist had any consistency: HOPE. This word appeared most often in three-dimensional lettering, blocky or bubbly, but sometimes shaped into odd representations: a clown juggling four balls that hovered above his open hands spelling out the word, another time four raindrops falling from a cloud said the same. I had always loved graffiti—it was a special way of remembering, of reminding the world of what has gone overlooked, been forgotten. Everyone gets caught behind a train from time to time, and though much graffiti is of the "i wuz here" variety, the true artist sneaks in a bit of style and optimism for the captive audience.

The caboose passed, the arms came up, and the few cars and trucks that were waiting pulled up the slight incline to mount the crossing. I got onto the tracks and turned north, hoping they would lead me to the Old Rail Terminal Mall, and once I got around the corner, past the grove of trees that must have been planted to conceal it, I was in the old rail yard. The tracks I walked split in two before me and that second set split into five that came to dead ends, where a number of train cars were parked. I thought I'd go climb up the ladders and look in the open doors of the empty shipping containers, images in my mind from old television programs of hobos hanging their feet out of the cars as trains chugged through the countryside, but I came up on another amazing piece, this one a sculpted mountain—no, a volcano—with a single rivulet of lava trailing through the ridges of the mountainside to spell out HOPE. It was a mishmash of browns and blacks and warm colors against the rusty maroon backdrop of the car but it worked. I couldn't look away. At the bottom corner were numbers: 6.6.97. I stepped to the car and touched the stream of lava, leaving a perfect fingerprint in the wet paint. The piece had been painted that day. June sixth. This artist lived in Holm. I reminded myself to keep an eye out for graffiti around town and cut over to the grocery store to see if I could find a cigarette, or at least a halfie in one of the ashtrays.

I wasn't built to love women—let me tell you that right away—I know that now, but over the years I have been drawn to certain people no matter their gender. Whether male or female, however, the mere thought of approaching someone made my heart quake and my eyes pulse but I couldn't stop myself when I saw the girl I'd come to know as Jenny standing among the cut flowers near the entrance to the More-4-You. She had a hypnotic quality that drew me, that pulled my words from me. Something inside had to come out, and it ended up being the stupidest, most awkward question I could have asked.

"Sniffing for butts?" I asked, leaning in next to her. This was what my father had said when he had caught me stalking ashtrays two years back. I regretted saying it before I had finished, my heart again entering panic mode, quaking in my head.

"More like sniffing for packs," she said, eyeing me up and down once before turning back to whatever she had been looking at before. I stood there next to her long enough to get a deep breath of the soft floral perfume she wore, roses and violets, and in that time she glanced my way twice but did not meet my gaze. Thinking she might not like me, might not like being approached, I took a few steps back to let her have some room and understood suddenly that I had done to her what the boys in the truck had done to me. I didn't want to make her uncomfortable and she had gotten there first, after all, so I tried to mind my own business for a while, tried to look away. I studied the roses and the chrysanthemums in their buckets, bundled into dozens by color, but I was drawn again and again to Jenny, her bold blue eyes, soft slope of a nose, and the way the slight breeze lifted her blond hair in wisps. I might have gone and left her alone if I hadn't seen in my stolen glances that she was sneaking looks my way too.

Before long, a Cadillac pulled into the lot and angled into the first row. A woman got out with a long, thin cigarette hanging from her mouth, the brand I associated with this type of older lady. Pantsuit, perfume, expensive car. Digging in her purse as she moved toward the store, I thought she was going to walk right in, cigarette and all, but as the electric doors opened she tossed it without looking in a flash of sparks on the sidewalk.

After the store swallowed the woman, Jenny looked around to be sure no one would see, then crouched and picked up the cigarette. She took a deep drag, then handed it to me and stepped off the curb into the parking lot. I leaned back against the store and puffed as I watched her approach the car, open the door, reach inside. After the car door slammed, she kept on in the same direction, past the next row of cars parked facing the store, but turned to me with her hand in the air to show me what she had gotten. It was the rest of the woman's pack, of course, and I would have laughed out loud if a car coming down the next lane of the parking lot hadn't come to a screeching halt, the driver laying on the horn as Jenny walked into traffic. She didn't get hit, but she did slap hard on the hood of the car.

"Watch where I'm going why dontcha!"

"Get outta the road!"

I had other, more important business in Holm but I couldn't look away. I should have stepped to the ashtray, sunk my cherry in the sand, and again took up my position on the wall to wait for another wasteful smoker—I was quite certain that this careless girl wouldn't lead me to my mother—but instead I called after her, ensuring everything that came later. She stopped and turned but didn't try to meet me, let me walk all the way to her with my heart pounding.

"Any chance I can get a square or two off you?"

She reached into her shirt and took the pack from her bra strap.

"Do you like music?" she asked, holding two cigarettes out for me, a white V from her closed fist.

"Music?" I hoped my face didn't show how odd a question I thought this was. "You bet."

"There's a concert at the fairgrounds tonight," she said. "Out past the Walmart."

I put one cigarette in my mouth and the other behind my ear. She flicked a lighter inside a chimney made with her left hand and I bowed to the flame.

"Are you gonna be there?" I asked.

"I might be," she said and walked away, rounding the corner at the movie theater without looking back.

I figured my laundry had finished, so I went back to the laundromat and moved my clothes into a dryer. To kill some time, I dropped a quarter into the Pac-Man machine and beat four levels, but the ghosts won eventually, as they always do.

It was past noon by the time the bedclothes were washed and back on the bed, so I stopped in for a burger at the Arlington. I got the one with a scoop of peanut butter like the super had mentioned—somehow more sweet and delicious than I had imagined—then I snaked a spiral through the west side of town. As my mother had told me in her letter, the Arlington stood at the intersection of Old Main and Center and the streets that crossed Center had been named after trees. Those trees grew along each street with the exception of Elm, whose trees had all been lost to disease. First Ash, then Birch, the middle school was on Cypress, followed by Dogwood and Elm, and Fern ran parallel to those for six blocks in either direction before turning eastward to meet up with Old Main making two grids, planned and predictable. The streets named for trees had no sidewalks; rather the blacktop broke into gravel near the edge of the road where grass then picked up, the lawns of wooden houses with peaked roofs or the occasional three-story brick apartment building. Churches here and there and nothing more to Holm than that. I took Fern north past where all the other streets ended and found the high school and beyond that the cemetery, and then turned around to take Fern south, ending up at the hospital and the government center. Beyond Holm to the west, the forest grew thick before it dropped off into the Spirit River, then came up just as thick again on the other side before it turned into farmland. Center crossed the river valley on a long bridge, became a four-lane highway on the other side.

A few hours after lunch I ended up at the library—the librarian was adamant that she had never heard of anyone by my mother's name and refused to check the records—then across the street in what passed for a park. I sat in a swing in a playground that shared a small square of grass with a picnic table, a couple of benches, and a water tower. I had talked the librarian into letting me take the newspaper outside and was reading about the recent conviction of Timothy McVeigh, guilty on eleven counts and likely to be sentenced to death by lethal injection later in the summer, when a young man stopped his truck, sauntered over, and introduced himself as Sven Svenson. Six feet tall, all field work and sunburn. Boots, hat, Confederate flag for a belt buckle. Cheek swollen with long-cut tobacco. As he approached, I saw he had one of the nicer trucks I'd seen in town, painted cherry red and fixed up with a shiny chrome roll bar. Hat in his hand, he called me ma'am, spoke softly, politely, then stood tall before me with his thumbs hooked into his pockets. Blue eyes and straight teeth on display, his similarity to McVeigh in the photo next to the article I was reading was striking.

"And if you like to get a little rowdy," Svenson said, pressing one of his nostrils closed with an index finger and sniffing, "well, I can take care of that for you, too."

I raised my head so that he could see my face. I didn't speak but when he saw I was no lady his smooth talk turned rough, making the bearded men in the Arlington and the boys in the passing truck seem like gentlemen. When he ran out of swear words he bent down and pushed my shoulders, sending me backwards on the swing and, unready for such force, I tumbled for half a flip in the air before I landed in the grass, the newspaper splayed out next to me, peeling away in the wind.

"I better not see you again," he said, hovering above me, holding his fist in the air between us. "There'll be trouble if I do."

I lay there for a time, thinking that every boy in this town might have a slight case of myopia, but decided in the end that they were merely desperate. I was in the habit then of making sweeping generalizations, defining large groups of people by a single shared characteristic. It was easy for me to do, since I had been so isolated for so long that by this point I always felt like I was outside looking in, even back in Grand Marais where I had spent my entire life. Holm, it seemed, would be no different.

When I finished gathering the paper and refolding it, I lay again in the grass to gaze at the sky and saw that I might have a friend in town, or at least a sympathetic ear: someone had climbed the rusted ladder of the water tower and spray-painted the word *sucks* after HOLM on the tank.

Past the laundromat and the railroad tracks, Center Street led me out of the planned part of Holm and set me on a path to the fairgrounds. To the north was the industrial part of town, where I found a green street sign that read BIG LAKE PLASTICS, my mother's old place of work, with an arrow pointing up East First. I'd be sure to make my way over there to see if anyone knew her but for the time I had Jenny on my mind so I kept on eastward. Beyond the plastics factory a few other smokestacks towered in the distance, and to the south was a run-down residential neighborhood, a few blocks of smallish square houses placed at odd angles on spotty lawns. Driveways here were gravel or dirt ruts in the grass. Broken walkways led to thin doors hanging loose on their hinges. No tree lines had been planted on this side of the railroad tracks, random oaks grew in a front yard here and a side yard there, marking out the makeshift gardens in the empty lots between houses. This went on until the sidewalk ended, then I walked the shoulder past a Pump 'N Munch and a short strip of businesses that faced the highway. After running across the southbound entrance ramp, I stepped up onto the curb and kicked through the knee-high weeds that grew through the cracks of the cement incline under the overpass, where country music and exhaust hung thick in the air around the idling cars and trucks. Beyond the highway the Walmart came up on my right, a cement box five hundred feet by five hundred feet with a parking lot somehow larger. It hung on the horizon for a while, by far the largest property in Holm that I had seen, not quite as tall as the Arlington but covering much more ground. A short while later I saw that the fairgrounds were on the other side of Center so I scurried across the road when the traffic grew thin.

The band was four guys with shaggy hair, mustaches, and beer guts and they only played songs by Lynyrd Skynyrd. I sat under a tree a good ways back from the stage with my eye out for Jenny. The wind was coming in over the horse stables and blowing straight through the concert so I watched the first couple songs with my hand over my nose. No one else noticed the smell. People had spread blankets in the grass and children ran from family to family waving and smiling. A man was selling beer and snacks in the shade near the band shell and beyond him was a gateway made of balloons, the entrance to a small carnival of games and rides.

After the singer told us what he hoped Neil Young would remember, a thin noodle of a boy about my age walked over to me. He was wearing a Twins hat pulled down so low that the bill hid most of his face and his clothes hung baggy on him, jeans sagging to the side. He sat down next to me and bobbed his head to the music, occasionally mumbling along with the lyrics between sips from a bottle that said MOUNTAIN DEW on the label but must have been mixed with something because the soda looked much darker than I remembered it to be.

The band went on break at the end of the song and many in the crowd groaned and stretched, went to buy beer or popcorn. The boy took off his hat and squeezed at the bill with his hands, bending the deep bow in the visor even further. His blond hair was short and stood up in tufts, a month or two of growth since his last buzz cut, but when he turned my way I saw a heaviness around his eyes that drove straight through me. He seemed on the edge of crying, as if he were doing all he could to hold back tears, and I felt my body lurch in his direction. My heart started up with the palpitations again, eyes pulsated—forces uncontrollable roiled my body. I couldn't speak but found I could respond.

"What do you play?" he asked.

"I used to play baseball," I said.

"No, what instrument?"

"Music?" I asked. "No, I don't play."

He took another drink, wiped the mouth of the bottle on his sleeve, then handed it to me.

"Black Velvet," he said, smiling in a way that pulled the sad corners of his eyes up a little.

I held the bottle to my nose. I had never drunk whiskey before but I knew the smell.

"You a singer then?"

"No."

"Then why do you look like you are?"

"I'm not sure."

"You ain't gonna make any friends looking like that."

I handed the bottle back without taking a drink, avoiding the boy's eyes so as not to be drawn in, then stood up and brushed off my pants. Unsure if I was fleeing what he said or how I felt, I looked off to the stables and then turned toward the midway, leaving the drunk in the baseball hat sputtering insincere apologies behind me.

The fair was like any other I had been to up around Grand Marais when I was younger. Maybe the same fair, they did travel after all. A round man fried doughnuts and sold popcorn from a red cart. Another had milk bottles balanced on blocks and taunted me with a "Looks like a girl, throws like a girl" as I passed. Young mothers were led from booth to booth by screaming, happy children. One boy followed his father closely, finger linked into the older man's belt loop, crying and red-faced, begging for cotton candy. Beyond the games were the rides: Alice's Teacups for the kids, the Scrambler for those a bit older, and the Ferris wheel for everyone.

"Hey you," someone called. "Hey you. Lucky!"

I don't know why I looked up—I didn't feel lucky. I turned to find a young man with his eyes closed to mere thin red slits. His hair was shaved up the sides but long on top, just to his ears. He wore a flannel over a T-shirt and jeans. I looked down at my own clothes—we wore the same outfit. Next to him was a girl wearing glasses with big red frames, her hair pulled into a ponytail so tight I thought at first her head was shaved bald. She hugged a large stuffed bunny to her chest and he held a thin plastic ring in the air between us.

"Our luck has run out," he said. "Will you blow on this?"

"What?"

"For luck," the ponytailed girl said.

"Okay," I said, stepping over to them, leaning in to blow a short breath at the ring.

They both turned back to the game, a table full of soda bottles a few feet away. He tossed the ring with a high arc and it came down a winner, then his girlfriend jumped with delight and wrapped her arms around him. I was happy I could help them win but, consumed with bartering the bunny and the winning ring for a new prize, they left me behind them and I folded back into the growing throng of Holmers.

As the sun was setting, the crowd changed from parents with small children to teenagers and young adults. Guys my age smoking cigarettes, arms around girls, none of them Jenny. A group in the shadows with tallboys wrapped in paper bags. The crowd thickened and I was afloat in a sea of cowboy hats, baseball caps, and teased-up hair. I thought I saw her a number of times but after a couple of hours I couldn't remember what she looked like beyond an undefined beauty and blond hair. The lights on the rides streaked across the darkening sky. I stepped out of the mass to get in line for a hot dog but I should have known better.

"I see you, faggot!"

It was a yell from above. At the top of the stalled Ferris wheel, the silhouette of a man in a cowboy hat stood against the darkening sky. Svenson. A moment later, the ride shook back into motion, almost tossing him from the car. A woman near me covered her son's eyes.

"I told you there'd be trouble!" he yelled, leaning out of the swinging car.

The vendor put my hot dog in a bag and I slipped back into the crowd, invisible again. Svenson was now stalled at the nine o'clock position so I turned back toward the game corridor, hoping it would lead me out of the fairgrounds, but I soon found myself at a dead end, a double-wide gaming booth where children kneeled on fake grass and plucked colorful plastic swans as they floated by on a twisted, narrow river.

I didn't look to see who owned the strong hand that came down on my shoulder. Rather, I slipped out from under it and ran down the lane of games to a chorus of *heys* and *fuck yous* from those I jostled. As I made my way through the concert, the singer bemoaned Tuesday's passing to a much thicker crowd—the open grassy field now checkered with blankets, a mass thirty or forty people deep around the stage, dancing and singing along. I had to slow down and sidestep to get back to the entrance gates where I picked up my sprint.

In the parking lot I heard quick footsteps behind me but they turned off before I reached the exit. I was running along the shoulder when I heard Svenson's truck. My heart was pounding from fear, as I had no doubt he would run me down right there, so I cut across Center and hurdled the median, stopping traffic in the oncoming lane with a screech. Svenson paced me, his head out the window, and another young man climbed out the passenger side, both yelling but their words were lost in the wind. I passed the Walmart on my left and then I was at the exit passing under the highway. Svenson sped ahead to turn back for me but got stuck at the intersection so I cut across the Pump 'N Munch lot and ran toward the long building that housed a few shops and a café. I looked for a sign but the only one I saw said HELP WANTED.

"Welcome to the Aurora," a man said. He wore a white chef's jacket and had long dark hair pulled into a ponytail. "Table for one?"

I held up my hot dog and took a few deep breaths. "Actually, I'm here to apply for the job."

An engine revved in the parking lot, then a siren sang and red and blue lights flashed through the window. The man who would become my boss and I turned to see an officer climb out of a car marked Holm County Sheriff on the side and make his way to Svenson's truck.

"Take a seat there," he said, pointing, then ran out the door.

I sat at the table for two near the window and watched him approach the sheriff and Svenson, who were now outside their cars. He must have called out because they both turned toward him and, after the sheriff reached into his open car window to switch off his lights, let him talk for a minute. Heads nodded all around before he shook hands with each man, then the sheriff and Svenson shook hands before they turned back to their vehicles. A moment later, he took a seat across from me.

"Where were we now?" he asked.

"You were just about to hire me," I said.

TWO

I was at the More-4-You again the next day waiting for another halfie when Jenny walked up, the morning sun shining around her updo, a golden halo. Her jeans flared wide and rolled up in the sleeve of her T-shirt was a pack of Marlboros.

"Sniffing for butts?" she asked, smiling, then handed me an unlit cigarette. Before I could stutter a response she continued, "Are you always going to settle for what scraps fall your way? Let's get out of here."

I took the smoke and the fire she offered, then she told me that she had looked for me out at the fairgrounds.

"I was looking for you too," I said. "But I must have missed you."

"That band sucked anyways," she said. "I hate cover bands. Write your own shit already."

"Fuckin' A."

We stood there a moment, smoking. She looked at me, caught me staring, then I looked away, embarrassed.

"Anyways, I'm glad you're here," she said. "I'm going camping with this guy and I know he only wants to fuck me. Would you want to come?"

Jenny's brash confidence was infectious. My plans for the day involved walking over to the plastics factory to ask people if they knew my mom but, with Jenny's company, that could be put off indefinitely.

"H-h-how do you know," I stammered, "that I'm not only out to fuck you too?"

She laughed a single loud "Ha," like a bark or a sneeze. "I wish," she said, "let's get out of here," then waved for me to follow her as she turned.

We cut over to the movie theater and took Old Main south from there, past the Arlington, where I pointed out my two windows on the third floor, then stopped in front of the empty shell of Kristina's Pet World, the store Jenny's mother once owned.

"There used to be a time," Jenny said, "when you could do all your shopping downtown, walking from store to store, hearing the different bells clang as you enter. People used to wave at each other on the street, but now we all drive out to the Walmart, fill our cars, and drive back home."

She went on for some time about the sadness she felt when her mother's store had closed, a little fire inside her that flared up with every new store closing, and said that it was nothing compared to how her mother had taken the news.

"You try to tell people there's more to life than low prices and a convenient location, but no one listens. For every closed store downtown, someone like my mother is wondering why their luck has run out."

We stood there staring at the papered-over store window for another moment before Jenny flicked her cigarette butt into the street and bolted down the sidewalk past the post office where the downtown business area petered out, giving way to wooden houses set on green lawns and shaded by leafy trees, bicycles turned on their sides along the stone walks that led to the front doors. A few blocks down, we came to a Dairy Queen with a steep red roof and Jenny turned down the road. In the front yard of the house just up Ash were two people I recognized, sitting on the grass beneath a towering willow, eating ice cream cones.

"Lucky!" the young man yelled and stood. His ponytailed companion stayed seated, focused on the ice cream melt dripping down her fingers.

"You guys know each other?" Jenny asked.

I shrugged.

"The name's J, just the letter," he said, putting his hand out between us. "And that's Mary. You should see the stuffed animal we got with your luck. It takes up half of Mary's room."

"Glad to help," I said, then told him my name and shook his hand. Mary looked up at me and we exchanged nods. Jenny said her hellos.

"I live here now," J said, hooking his thumb over his shoulder at the two-story wooden house with a peaked roof behind him. It was like all the others in town, but a little more unkempt, like it belonged on the other side of the tracks. The white paint was peeling, window screens were hanging at odd angles, the grass grew in tufts or not at all.

"If I lived next to a DQ," I said, "I'd weigh three hundred pounds."

"I haven't moved my stuff in yet, but give me some time and I'll see how much ice cream I can eat."

"So you're new here?" Mary said. "I haven't seen you around. Before last night, I mean."

"Got here yesterday," I said.

"Of all the places in all the world, why would you come here?" J asked.

"I'm looking for my mother," I said. "I thought she lived here but I found out yesterday that she moved. I've talked to a couple people who knew her, but I don't know what I'm going to do. I have no idea where she went. Jenny asked me to go camping, so here I am."

"Great," J said, cutting a squint at Jenny, "the more the merrier."

"You don't know where your mother is?" Mary asked.

"My parents divorced when I was young," I said, "and I didn't see my mother much after that, only once. She sent me a Christmas card a few years back."

"What about your dad?"

"He's dead," I said, not wanting to go much further with it. "That's why I'm looking for my mom."

"A sleuth," Jenny said. "Following leads, sniffing around. Fun! I'll help you."

"So, you've been here long enough to see the whole place," J said. "What do you think of Holm?"

"Well, you guys seem cool," I said, "but most of the people in this town are assholes."

J laughed when I said this but Mary recoiled, as if what I said had stabbed her in the stomach. I asked J if he had problems around town, if he had ever been called a faggot by a group of guys passing by in a pickup truck. Though he did have pretty-boy looks—big brown eyes and a confident, if slightly uneven, smile—his hair wasn't quite long enough for him to be taken for a woman, and the hints of tattoos on his arms, peeking out from under the half-rolled sleeves of his flannel, gave him a jailhouse look. My guess was he had been spared the humiliation thus far.

"I'd kick a guy's ass if he said that to me," he said. "Do you need me to do that for you?"

"No," I said, "I can handle it. I was wondering if it was only me."

"Let me know," J said.

"Anyone with hair like that would get it," Mary said. "People here are very conservative. They wish it was the fifties. Why don't you cut it?"

"Because that would be giving in," Jenny said. "Why does some asshole have the right to tell him how to wear his hair?"

"If it's easier . . ." Mary said, trailing off at the end.

"Do you live your life by what other people expect of you?" J asked. "Do you always do what's easiest?"

"I guess I do," she said.

"That's sad," J responded.

This put Mary in a sour mood, so she averted her eyes and stopped talking, but a few jokes and gentle nudges got her back on J's side again. Soon we were all laughing and J pulled a beat-up cigarette pack from his pocket, dug deep inside it with his finger and thumb, lit what he found, and passed it around. Shorter and unfiltered, it wasn't the same kind of cigarette Jenny had given me earlier. I didn't mention until we finished that I had never smoked marijuana before.

"Shit, man," J said. "Would you jump off a cliff if everyone else was doing it?"

"No, no," I said and laughed.

"I mean it," he replied. "That's where we're headed. It's right on the way to the campground."

The St. Croix ran through a craggy canyon and the cliffs on each side were two hundred feet high in places. We had been on the road for an hour, through cornfields, small towns, the occasional forest, and I had assumed we were on our way to a small rock quarry but the river was immense and I lost myself in the blanket of diamonds the sun lay on the water as we passed out of Minnesota and into Wisconsin.

"We're going to jump into that?" I asked, hoping the fear in my voice was contained.

"Yep," J said, "right over there."

J pointed out a ledge from the bridge and Mary turned her long brown Buick north on the far side of the river. Signs that read No CLIFF

Jumping and No Parking were posted every hundred feet along the road.

Mary pulled onto the shoulder when she thought we had reached J's cliff and turned on the flashers. The road had veered a ways off from the river so we had a good piece of forest to walk through. The brush was thick but we made our way with J leading, lifting low branches for the rest of us to duck under. Then we came up to a fence that had been put up around a large, deep crevice. Trees and other brush grew out of the rocky hole.

"I think we should turn back," Mary said. "Those signs on the road and this fence. We could get in trouble."

"It's a swallow hole," Jenny said. "It means there are caves below us."

"But couldn't the whole cliff face fall off at any second?"

"It will fall eventually."

"Eventually. The earth will be swallowed by the sun eventually," J said, making his way around the fenced-off area, "but not today."

He disappeared into the woods and I followed. After a moment, I heard Jenny and Mary crunching through the brush behind us. The trees thinned out and then we were on the cliff, the river below and the other cliffs on both sides of the river overgrown with the same scrub trees and pine as far as one could see. Before I could say anything J, suddenly barefoot and shirtless, emptied his pockets and ran, jumped without even looking for safe landing.

"WHOOOOOOOOO-EEEEEEEEEEEEEE."

Stepping to the edge, I expected to find J's broken body on the rocks below but saw instead that the cliffs dropped straight into the water. I didn't see him at first but after a moment J came up for air, a tiny face looking up at me and waving, treading water in the weak current. It was a long ways down, but J had survived so I kicked off my shoes and stepped to the edge.

"I don't think you should jump wearing those jeans," Mary said.

"Or your shirt," Jenny said.

"And you might want a running start."

But I paid them no mind. I wasn't one to undress in public and the joint we had smoked earlier hadn't left me exactly clear-headed. An odd leap later I was in the air over the St. Croix, breaking into a clockwise spin as I fell. Seeing the worried faces of Mary and Jenny looking down at me gave me a sharp sense of regret but the spin continued. Downriver I could see the bridge we had crossed. Upriver, in the distance, another bridge. Just before I hit the water I saw a group of four sunburned people floating in inner tubes, a beer cooler taking up the rear in a fifth tube. *Splash.*

The river was very deep. Ten or fifteen feet deeper, J had mentioned, than the usual forty. Underwater the whole scene turned blue, the sun illuminating the thick forest of weeds that grew along the river bottom. My corkscrew descent continued as I sunk, so I turned back toward the cliff, swimming, but I kept sinking. I kicked but a weight held me in place. Mary had been right about my jeans.

As I continued to sink I undid my pants and pulled them down, off my legs. Unsure what to do, I bit down on a belt loop and began to swim again but then my head was sinking and I could no longer keep my eyes open. It was a great relief to let go. Light as smoke I rose upward and cliffward, reaching the rock wall first. Blindly feeling along the edge I moved slowly toward the air. To hit a jutting rock with my head now would be trouble. I came up safe but opened my eyes in darkness.

There was no place to go but I could breathe. I coughed up the water I had swallowed while I held on to a submerged stalactite and a moment later my eyes adjusted. A dim blue light shone from beneath the water reflecting barely visible twinkles on the rock ceiling not more than two feet above me—I had swum into a cave. I remained a moment, treading water while holding on to the wall with my hand, and watched the way the light split, the odd reflections a web dancing over all I could see, like the battle between the sunlight and the flashing traffic signal on the wall in my bedroom.

A strong kick popped me out of the water high enough to graze my head on the cave ceiling. Had the river been that much higher I would have drowned, my lifeless body trapped in this pocket until the river came down in a few weeks, and no one would've known, the only evidence I existed the shoes I had left with Jenny and Mary and the backpack on my bed at the Arlington. A streak of laughter rose up in me then, my body convulsing in its only defense against fear, until the hanging rockcicle onto which I held snapped off, dropping me underwater again, into a thrashing of blue light and darkness until I came up with another rocky handhold to keep my head above the surface.

The way I had come was the only way out so, after calming to the idea that I could have died, I took ten deep breaths and swam toward the light until blueness was all I could see. I rose to the surface to hear my name being called from all around. J was treading water about fifty feet away, screaming. Jenny and Mary were shouting from the cliff. The group of people in inner tubes must have heard my name and added their voices to the search.

"There!" Jenny yelled from up on the cliff. "Shane!"

"I lost my pants!" I hollered back. It was all I could think to say.

A man jumped out of his inner tube and swam over to me. He took me like a cape and draped me over his back then swam us over to his friends. He put me in his tube, then swam next to it, guiding it down the river. The lady a tube over handed me a beer and we floated to meet J.

"Goddamn, Lucky," J said with a gaping smile as he hung on to the side of the tube. "You're really pressing it. Let me get a sip of that beer."

J took a long drink from my beer, then handed me back the empty can as our new friends in the inner tubes led us to the nearest place we could climb the cliff—the long incline under the bridge we had crossed from Minnesota. We zigzagged back and forth up the rocky valley wall toward the abutment and when we got to the top we found Jenny and Mary waiting with the car.

"That's it," Mary said. "No more cliff jumping."

"No shit," J said.

"Nice shorts," Jenny said, pointing at my plaid boxers, red, white, and blue. "Very American."

Jenny handed me a cigarette and we saw my hands were shaking but no one mentioned it. J had Mary pop the trunk and he dug in there for a while before coming up empty-handed.

"Thought I had some pants in here but it looks like you'll have to wear your undies."

The campground was more of a party than a rugged experience of the outdoors. A three-day music festival was taking place at the adjoining amphitheater so tents were popped wherever they could fit. It was not the quiet isolation I had been expecting, having imagined that we would be alone in the woods, the only tent for miles. Mary was quite upset and grumbled about how crowded the place was as she steered the car through the masses.

"You knew this was happening, J," Mary said. "We could have gone camping anywhere but you tricked me into driving out here so you could buy drugs."

"I'll find us some tickets," J said, "if you want to go."

"Four tickets? Yeah, right."

"You think I can't?"

"You can, but I know you won't."

As they went on bickering in the front seat, Jenny tugged on the sleeve of my shirt.

"Wait until tomorrow morning," she said. "You'll see. Once everyone goes to the concert, all of this will be ours."

Mary found a spot way in the back of the field and J set up our tent. Even in our isolated corner the sound of the campground was a dull roar that grew louder and louder as the other campers filed into their spaces, leaving hardly a spot of grass between the pop-tent bubbles and the other multiroom canvas houses. People walked the road through the campground selling drugs and firewood, yelling whatever they were selling to anyone listening. Cocaine, weed, one guy was even selling balloons.

"Balloons?" I asked Jenny.

"It's not what you think," she said. "Do you have ten bucks?"

I unbuttoned the pocket of my flannel shirt and pulled out my spending money, a ten and a one still wet from my jump in the river, then we walked off after the balloon guy and when we caught up with him Jenny asked him for two. He wore a tie-dyed shirt that read *Not Fade Away* across the front and had long blond dreadlocks tied into a bundle behind him.

"Are you two excited to be alive today?" He smiled two rows of perfect teeth, straight and white.

"He almost died jumping in the Saint Croix," Jenny said.

"That's crazy," he said. "I met the guy who pulled you out an hour ago. You are damn lucky."

"People keep saying that," I said.

"What happened?"

We sat down in the grass and, while I told him about my jeans and the cave, he prepared Jenny's balloon. He spun a gas cartridge into a silver cylinder, then fit a balloon onto one end. A slight twist of his hands caused the balloon to inflate to the size of a beach ball. He pinched the balloon by its neck and handed it to Jenny. Then, after throwing the spent cartridge in the grass, he prepared the next one for me.

"Why were you wearing jeans? It's hot as fuck and you were going swimming."

"I don't wear shorts," I said.

"There are nice shorts out there," the guy said, looking down at my boxers. "You just have to look."

The hiss of the canister came to a stop and he handed me my balloon. I tried to give him my ten, but he waved his hand between us.

"No charge for these, my man, I want you to enjoy being alive."

I put my money back in my pocket as the young man walked off, dreads swaying behind him, and then Jenny told me to watch her. She took a deep breath and held it in as long as she could, exhaled, and did it again. When the balloon was the size of one last breath she took it all down, but instead of exhaling into the air she refilled the balloon and then emptied it again, an external lung. A couple cycles in, the balloon fell from her fingers to sputter through the air, then her head rocked back on her neck and she stared up at the sky. I brought my own balloon to my mouth and followed her lead.

The world inside the balloon was a place I couldn't remember once I left, only the feeling of having been home remained, of having truly existed, as if the world where I lived in Holm was the dream and this other place real. A siren in my ears called me to constant attention, *woowoo-woowoo-woowoo*, an awareness so keen that I could do nothing but remind myself that I had to remember this, only this, so I could tell Jenny upon my return. That clarity was lost once the real world came back into view, leaving me with the feeling of having forgotten something important. Back from such a serious space, the setting around me seemed trivial. I looked over at Jenny coming out of her trance as well and when our eyes met I felt the hilarity inside me, an ache in my gut I had to hold with both hands as it made its way through me. Laughing then, in the grass with my beautiful friend, there was nowhere I'd have rather been.

When we collected ourselves, stood up, and walked back toward our camp, I saw that by Holm standards the parade of people walking by had become a freak show. Pierced noses and lips, plugged ears, tattoo sleeves. A pair of twin boys with matching braids so long that they tangled up in their ankles as they walked. Jenny tried to stop anyone who came by with the story of my near death in the hopes of getting more free stuff.

"He almost died," Jenny said to a boy who was maybe fifteen.

"I spilled beer on myself," he said, holding up his can to show us the label. Budweiser.

By the time the sun turned the sky pink and red, we had a bag stuffed full of weed and a pile of firewood. J splashed the logs with Wild Turkey and threw in a match, then passed the bottle to Jenny. Mary made a choking sound, crossed her arms, and stared deep into the flames.

"What's wrong, babe?" J asked Mary as Jenny tipped the bottle.

"Nothing," she said.

"I know that 'nothing,'" he said. "That means something."

"Can I have the whiskey already?"

Jenny wiped her mouth and passed the bottle, then moved away from J, taking a seat on the grass next to me. Mary took a long drink and we sat there watching the fire for a while, until J stood and unzipped his pants, then turned and peed into the long grass.

"I need to use the restroom too," Jenny said.

"You could go here," J said, head turned back toward us. "I won't look and there's TP in the car."

"Would you stop being such a crude prick?" Mary said before she led Jenny into the darkness.

J finished his business and sat down near the fire again, unaffected by Mary's accusation. The fire crackled, a pine knot popped.

"So how was that balloon?" J asked.

"It's like hitting the reset button on a video game," I said after searching a moment for the comparison. "You know what I mean? The way the image on the screen squiggles then cuts sharp before you're back on the start screen again."

"I know exactly what you mean," he said. "I'd give anything for an old Nintendo."

"I have one," I said, "but I don't have a television to play it on. You could have it if you—"

"Any of you faggots want to buy some powders?"

The owner of the interruption walked into the ring of light cast by our fire and I thought it was Svenson but he was shorter and fatter and balding. A minute later, the Svenson I knew showed up to stand beside his older brother.

"Figures we'd find this fucking longhair out here," he said and kicked at my leg with his boot. "Fortunately for you, we're here on business."

I didn't answer or acknowledge him. Instead, I stared deep into the fire, watching the tongues of flame lick away the outer layers of the wood. My uncle was a small-town tough like Svenson, right down to the pickup truck and the bad attitude, and I understood Svenson because I understood my uncle—they were both out to prove their size and power in the world. If I ignored him long enough and stayed out of his way, thereby conceding Holm to Svenson, he would stop bothering me. As long as I could survive until Svenson got tired, I thought, my life in Holm would be just fine.

"Enough chitchat," Svenson's brother said. "Y'all want some shit or not."

J dug in his pocket and pulled out a five, held it up. Svenson took it.

"Five lousy bucks? What is this, middle school?"

His brother stepped over to J and pulled a small plastic bag from his pocket. He dipped a long spoon inside, then held the tip to J's nose. J sniffed and his eyes went wide. He put his hand to his heart and then exhaled deeply.

"Damn," J said. "Can I get your phone number?"

The elder Svenson pulled a small notebook from his pocket, scribbled on a page, and handed it to J. "If you're going to come to my house, you'll need to come alone," he said, then pointed at me. "Don't bring this freak show with you."

J agreed and slipped the note in his pocket. Svenson and his brother made their exit, or we thought they did until there was a loud pounding on metal, Svenson slapping the hood of Mary's Buick.

"So this is the car you're cruising around in?"

No one answered and soon we heard the older brother asking the faggots at the next fire if they wanted any powders.

"That's the guy you were talking about back at my place?" J asked. "What a prick. Good shit, though, real good shit. If I had a little more I bet I could beat his ass even though he's a foot taller than me."

Jenny and Mary returned then, and Jenny asked, "Was that Sven Svenson?"

"Where?" Mary asked.

"Just there," she said, pointing. "I can hear his stupid voice from here."

"Oh," Mary said, sounding disappointed. "He's gone already?"

"You're into that guy?" J asked. "Holy shit! That guy, Mary?"

"No," she said, but it looked to me like she was. "I know him, I mean, we used to go to Young Life together."

"He is a horrible person," Jenny said.

I didn't like where this was going and I didn't want to ruin the good time we had been having before Mary and Jenny had left for the bathroom, so instead of talking more about Svenson I told them about the last time I had nearly drowned, jumping off the high dives built on the old loading docks in Grand Marais.

"The big swamp?" Jenny asked.

"*Oui, oui, mademoiselle,*" I said. "*Parlez-vous français?*"

"No," she said, "but I recognize it."

Jenny had done a circle tour of Lake Superior with her mother, she told us, stopping at all the lighthouses as they traveled through northern Minnesota, Canada, the Upper Peninsula of Michigan, and Wisconsin. Then she moved on to other trips she and her mother had taken and I was off the hook. J passed the bottle and Mary rolled another joint while Jenny described for us the Grand Canyon, the Badlands, and Yellowstone National Park.

"That's enough about you and your mother," Mary said. "Tell us about yours, Shane. You only saw her once after she left?"

"Naw," J said, "don't make him talk about that sad shit now."

"I want to know, too," Jenny said.

"A-a-all right," I said and stuttered through the first few lines but soon found my rhythm.

One rainy day my father brought me home from school and put me on his knee at the kitchen table. We sat there for a moment, silent, then I put my head down on my arms and cried. I watched *Divorce Court* on television—I knew what was happening.

That fall I moved into fourth grade, the year we stopped having desks and instead were assigned seats at long tables in groups of four. Across from me was the beautiful red-headed Natalie, my first crush, but I knew I had no chance when she told this story to our group.

"Every day I go home after school and see a pair of arms in the upstairs window of the house across the street. Covered in tattoos. One arm puts a beer can on the windowsill, then the other arm slams the window down to crush it and the first arm throws it into the yard. There's a mountain of crushed cans down below the window. A woman inside thinks this is so funny, she laughs so loud we can hear her inside my house when the windows are shut."

Natalie looked at me and pointed her short finger.

"And that woman is your mother."

That surprised me. Not that the story was about my mother—it sounded exactly like her—but that she had only moved across town. I hadn't seen her for months.

"My mom says that your mom is trash," Natalie said. "She said only common trash would think that's funny."

I followed Natalie home that day. Across the street from her house there were beer cans in the yard, but Natalie had been exaggerating when she said there was a mountain—I counted no more than thirty. Around the side of the house was the entrance that led to the second floor. I climbed the stairs and rang the bell.

"Who is it?" my mother asked through the closed door.

I answered with my name but she asked again.

"Who?"

"Shane," I said. "Your son."

No answer. I heard a man's voice and she said something about her fucking kid and how he should put that fucking shit away so she could let me in. The voice told her I wouldn't know what it was and she told him that she didn't fucking know what I was doing there anyways. A few minutes later, the door swung open and there she was, wearing the same beat-up pink sweatsuit that featured in the long, lazy days we spent at home before she left, but I hadn't seen my mother for so long that her face had gone soft in my mind. I'd remembered that her eyes were the same deep brown as her hair, but I hadn't understood until that moment just how different that made her from me, very much my father's boy with my blond hair and blue eyes.

"Hiiiiiiiiiiiiiiiiiiii," my mother said in the way I knew meant she didn't want to see someone. It was musical. The first part had a nice high tone and it dropped as it moved on.

"Hello, Mother."

"I'm so glad to see you," she lied. "Go have a seat in the living room."

I followed her down the hall, past an open door. Inside, a mattress sat on the floor without sheets, the pillows and a blanket bunched up near the foot of the bed. Another matching blanket hung from nails to block out the light. Past a closed door the hallway opened up into the living room, where I found the tattooed arms attached to a bearded man with long hair. He looked at me. I looked at him. He lit a cigarette. I sat down next to him on the couch. My mother went into the kitchen and picked up the phone. I lifted my eyes to meet the gaze of the tattooed man when her voice floated into the room.

"What's he doing here, Ole? If this is some kind of ploy to get me back—"

The man tried to distract me with his tattoos. He raised his right arm in the air and showed me the skull on his elbow. The jaw was below the joint and the cranium above so when he moved his fist forward and back the skull would open and close its mouth. He told a joke and the skull laughed. He held his cigarette up to his elbow and the skull coughed. When his eyes veered off toward the kitchen, I followed them to see my mother, still on the phone, pulling the long coiled cord into the living room so she could look out the window. I'd always thought of my mother as a towering figure but there, in the afternoon sun, she yawned, arms stretching toward the ceiling so that the sleeves of her sweatshirt slid down to reveal her tiny wrists, and I couldn't remember if my mother had always been so thin, so small.

"Yeah, yeah, yeah," she said, raising a hand to the glass, tapping with a finger before turning back to the kitchen and slamming the phone down into the cradle. A moment later she was standing over me, smiling the almost straight smile I'd see on my own mouth a few years later.

"Look, we'd love for you to stay, Shane," she said, "but we have plans. We're very busy. Next time, you should call first."

I looked down, studied the table. An ashtray. Two beer cans. A lighter. A small book with the word ZIG-ZAG on the cover. A pair of scissors with a clamp on the end instead of shears. All under a layer of dust.

"Did you hear me?"

"I don't know your phone number," I yelled. "I didn't even know where you lived until today."

"Don't talk to me like that. I'm your mother." She took me by the arm, dragged me to the door, pushed me outside.

"How can I call when I don't have your number?" I asked quietly, politely.

"I'll call you," she said and shut the door.

"That call didn't come for a couple of years and when it did it was the last time we spoke," I told the group, finishing my story.

"That's horrible," Mary said.

"It sounds like she might not want you to find her," Jenny said, a thoughtful sadness in her voice.

"I told you," J said.

"Oh, I don't know," I said. "She was so young. You can't blame her. What would either of you do if you got pregnant now?"

Neither Jenny nor Mary answered, all of us staring into the fire, wordless. I thought for a moment that I had killed our good time for the night, but soon J said something, then Jenny and Mary, and after some time we were laughing and happy again. I'm not sure if it was the whiskey or the weed or the festival itself, or it could have been getting that story about my mother off my chest, but after a time I found that talking came a little easier, that the pressure I usually felt to restrain myself, to hold back my words, was gone. My mouth started moving, and Jenny, J, and Mary all turned toward me with curious looks as I spoke. I had a sudden understanding of the stars above us, the Milky Way being particularly vivid that night, and us down below, stars in our own right. Jenny again took up my words and made them her own, adding at some point that the iron that runs through our blood was made in stars like those, millions of years ago.

"Everything is starlight," she said, and I felt that this was so close to my point, that she had understood me so finely, that I reached out and put my hand on her leg. She put her hand over mine, cocked her head, and squinted in a way that made me think she was confused, but then went on: "The nature of the universe is dependent on these chemical reactions, these constant explosions propelling matter to collide in new and more complicated ways. We are the accidental result of the slapping together of a few elements from here and there in the universe. Some of us must explode and die so others can go on."

"You don't think God has anything to do with it?" Mary asked.

"Don't be messing with my God now," J said, suddenly serious. "He's all I got, you know."

Mary's and J's words grew garbled and hard to follow once they started grilling Jenny about religion and soon after that I began having trouble keeping my eyes open, so I stumbled over to the tent and fumbled with the zipper until Jenny came and helped me get it open. I thanked her and fell into the tent but she climbed in and lay down next to me, shaking me out of my stupor. I wasn't sure what to do so I didn't do anything. She nuzzled in close and looped my hair behind my ear with her finger. I opened my eyes to find her face before me, our noses nearly touching, her arm resting against my neck, hand at the back of my head. Outside, J's and Mary's voices grew loud.

"Come to bed," she yelled, standing outside the tent. "You don't need any more of that shit."

Point made and ignored, Mary zipped us in and dove over us, landing next to Jenny before rolling to the side, leaving a wide space between her and Jenny for J to take if he ever came back.

That night I had a dream that had been recurring all that year, but this time it was set in Holm. Legs locked beneath me, I stood in the middle of the More-4-You parking lot unable to go any farther. I wanted to move—I had been on my way to the store before I had become trapped in this position—and I did my best to get my feet off the ground but a tremendous weight held them immobile. I could only stand there as the world moved around me, shoppers coming and going, hoping that no one would come careening my way, unable to stop.

"J, no," Jenny said, "you drunk motherfucker. I'm not Mary. Stop it."

Her words penetrated my sleep, her voice entering my dream over a loudspeaker in the parking lot, and then her knee came down hard on my stomach as she tried to climb over me, bringing me back into the world. The sun hadn't yet risen but the sky was lightening, the tent barely bright enough to see. Four, maybe five, in the morning.

"I know who you are," he said. "I thought you were into it."

"I was sleeping," she said. "How can I be into it?"

Jenny folded herself into the corner of the tent so that my body lay between her and J. We settled back into silence until the pulling of a zipper and the shifting of fabric.

"Baby," J said. "Baby, get up."

I opened my eyes to see J on his knees between Mary's legs, her pants pulled down to her ankles. He spit on his hand, rubbed it where he needed it wet, and then moved into her. Mary groaned. The rustling of blankets and clothes grew into a steady rhythm. The bubble of the tent swayed above us.

"No, J," she said. "J. No, stop it. J. Oh, oh, J."

Jenny leaned up on her elbow and tried to look over me at their coupling, watched for a while before she put her head down on my chest and fell asleep.

It wasn't her voice that woke me but the first thing I heard the next day was Mary apologizing to Jenny. They were outside the tent, Jenny having climbed out at some point without me noticing.

"I thought it'd been a dream at first, but now that I've got this shit leaking out of me I know it wasn't," she said. "I'm sorry you had to see that."

"Nothing I haven't seen before."

"Really? How old are you?"

I didn't hear Jenny's answer. A car door slammed and then another. That second one could've been the trunk.

I rolled over to find J facing me, nose as near as I had found Jenny's the night before, a trail of something blue leaking from his mouth. Startled, I sat up. My head throbbed and my vision grew dark around the edges, narrowed into two long tunnels and returned. I reached for my shoes.

"So Mary, what are you going to be when you grow up?"

A crackling sound came from the direction of their voices and the first wafts of bacon seeped into the tent.

"A secretary," Mary said.

"A secretary?" Jenny asked. "That's different. Most people want to have a secretary, not be one."

"I'm not most people."

J made a soft choking noise and coughed, spraying blue over where my head had been a moment before.

"I want to get away from Holm as soon as I can," Jenny said. "I hate that place."

"But you've lived there your whole life. How could you move away?"

"Don't you want to go to college? Meet new people? Didn't you graduate from high school the other day?"

"There's a college in Holm. And I meet new people all the time. I've lived there for eighteen years and I still haven't met everyone."

I unzipped the tent and climbed out into the morning. The sun was screaming white so I held my hand to my forehead like a visor to look around. Mary had a two-burner gas grill set up on the picnic table and Jenny was standing next to it, smoking a cigarette. The morning sun lit the campgrounds in a way that made it all look brand-new, a warmth in the air that I wasn't used to so early in the day. Aside from the three of us, very few people remained among the canvas bubbles and parked cars. Most were packing up their sites, though no one seemed to be leaving.

"Where is everyone?"

"The concert is getting going now," Mary said. "How do you like your eggs?"

I told her I'd take mine over-easy and she poured a little bacon grease into a frying pan, then cracked two into it. My joining Mary and Jenny killed their conversation, so while my breakfast crackled and popped in the pan, we watched the stragglers from the other campsites rise and move eastward to where the entrance to the concert must have been.

After we ate, Jenny took me car shopping. She was never happier, she told me on our walk, than when she was stealing. At the first camp I was afraid of security systems, but Jenny lifted the handle to show that it wasn't even locked.

"If it wasn't for dickheads like these, there wouldn't be any thievery in this world, would there?" she said, then looked at me expectantly.

"Umm, no," I said.

"You've never seen that movie?"

"I guess not."

After that, we tore into every site we passed, except for the ones other scavengers, or possibly the rightful owners, were occupying. Within an hour we had half an ounce of weed, a six-pack of beer, and seventy-five dollars. I found a new pair of jeans, the same brand and size I had lost in the river except strung through the loops was a braided leather belt. I pulled them on over my boxers and then grabbed the bundle of firewood tied up near the fire pit. Our hands full, we turned back toward our camp.

"I think this small-town living is bullshit too," I said, breaking the silence between us. "I heard you talking to Mary earlier and I think it's crazy she wants to stay in Holm."

"It's not her opinion," Jenny said. "It's her father's probably, but you can't convince anyone of anything. People need to realize this stuff for themselves."

"There's more to life than Holm," I said.

"For some of us."

J was walking away from the campsite when we returned, Mary yelling after him. He stuck his middle finger up in the air, then vanished into the sea of tents without looking back.

"I knew he would only get a ticket for himself," Mary told us. "He's going to the concert but he can find his own fucking way home. I'm leaving. You two are welcome to come with me but he can walk for all I care."

We rolled up the sleeping bags and took down the tent. Once we packed the car, we sat in the grass by the smoldering remains of the previous night's fire and smoked one last joint. Mary kept looking around the whole time, hoping that J would come back, but in the end we left without him.

When we got back to Holm, Jenny asked Mary if she could drop us at the Walmart, which was fine with me, but once we got there she stuffed all the stolen drugs in my pockets and made me sit on a bench near a child riding an airplane. The plane looped up and down in a way that planes are not supposed to move while the toddler cooed at his mother and slapped his tiny hands at the sides of the ride. A real airplane flew over us and he pointed at the sky.

"Pane," he said. "Pane, pane, pane."

After ten minutes that drew out into an eternity, Jenny came out of the store with a bag of candy. She sat down next to me, ripped open the bag, and handed me a lollipop.

"They stole from us, we steal from them," she said, then went on to tell me that shoplifting at Walmart was one of her favorite things to do in town. She claimed they deserved it, the Waltons, for moving into Holm and taking away people's livelihoods, then told me again about her mother's store.

"You had us dropped off out here so you could steal a bag of candy as revenge for your mother?"

"No, I bought these suckers," she said, then handed me what she had taken. "Diamond-tipped drill bits. Small but expensive."

They were in six thin packages with price tags reading twenty bucks each. After we sat on the bench for a while, she told me that I was to go in and return them for cash. We had another lollipop each, both Jenny and I forgoing patience and crunching down with our teeth after a minute before tossing the sticks into the parking lot. My heart began racing then and didn't stop until I lied to the cashier at the return counter.

"I'm sorry," I said. "My dad sent me out here to get drill bits but I got the wrong kind."

"Do you have a receipt?"

"No," I said, not looking her in the eye. "I didn't think I'd need one."

"Be a little more careful next time," she said, then slid six twenty-dollar bills and some change across the counter.

Three

That Monday, I worked my first shift washing dishes at the Aurora, breakfast and lunch, and once I punched out, I ran to the post office to see if my mother had left a forwarding address for her mail. Of course she hadn't, and I was sitting with my head in my hands on the stone steps out front, pondering the pointlessness of my search for someone who did not want to be found, when the sputtering drunk from the fairgrounds walked up, Twins hat in his hand, feet kicking at the loose rocks on the sidewalk as he asked if he could apologize. Russell he said his name was, and he lifted his shirt to show off an odd bulge in his pants, the neck of a glass bottle sticking out of his pocket.

"Let's go do something with this," he said.

I didn't want to go with him after what he had said at the fairgrounds but his eyes persuaded me. Those sad glances made me want to take him in my arms and hold him. I couldn't have explained it then, this feeling that drew me to Russell, but I needed to give him a second chance. If my mother deserved one after what she had done, then I could give one to this boy whose only fault was that he had told me the truth.

We walked a couple blocks in silence, awkward silence I thought, before he pointed out the playground across from the library and we each took a swing beneath the water tower still adorned with the words *Holm Sucks*. I kicked my legs until I was swinging and Russell sat with the bottle between his knees, turning in circles so the chains above him twined together until he finally let go and spun the opposite way, the bottle flying into the grass. When the chains straightened out again, Russell stood, stumbled in his dizziness, and fell to the ground near the whiskey, where he uncapped the bottle and told me he'd had a job for a day. Training as a bar back at the Holm Bar and Grill on Saturday night, he'd slipped the bottle into his backpack the first time he was sent to the liquor room for stock. No one noticed before his shift ended, but he got the call the next morning telling him he need not return.

"Fuck it. Free whiskey," he said, then put the bottle to his lips and turned it upside down. "They didn't say it was because I stole, but you know it was. It doesn't matter. I've got other prospects anyways."

He told me about a party he had heard about, a field party, though he hadn't necessarily been invited. I had my doubts, which grew into sneaking suspicions, which grew into fear. My first thoughts were that someone had put Russell up to this, possibly bribing him with this bottle to trick me into going to where no one would hear my screams. I mentioned that I hadn't gotten along too well with most other kids in town, but Russell told me that we could leave as soon as I felt the need so I followed him down Center, past the middle school and the old folks' home, over the bridge that crossed the Spirit River to where it became the highway. A couple of trucks blew by us but no one whistled or called—they must have thought I was Russell's woman.

We turned onto a two-lane road that ran between cornfields. Stalks as high as my eyes with no end in sight. Russell handed me the bottle and I took two small sips. He called me a pussy so I took two more. A pinching tightness developed between my shoulders and a looseness behind my eyes. Russell had no problem with it, and with each pull he smiled wider and talked louder. He could drink whiskey faster than I could drink water, moving alone through the bottle as quickly as the four of us at the campground. I wanted to throw up just watching him.

The road curved toward the setting sun, more an inconvenience on this cloudless day than an occasion of beauty and wonder, so we walked toward it with our hands in front of our faces like shields. I pointed out the thin dirt roads that occasionally split off from the pavement, often no more than wheel ruts that disappeared into forests or fields, and Russell claimed to have lived on a farm for the first ten years of his life. He told me that these were mostly access points for tractors and harvesters.

"But some of these rednecks live down roads like these," he said. "Houses deep in the woods, barns full of guns."

We came up on a pair of bridges that led over the Spirit, one the road we walked would cross and another set lower on the valley walls, narrow and old. I veered off on a gravel path that cut back and forth down the slope, leading to an orange sign hanging on a chain. DANGER: NO TRESPASSING! A plaque mounted on the portal strut read 1888.

"Hey, what's the plan?" Russell called from the road.

I told him I would see him on the other side and crouched under the chain. The bracing looked safe enough, a little rusty but intact. The wooden deck was rotting away and, as I carefully stepped around holes so large I could have fallen through without touching the sides, I could see that the the concrete pillar that held the bridge in place was crumbling into the water below. The river ran slowly, indifferent to my peril.

On the other side of the river was more corn. A lot more corn. We were in the middle of nowhere. I again grew worried that Russell was setting me up. He handed me the bottle and smiled, proving my suspicions. How did I let myself come to be alone with this guy I hardly knew? I felt a bit better when the corn gave way to soybeans because they were so low to the ground that I could see no one was hiding in the field, but those feelings were short-lived as we moved past the soy and back into cornfields. The sun set and the stars came out, so many that I asked Russell if he thought there were as many stars in the sky as there were ears of corn in the fields.

"Someone should harvest those," Russell said, now drunk, pointing at the Big Dipper, then turned toward an orange glow in the distance. "There's the party."

We stepped into the field and followed the rows until we could hear the crowd. Russell knelt down and laced his hands together. I stepped in and he lifted me above the corn so I could point the way to the party, then we walked for a while at a sharp diagonal, trampling cornstalks.

We came out of the corn to a half circle of parked trucks, headlights pointed at a crowd of people milling in pairs and small groups, most of them holding red plastic cups. A bonfire, the orange glow we had seen in the distance, burned between us and them, and next to that, a girl pumped beer out of a silver keg, five people behind her waiting for refills. One of the trucks played what might have been Led Zeppelin. I thought I recognized a couple of the guys from the streets of Holm but I couldn't be sure—the only person I knew, by truck or by face, was Svenson.

"I don't see my guy yet," Russell said, then led me over near the fire.

Russell drank from the bottle and then passed it to me. No one had yet noticed who I was, but I was certain that someone soon would. I was about to suggest we slip back into the corn when a girl wearing overalls and pigtails, obviously drunk, stumbled up to the fire and yelled, pointing beyond us at a set of headlights on the road from where Russell and I had come.

"That's them!"

The lights rolled past the party and turned back toward us at the next road. A few guys climbed up into the beds of their trucks, taking turns whistling with two fingers in their mouths. We all turned toward the entrance, if you can call a path of trampled corn an entrance.

I took three steps back when I saw the truck was cherry red. Russell turned and I signaled for him to ease away from the crowd. We were at the edge of the standing corn when three ghosts got out of the truck to whooping cheers from the party. When the newcomers moved toward the fire I saw that they weren't dressed like ghosts. They wore white robes and masks with tall pointy hats. On their chests, above their hearts, were red circles with white crosses. The first Klansman put his hands over his eyes, the second over his ears, the third over his mouth. This must have had some meaning beyond what I associated with it because the crowd grew very loud, a chorus of cheers and laughter. Cameras appeared and the partygoers posed with the costumed newcomers. Flashbulbs popped in the night. Rifles and shotguns were fetched from trucks and given to the Klansmen. "For authenticity," someone kept yelling.

I pulled Russell into the corn and turned back the way we came.

"Hey, where are we going?" he called from behind me, but I didn't turn back. "That was my guy. The party was just getting started."

I stopped to wait. Russell caught up and handed me the bottle, now less than a quarter full.

"What happened?" I asked. "Did you spill some of this?"

"Spilled it right into my mouth."

Russell had drunk more than half the bottle but was still walking straight and making sense when he talked. I wasn't sure what he would have to gain by pouring out the liquor and claiming to have drunk it, but it worried me more that he could drink this much and still function. I choked down a big swallow, more to keep it from Russell than from any desire to keep drinking, and held on to the bottle as we walked.

"What was going on back there?"

"They're trying to be their fathers," Russell said, "just like anybody else. Makes me wonder what your father is like with you running away like this."

"Better to run away than to be that," I said.

"They ain't really KKK. They don't mean it."

"What is it that they do mean?"

"They like to dress up," Russell said. "Boys'll be boys, ya know? It's not a big deal." And then, when that line didn't get the reaction he wanted: "Look, they're idiots. They don't know what they're doing. It's not like they burn crosses or anything."

"Let's talk about something else."

Russell caught up and moved into the row next to me, corn tassels rustling against our arms as he told me about his uncle, who had lived for a time with him and his parents on the farm. He had seemed like a nice enough guy, to Russell anyway. An early riser and a hard worker, he was a great help with the morning chores, and on those lazy afternoons afterwards, he taught Russell how to throw, how to play baseball. But on weekends he underwent a mysterious change—when he would go out for an evening on the town, he came back a stranger. In one rage or another, he returned from wherever he had gone in a fit of yelling, punching holes in the wall, kicking chairs. Broken glass, usually plates or windows, often featured in those Sunday mornings, Russell and his father tiptoeing around the house as Russell's mother tried to calm her brother. The last time he would see him, Russell awoke to find his uncle passed out in the dining room, cheek flat on the table, eyes open and staring but seeing nothing. A large bowl of coleslaw was overturned on the floor and strands of cabbage were strewn around the house.

"I didn't know he was a drunk until much later," Russell said. "I thought he was crazy."

We reached the end of the cornfield and then walked along the road. Darkness had fallen hard and, since there were no streetlights, the stars and moon were left to guide us back to town. Crickets sang the melody to the rhythm of our feet in the gravel.

"They kicked my uncle out after that thing with the coleslaw," Russell said, "told him never to come back. Said he was no longer part of the family and acted that way too. Took his pictures out of the photo albums, tore up his letters, refused his collect calls. When I bring him up they act like I haven't said anything."

"That's how it was with my mom, too," I said. "Once she was gone, my dad acted like they had never met."

"My uncle had this darkness hanging over him," Russell said, "but sending him away was the worst thing we could have done. My mom doesn't listen when I tell her that. 'Tough love,' she says, 'someday you'll understand.' But I won't. If anything, I'll be the next one kicked out of the family."

At the pair of bridges, Russell grabbed the bottle from me and ran down the hill, out onto the abandoned bridge. I yelled for him to turn around and take the safe way but he wasn't coming back. Drunk as he was, I figured he would end up in the river so I wasn't surprised when I found him dangling from the edge of the first big hole in the deck. It would have been a short fall but the river was very shallow. A rock in the wrong place would break his leg if he were to drop.

I grabbed him by the armpits and pulled him up, falling down on my ass as he came out of the hole. The forward momentum brought

Russell down on top of me, drunk and flailing from the fear of falling, or so I thought until his open mouth came down on mine, his hands behind my head pulling me to him. We tangled there for a long moment, inexperienced and unpracticed, my hands on Russell's waist as he reached under and over and around to feel what he could, to pull me closer to him, until his hand went between my legs and I pushed him away.

We lay there on the bridge next to each other for a while, staring up at the stars, neither of us having the words to talk about what had just happened, my desire having grown into a dark yearning that I didn't understand, a shadow of myself twice my size, hungry, and barely under control. I wanted another drink but the whiskey was gone, Russell having dropped the bottle in the river in his scramble to stay out of the hole, so my buzz was beginning to wear off. Russell had drunk so much that he was still quite tipsy but somehow still awake. As alert and aware as when we had first met up that day.

"So, what else happened on that farm?" I asked.

"Every once in a while we'd get a brood of like fifty chicks and I'd get super excited, really, more excited than I've ever been since, for sure. They were little and yellow and soft. Once when I was like seven I wanted to keep one but my dad told me we'd have to leave it in the incubator for a few days so he gave me a marker so I'd know which one was mine. They all looked the same so I should have waited until they were more mature to choose, but I picked one up and drew a big red dot on her forehead. That night I couldn't even eat dinner I was so excited about my new pet, and I couldn't go to sleep until I saw her again, so I waited for my parents to go to bed and snuck out to the barn. You probably know where this is going."

"No idea."

"When I got to the incubator her head was split open and the other chicks were pecking at her brains. I screamed loud enough to wake my parents and they came and got me and put me to bed."

"That's horrible."

"Others were pecked to death for much less—we couldn't even figure out why some of the chicks had been attacked. As far as we could tell, some of them were perfectly normal."

"Boys will be boys, I guess."

"Ladies in this case," he said. "These were all egg-laying hens."

There was screaming in the distance and the sound of engines. Svenson's truck was the first to cross the bridge, the other two Klansmen standing in the bed, holding on to the roll bar with one hand, red plastic cups in the other. The rest of the party followed, more tame than the leader.

"It's good we aren't up on the road now," Russell said.

Four

I ate breakfast at the Arlington almost every day that summer, sitting with coffee while the old-timers came and went, the strong gray-haired men wearing flannel work shirts under insulated vests who would show up early and read aloud the newspaper stories about welfare and immigration. They reveled in the accomplishment of Timothy McVeigh. These men had the same swagger and attitude as the boys on the streets, the same confidence and misconceptions about how people should treat each other, but they also shared a general feeling of disgust with the way the world was heading. They came to the Arlington to complain and to tell each other that their complaints were justified.

"I mean, it's my money," I heard that first morning I had breakfast alone. "Why's some raghead Somali going to spend it in Minneapolis?"

"I don't know why we keep letting them in the country."

These men lived in Holm or the nearby towns of Karlstad, Mora, Chisago, or Lulea, and many in the rural lands between, and they were all Swedish, of Swedish descent anyway, the remaining shreds of that heritage being the long vowels in their speech and the annual trip to the Holm Swedish Festival.

I stirred sugar into my coffee and listened with my head cocked, staring off into a corner or out the window as if I wasn't there, but I saw it all. They tipped in coins, some leaving a single quarter on the counter, and assumed this bought the right to pinch Karen's ass on the way out the door, every last one of them. When the old men left, the whole mood of the Arlington would change. The waitresses were quick to bring the discarded newspapers over with the coffeepot. Laughs were a bit easier to come by. Life got less serious once all the rednecks cleared out.

Later in the summer the old men caught me listening, noticed I was a little off, sitting at a table near the counter, alone, looking like a girl, but those first days I heard everything, unedited and unfiltered. They sat nearer each other at the counter after that and, voices quieter, always with their backs between me and what they were saying. It was easy to see where Svenson got his attitude.

The shiny chrome pipe Jenny bought with her drill bit money was a foot long and she wasn't afraid to whip it out. After a long morning of coffee and newspapers, I found her leaning against the wall of the Arlington, bowl sunk deep into a plastic baggie, corralling green crumbs.

"Couldn't we at least go up to my room for this?"

"Most people wouldn't understand," she said. "And even if they do know, who are you trying to impress? You're heading off to college at the end of the summer—you'll never see any of these people again."

She put flame to the bowl, holding the long stem to her chest as if she were doing nothing more than adjusting a pendant, then we walked off down Center trailing sour clouds behind us. Until then I thought Jenny was reckless and a bit edgy. I admired her blatant disregard for the rules but it became clear to me that she wasn't testing boundaries with her nonstop shoplifting and public smoking and stealing from cars, rather she was trying to get caught. I couldn't say why then but every one of Jenny's actions seemed to be directed toward getting arrested. The only thing I could get her to do that didn't include at least the threat of arrest was look for my mother.

The plastics factory was a fortress of ugly: three stories of reflective silver metal and two blocks long, in the same spot as the strip mall that housed the More-4-You but on the wrong side of the tracks. We had no luck at the front door where two security guards checked appointments and IDs and, since neither of us were old enough to work there, they wouldn't even let us in to fill out an application. Outside, I started back toward the Arlington but Jenny stopped.

"You aren't very good at this, are you?"

"No, I guess I'm not."

"Follow me."

She turned us around and led me down a sidewalk that ran the length of the factory. Noontime beat down on the building's facade and up from the hoods of the parked cars, catching us in the middle with the heat of three suns. At the end of the building was an area fenced off with chain link, picnic tables lined in rows shaded by big square umbrellas.

"How are we going to get in?" I asked. "Climb the fence?"

She reached in through the neck of her blouse to take her smokes from her bra strap, tapped two out and lit them. "We don't need to go inside," she said, handing me a cigarette.

We puffed for a moment before the lunch whistle sounded and soon the door crashed open, the picnic tables filled with men and women in matching gray slacks and collared T-shirts, unrolling brown paper bags and lighting cigarettes. They grouped themselves by age, a few old-timers together at one table and a few that may have just finished high school at another, but all the other tables were taken by people my mother's age. I half expected to see my mother herself but she wasn't in the crowd. The sound of chatter and laughter was loud but Jenny yelled over it.

"Does anyone know this boy's mother?" she shouted. "She used to work here." She called my mother's name a few times and soon a woman seated at a picnic table went inside and came back with a stocky man carrying a clipboard.

"You kids can't hang out here," the man said.

"My mom—"

"Look, kid, your mother was a fuckup," he said, "and it'd probably be better if you stop looking now and get on with your life."

My face must have dropped to the ground because Jenny looked at me and then snarled through the fence. "You fat fuck," she hissed. "You come out here and say that."

"I don't have time for this," he said. "In any case, she worked the night shift and I fired all of them. Every last one. Bunch of drug addicts, your mom included."

He turned and walked back inside. Jenny stuck her fingers and cigarette through the fence and flicked her butt at the man but it fell short.

I turned back the way we came and Jenny followed, taking my hand in hers as we made our way back downtown but I wasn't looking to be consoled. I had known it wouldn't be easy.

"All the money I have, I got from my mother," I told Jenny after I recounted the day I had graduated from high school, the note from my uncle, and the bus ride to Holm. The Christmas card that led me here had a hundred-dollar bill inside. I got so excited when I opened it: a hundred dollars—I was thirteen then and had never seen so much money at once before, let alone a single crisp bill. My father and my uncle were my whole family in Grand Marais and sitting around our Christmas tree I told my father all the things I wanted to buy—bike parts, video games, candy—but I didn't see the tears in his eyes. My father was so softhearted that he couldn't speak up as I kept talking and talking until my uncle stood, towering over me, and yelled about all the times my mother had crossed my father, all the times she had ignored me. He listed her boyfriends' names from both before and after they were married, the long nights when she had left us alone, one of them a week after I was born. "She flashes a hundred-dollar bill and you forget all of that," he screamed into my face. "You're just like her!" And now I don't know if it was his rage or my final understanding that my mother abandoned us that sent me into a sadness days long, ruining my winter vacation. In the end, I stuffed the bill back in the card and promised myself I would never use the money, but having nothing and nowhere to go after my dad died, I needed it.

"I'd be sad if my father died too," Jenny said when I finished my story. She moved her hand to my shoulder and I tried to smile at her.

"It isn't my father's death that makes me sad, but that he never lived," I told Jenny. "He spent his whole life in Grand Marais: finished high school, met my mother, had me, and then raised me until his heart gave out. My mother went out to see the world, if you can call Holm and wherever she is now the world, and my father stayed home with his responsibilities."

We had made it back to the Arlington by the time I finished my story but instead of going upstairs, I rang the super. He came out in the same paint-splashed jeans he had been wearing when we had breakfast.

"Did you find her?" he asked.

"Not yet," I said. I dug out my money and gave him two twenties, stuffing the single dollar that remained back in my pocket. "So it'll be twenty a week through July too? And August if I stay?"

He told me I was right about the price, then told me to wait and ambled off. He returned with a square of paper, the words RENT RE-CEIPT across the top in blue, and a spare key. Unsure what to do with the spare, I held it out to Jenny and she took it without a word.

"I can see why you're staying in town," he said, hooking his thumb at Jenny. "What a beautiful woman, no? If you don't find your mother, at least you found her."

Five

Sisyphus was large and round and sat at the end of her chain's length, head tilted, watching the cars and people pass on Ash. Lucifer was much smaller. He was allowed to run free but never went far from his sister, who was tied to the trunk of the willow tree. Like any pair of pit bulls, they looked ferocious and were capable of ripping a person apart, but Sissy and Lucy were soft and gentle and friendly. The huge willow stood between us and the sun, the slight wind blowing the fronds of the tree so the long ropes of shadow swung back and forth across the four of us as we lazed about.

J and I were sitting on lawn chairs that I would never see again— apparently, there were many things that disappeared from this house— while he told me about the short time he and Mary had spent apart. The best three days of his life, he said, and then she was back, knocking on the door, waking him up at the crack of noon, apologizing. It seemed to me that it should have been J who said he was sorry, but it doesn't matter who is wrong in situations like these, J told me, rather, who wants the other person more.

J reached down between our chairs and pulled out of the grass what looked to me like a long gray icicle, then threw it so it flew end over end into the street. Lucifer jumped up and ran for it, dashed into the road without looking, picked it up in his teeth, and brought it back to J. He kept throwing and Lucifer kept fetching, bringing it right back to J's hand until finally he dropped it at our feet before turning back to his sister and lying down next to her. I climbed out of my chair and picked up the icicle. It was solid but very light, dotted with tooth marks up and down.

"What is this thing?"

"No idea," J said. "I found it here—there's a bunch of weird shit like this kicking around the house. Lucy loves it though. He snaps through regular sticks, even branches, with one chomp. I call it the Indestructible."

I turned the stick over in my hands a couple of times, found no name brand or other markings, then dropped it back into the grass before sitting back down.

"So why do you stay with Mary if you aren't really into her?" I asked.

"What's your favorite sandwich?"

"Peanut butter and butter," I said without hesitation.

"PB and butter?" he asked. "Really?"

I nodded.

"Two kinds of butter?"

"Yes."

"Well, that's different," J said, "but anyways, let's say that you've eaten lunch and someone walks in with a tray full of peanut butter and butter sandwiches, sets them right in front of you and tells you to eat. Do you eat? Or do you let them sit?"

Lucifer was a jumper. Up and down, over his sister, running circles around her. Sisyphus, big and slow, snapped her jaws at Lucifer, reached out with a paw and missed.

"I'd definitely eat," I said. "But I don't see how this works. Is Mary the lunch or the peanut butter sandwich?"

"C'mon, Lucky, you know what I mean."

I knew from the beginning that J wasn't nice, wasn't a thoughtful person, but he had developed some sort of attachment to me, and I to him. I was like some sad cat he had fed once and, as with strays, when I had nowhere else to go I would wander back to see if he had anything else for me. Not that I didn't like J, he was friendly to me, but I was aware of how badly he treated others.

"I usually don't think of women as sandwiches," I said.

"Clearly, you think too much."

We sat there silently for a while, my comment a nonissue, then he pulled a small plastic bag and his keys from his pocket. He dug a key into the bag and the tip came out with a small pile of an off-white powder.

"Hey, try this," he said. "Maybe it'll stop that overworked mind of yours."

I may have been a bit naive but I didn't think J would give me anything that would hurt me. When he brought the tip of the key to my nose, I sniffed back and felt good instantly. More than good. Great. The best I had ever felt. My heart pulsed in my eyes, I inhaled to deep parts of my lungs I had never used before and, with a wave of tingling pins and needles that moved over the top of my head and down my back, a tremendous sense of relief washed over me.

"What was that?" I asked, though a tension in my jaw made it difficult to speak. "I feel like I could do anything."

"It's got a lot of names," he said. "Sprack, I guess they call it now, speed."

"You aren't going to do any?"

"I did a little earlier," he said. "You should see what this stuff does to Mary. We were busy for six hours last night."

He made some lewd pantomimes while he rocked his hips and I wasn't sure what to say to that so I let it be what it was. Feeling the way I did then, letting go was very easy. I smiled violently. It hurt my cheeks to sit there and be alive, merely looking into the grass, watching the dogs. The sounds of the world became a symphony: the wind through the trees playing percussion and the distant traffic pairing with birdsong to make a soft melody.

"I love my fucking dogs," J said after a while, maybe a few hours. "They're big and mean-looking and everyone is scared of them." He got out of his chair and ran at Sissy, tackling her near the tree. Lucy jumped in and bit at J's pants and shirt. They rolled around on the ground for a while until J played dead and the dogs took to whimpering and tried to lick him back to life.

When he came back to sit down I saw a chunky streak of brown slime across the back of his flannel.

"Dog shit," I said. "You got dog shit all over your shirt."

"You're either ankle-deep in shit or you're lonely," he said, taking off his flannel and inspecting it before throwing it to the ground. "My dad used to say that."

J settled back into his chair and grew silent except for the loud sighs he let out every few minutes and the near-constant gravel of his grinding teeth. We didn't speak again for hours, sitting there in the waning day with the dogs until sunset, dusk, dark, when we were nothing more than two glowing embers in the night, the fiery cherries at the ends of our cigarettes.

Another quick sniff and I found myself climbing a ladder behind J, the metal creaking against his house as we made our way to the roof, and when I got there it was as if I had never seen the sky before. More light than dark, I thought maybe dawn was about to break so I looked to the east but J grunted and I turned to find him pointing at three green wisps, hundreds of miles long, glimmering, cracking like slow whips in the sky.

"Is this really happening?" I asked.

"I'm not sure."

Late that night, the wall in my room rippled in the same way, just like the barely visible twinkles on the ceiling of the cave on the St. Croix. The red light outside threw color through the window in rhythm with my heart, carrying me into the darkest part of the night, and then upon the lightening of the morning the colors blended into images of men and women passing along the wall carrying all sorts of vessels and statues and figures of animals made of wood and stone and various materials. Some of them talking and some of them not. I felt for a moment that I was a prisoner of these people until I began to name them. With that act, I became their leader and when they congregated in a colosseum I climbed out of my bed, took to its stage, and spoke. This, I told them just before dawn, is the life.

The world swayed and my vision narrowed and I stumbled to my desk to hold myself up until my senses returned. I couldn't tell if I had slept or not, though I had lain in bed with my eyes closed for a time. My body was weak, but I was awake and there was no point in trying to deny it. Down at the Arlington Karen asked me if I wanted the usual but, with my stomach in a tight, empty knot, I told her I'd have only coffee.

"How goes the search?" she asked when she returned with my cup and the coffeepot.

"I got nothing," I said. "I met some people who knew her but no one knows where she went."

"It doesn't surprise me," she said. "If the police haven't found her I don't see how you could."

"The police?" I asked. "Why would they be looking for her?"

"She's missing, right? Didn't you file a missing persons report?"

How had I not thought of that? I thanked Karen, tossed back my coffee, and left a five on the table.

My heart pounded like a bass drum as I walked down Old Main toward the police station, the coffee having kickstarted whatever residue was still lurking in my body from the previous night. My mouth grew dry, my tongue like sandpaper as it flailed around of its own accord. I felt my insides coming apart with each step I took through the morning so fresh that dew still sparkled on the lawns. Smells attacked me as I walked—animal droppings, garbage, exhaust—each of them pulling the liquid contents of my stomach closer to the outside world.

The police station was a relic of times past, a stone cube with a peaked roof and the words COUNTY SHERIFF AND JAIL emblazoned on a sign that hung over the door. It stood alone, across a wide parking lot from the more modern government center, three stories of steel and glass housing the courts, jail cells, and probation services. A bell rang when I pushed through the door and a woman with a mop of curly dark hair stood up to meet me.

"My," she said, "are you feeling okay? You look like you've seen a ghost."

"I could use some water," I said, my voice a squawk from lack of saliva.

The woman pointed me to a seat and then turned to get me a cup of water from the cooler behind her desk. Beyond her, inside an old jail cell from which the barred door had been removed, a man in uniform was reclining in a chair with his feet up on his desk, eyes closed. The woman whispered something to the sleeping man and he startled, sat up, and shuffled through the papers on his desk before he stood, took the water from the woman, and walked my way. He was a tall and thin man with a bushy blond goatee and blue eyes that stared right through you. The name tag pinned to his chest read SHERIFF BRAUN.

"You're new in town, aren't you?" he asked, handing me the cup, which I took and drank to the bottom before responding. I could feel the moisture as it hit my stomach, then the battle as it attacked the dryness of my body, radiating out from my center until it reached its limit. I was far from feeling better and it began to affect my mood.

"What's that got to do with anything?" I snapped.

"Nothing," he said. "But this town has very few pedestrians. Hard not to notice when a new one arrives. Did I see you walking with Jennifer Freya the other day?"

"Jenny? Yeah. We're friends."

"That's nice. She and I go way back. Lord knows, she needs some good friends. Anyways, what can we do for you?"

"My mother," I said. "She's missing."

"A missing person. I see. Is that why you look so upset? It's like you haven't slept for a week. Claire, bring me a missing persons form!"

His assistant brought the form and we went over all the details. Height and weight, hair color, birthday, but we stumbled when he asked me when I saw her last.

"I think it was 1988," I said.

"What?"

"Nineteen eighty-eight."

"That was nine years ago."

"But she moved away from here less than two years ago."

The sheriff grew flustered but I couldn't understand why.

"I'm sorry," he said. "She may be gone but she is not missing. She's an adult and can do what she pleases. Unless you can prove that she was abducted or had some crime committed against her or she has some sort of mental illness that would cause her to wander off, but it seems to me that none of those conditions are true."

"But," I said, "she's gone. What am I supposed to do?"

"You shouldn't get your hopes up," he said. As he spoke of filing paperwork and running her name through the database, a subtle rage built inside me. My muscles tensed and my stomach contracted as I tried to contain my anger at my mother for leaving, at the sheriff for his inability to help, and at myself for caring so much. I could have taken that hundred dollars and done anything else but here I was, chasing down someone who didn't want to be found. Tears welled up in my eyes, though from where my body took the moisture I'm not sure. The sheriff went on talking as I made my decision to give up on finding my mother and, with the release of this tension, I leaned forward and vomited coffee and water all over the floor.

I apologized and asked if I could clean up, but Claire wouldn't have it. She told me I needed to go home and get some rest and that's what I did. I was back in bed by noon and didn't wake up until the next day.

J's house was unlocked, so I stepped in and shut the door. It was dark. I flipped a switch but there was no light. Upstairs, two doorways were curtained off with bedsheets, at the end of the hall a bathroom, also newly doorless. My face in the mirror. I wondered aloud where the doors had gone.

"Who cares about doors, Lucky," J called from his room. "Where's my fucking Nintendo?"

Behind the curtain I found J sitting naked on the edge of his bed, tracing the tattoos on his arm with his fingertip. An outline of an eagle and below that, in an uneven hand, the word *Dad*. He had grown thinner since the day I met him at the fairgrounds but he looked good, so lean that the muscles on his stomach and arms stood out in high definition, his face all sharp angles and cheekbones. Next to him, under a thin blanket, Mary slept.

"If you don't have it, you better have some other way to make yourself useful."

He had been telling me that he wanted to trade me something for my game system since he found out I had one, but I kept forgetting to bring it. To make it up to him I found the rolling tray, emptied my pockets onto it, and went to work with the last of my weed in the chair near the window, trying to stop my casual glances over at him. Outside, Sisyphus and Lucifer stood like statues. J rose from the bed and dressed in clothes that he found on the floor. Mary woke and asked J to get her a shirt, then took it under the blanket.

"Why so self-conscious, babe? It's only Shane and he's asexual. He slept right next to Jenny and didn't even try to fuck her."

"I can't do this now," she said, "I have to go to work." She threw the blanket aside, stood up, left the room.

A few minutes later, we found her downstairs in the kitchen, dressed in her work uniform, trying to tune to a station on the television. J pulled a string that hung from the ceiling. The fixture clicked but nothing happened. He opened the refrigerator, no light in there either, took three cans, and passed them out.

"If that fiend is going to keep stealing the lightbulbs," J said, "we're going to drink his pop."

Mary slapped the top of the television.

"Half the antenna is missing," she said. "What the hell do you do with half a TV antenna?"

J cracked open his can, then walked past me and Mary, went outside to see the dogs. Mary switched off the television and we followed him. Lucy and Sissy whined and barked like little puppies when they saw J, standing on their hind legs to paw at his belly and lick his face. He grabbed their ears and patted their heads and crouched down to kiss them back.

After we dropped Mary at Taco John's, J took the wheel, I climbed into the passenger seat, and we drove back to the house to pick up Sissy and Lucy. The dogs weren't allowed in the car because they left thick black hair all over and they took turns chewing the corners of the front seats. The upholstery was shredded and most of the underlying foam was missing, but when Mary brought up these examples J merely denied that this was proof that his dogs had been in the car.

"Mary missed her period," J said once we were heading south on the highway, then turned up the radio to sing along with the band, shouting the reasons why he took so many pills. Outside my window, sod farms rolled by. Wide green fields split by thin patches of leafy trees and bushes, other people's grass before it was cut into squares, made into lawns. A single telephone line rose and fell along the road. I lit the joint I had rolled back in J's room and passed it to him. J sang on: *Everything, everything, everything, everything.*

"What are you going to do?" I asked, knowing full well Mary wasn't the type to get an abortion.

"It's still too early to tell, too early to even take a pregnancy test, she said, but if there's really a baby in there she's going to keep it."

She, he said, not we.

"Are you happy?"

"These things happen," he said. "I'll deal."

He slumped in the driver's seat, defeated, suddenly not the person I thought I had known, and I was reminded of a picture of my father and my uncle from when my father was a senior in high school. My father, dressed head to toe in denim for some reason, stood next to my uncle, who carried on his shoulders his daughter, my cousin who was taken away from him before I was born. The confident smile on my father's face in that photo had been something foreign to me when I first saw it, as well as the golden curls that framed his eyes. This is not to say I had never seen my father smile, we had happy times too, but these were only brief respites from his greater burden, the weight of the world, my weight on his back. This had now found J, the gravity of adult life, the consequences of his wild youth.

J turned off the highway, stopped at a Pump 'N Munch, and asked me if I had any money for drugs. I took two fifties out of my pocket, most of my paycheck from the Aurora, and handed them over. When J got out to pump fuel, the dogs shifted in their seats and watched him through the back window. He went in to pay and came out with a small bag. A pack of cigarettes for me, another for himself. He unwrapped a piece of beef jerky, broke it in two, and threw one of the pieces over his shoulder. The dogs fought over it and after Lucy won, J put the other half in Sissy's mouth.

"I do know one thing," J said when we were back on the road. "The next eight months will be my last chance at a real life."

"Then?"

"The little guy comes."

We rode without speaking for a while. I reached back to pet the dogs. Sissy had fallen asleep and Lucy was quietly chewing on my seat. J pulled off the highway again and parked on a side street. The dogs barked and squealed when he got out of the car and walked around the corner. I dug in the grocery bag, found another stick of beef jerky, and split it for them.

A few minutes after J left me, a familiar vehicle appeared at the end of the road, rolled up to the car, stopped. Svenson. He must have left his brother's house when J arrived, knowing that he'd find me hiding out somewhere nearby. He angled his truck so no cars could pass and got out. The dogs sensed a change in my mood—Sissy let out a low growl and Lucy joined her.

"Look what we have here," he said. "The faggot longhair who wishes he was a woman."

The growling grew louder as he came up to my door. He reached through the window, took some of my hair in his hand.

"Just like a bitch," he said, then pulled my hair so hard that my head hit the doorframe.

Loose from his grip, I scrambled into the driver's seat to get away from him and Lucifer lunged over my seat, closing his jaws around Svenson's wrist. He shook the dog off and took two steps back. Blood ran down his arm and dripped from his elbow onto the street. Lucy barked, head out the window. Svenson walked backwards to his truck, eyes on me. Stood there staring until a horn sounded behind him.

"You're going to pay for this," he said.

After the horn sounded a second and third time he climbed into his truck and went on his way, bloody arm out the window.

J came back and wouldn't stop talking. He kept saying that I wasn't going to believe it, that I had to try it, over and over. He wouldn't shut up. I couldn't get a word in edgewise, let alone tell him about Svenson. When I finally told him to get to the point, he pulled over and showed me, and I was happy to see what it was. I longed for the contentment that my last night with the powder had given me and the mere sight of it in J's hands cleared my mind of my problems with both Svenson and my mother. We could focus only on the task before us.

J didn't ask me how I wanted it, grabbing a take-out spoon from among the garbage on the floor of the car and going to work. I looked away when it happened—he told me to hang my arm loose and then flex it and then it was done. All that remained was a small red dot in the crook of my elbow. A chemical taste bloomed inside me, vapors filling my lungs, and with these first breaths I had the feeling of smoking but backwards, the sweet taste of the drug mixed with an earthy flavor, a meaty, animal taste. Blood, sweat, salt, me.

I looked up from my arm to see that an awesome wave had formed on the horizon and was moving toward us. Strong winds blew fallen leaves and small animals around the car. My flannel and hair were flapping and I ran my hands down my chest to keep my shirt in place. The wave was moving with great speed, throwing houses and trees and telephone poles into the air and letting them fall where they may. Heavy raindrops exploded like bombs on the hood and windshield as the wave neared. I closed my eyes and felt the car fly up. I flailed with both arms to hold on to something, anything, but we didn't tumble or tip—the car landed right where we had been. When I opened my eyes the wave was gone, the rain had stopped, and the wind was dying down. In my right hand was the door handle and in my left, J's right. The taste remained.

"Maybe you aren't asexual after all," J said.

We sat there a moment, hand in hand. The day had taken on a dead calm, the sun beat down on the blacktop. I looked up at J, then down at our hands, then up at him again before pulling mine away. Embarrassed, I stared out the windshield. One of the dogs whimpered.

J started the car. Lit two cigarettes, gave me one.

"I was scared my first time too," he said, pulling back onto the road. "You don't need to feel bad."

I didn't speak. I couldn't. The clarity I felt was too strong; my mind couldn't keep up. I took long, deep breaths while my cigarette burned away in my hand. Feeling a bit better by the time we got back to J's,

I found a pen and a scrap of paper and sat in the chair near the window, trying to describe the wave while he split and measured the rest of what he had picked up. It was a huge pile. I wasn't sure what he was planning to do with it.

First, J gave me my hundred's worth and took the same amount for himself. Then he chopped the rest into a pile on a round mirror before he left the room and returned with a bottle of vitamins. He took two pills, crushed them to powder, and mixed that into his pile of drugs. Then he put small amounts of the mixture on little squares of paper that he folded into envelopes.

"Let me know if that other friend of yours would be interested in this stuff."

I shrugged and exhaled deeply.

"And if anybody asks," he said without looking up at me, "you don't know anything about any vitamins."

We didn't sleep for days that time. Running we were, hiding, J from his upcoming fatherhood and I from my mother, stringing ourselves along dose by dose, withholding long enough to let the withdrawals have their effects as well. The right amount of darkness caused the world to fold in on itself, the secrets of the universe spelling themselves out across the wall of my room at the Arlington, this window zooming in on the foreign world of which I had only caught glimpses previously.

J and I spent a couple afternoons cruising around Holm in Mary's car selling J's mixture of vitamins and crystal meth, telling people where he lived, and before long they started showing up at the Dairy Queen looking for us. Scary people. Twitchy eyes, pockmarked faces, missing teeth. These people were not happy, this parade of stick figures in clothes two or three sizes too big, a march of zombies. They were not riding waves when they got high, rather raising their heads out of the water for a single breath, a gasping for life, before dropping back into an abyss of darkness and bodily pain. J told me that we weren't like the people who bought most of his product, that we would know when to stop, that we were too young to end up like them. I'd hang outside with the dogs while he went in and out of the house with his buyers and then when the sun went down we would move into J's room and fix up ourselves.

"To infinity," J would say, quoting some movie I hadn't seen, "and beyond."

It is difficult to pull specific events out of the fog of this first week-long drug binge and those that came after. There are, of course, those common to all: the grinding teeth, the shifting shadows, the marathon masturbation sessions when I found myself alone for the night. More than once I walked the streets until the sun rose, the streetlamps guiding me with their yellow cones of light in the darkness. But in my memory it all folds back into a single thread, one long night punctuated by bursts of sunlight. At some point, I brought over a couple of notebooks and we each took to them with pencils. J drew and I wrote but neither of us were very good at what we did. My poetry narrated our lazy days in the sun, the waves washing over us, and J drew abstract designs that grew more and more complicated as he worked, until the page was a solid block of inky darkness, a monument to the energy bound up inside both of us.

At home late at night, the men and women on the wall stopped working and turned their attention to each other. Ancient rhythms of the heart and body. Every angle the neck can twist to take a kiss while holding the sacred contact. Every possibility of the shuffling of limbs. Yet no matter my efforts, I was trapped in the rocking. Pulling and groaning to no climax. Until sunrise. Then up with my pants and off to work with no rest.

I was working a dinner shift, awake for the fifth day in a row, when my last hit of speed wore off and the waves receded. That was when my fear returned, when my dreams crept into my waking life. Customers peeked around corners to give me dirty looks. The waitress walked up to me and looked down at the crook of my arm. "You disgust me," she said. "Wash the silverware and bring it out to the dining room."

I did as she asked.

"He's got tracks," someone said in the break room. I ran to the doorway but no one was there.

I worked with my head down. Dirty dishes were brought to me in tubs. I took the plates and bowls and stacked them on the counter, dumped the liquid from the glasses and put them in the slots overhead. The silverware was tossed into soapy water to soak. I loaded the plates onto racks and pushed them into the dish machine. Ninety seconds later they came out the other end. Thick clouds of almost invisible insects swarmed. I swatted them away from every white surface. I worked and worked and soon there was no more work to do. All the dishes were washed and stacked and brought to the line, and the bathrooms were stocked with paper towels, hand soap, and air fresheners.

"Hey, dishrat," the cook yelled. "Bring me a pork chop."

I went to the cooler to find one and came back.

"What are you doing with that?"

"I brought it for you."

"Is it my birthday?"

"You called for a chop."

"You need to lay off the drugs, dishrat, you're losing it."

The cook turned back to his work. On my way to the dish room I heard him mumbling so I peeked back around the corner. His features had disappeared, his face was flat and barren like the pad of a thumb.

"What the fuck are you looking at?"

I ran back through the dish room and into the break room. I put the chop back in the cooler, then sat down and lit a cigarette. The cook's voice floated through the doorway, a whisper, but I knew he was talking about me.

"Knives," the waitress said.

I jumped up and ran to the doorway.

"Act cool," the cook told the waitress. "I think he heard us."

I snuffed out my cigarette, then snuck up to the cook's line where the cook and the waitress stood, bored, as if they hadn't been talking about me. A chef's knife and a serrated sat on the cutting board.

"Do you need anything?"

"No."

"Your knives could use a quick wash."

I took them to the dish room and set them in the sink. From the drawer where we kept the kitchen utensils I took the other knives and the sharpening steel. I wrapped it all up in a white towel, brought the bundle to the walk-in, and hid it in a box of lettuce. I walked out of the cooler calmly, as if I weren't being threatened, and when I saw that no one had seen me go in or come out, I took off my apron, threw it in the linen hamper, and ran out the back door.

Minutes later I was knocking on J's doorjamb, the bedsheet flapping out around me on the breeze.

"Who is it?"

I answered.

"I was sure you were the cops, knocking like that," he said, weathering paranoia similar to mine. He sat in his chair smoking a cigarette while a single candle burned in the window. The room was dark and

I thought I saw someone sitting in the corner but when I turned and looked I could see that no one was there.

"Man," I said. I didn't know what to say. I looked again to the dark side of the room, then I sat down on J's bed. "So, where's Mary?"

"She went home. I thought she said something but she didn't. I don't know."

"I hear you," I said. "I can't tell what's real anymore. That's from the drugs, right? Withdrawal?"

I was so desperate for him to tell me this—my fear had drawn all of my muscles tense, ready for battle or, more likely, flight—that when he nodded I could feel my body expanding into its natural form, the relief was so great.

"I don't have any of the pure shit left," he said, "only a couple folds of the vitamin mix. You should try to get some sleep. That's the best way to send the shadows back where they came from." He held out a small plastic bottle with squared-off corners, shook it so it rattled, handed it to me. SLEEP AID, it said on the label. "Six of those will put you out no matter what."

Afraid that I'd fall asleep on my way home, I didn't take the handful of pills until I made it back to the Arlington, tossing them in my mouth as I creaked up the stairs and taking water straight from the faucet in my room to wash them down.

I had felt much better after talking to J but it wouldn't last, because my visions again turned on me when I looked into the shadows on the wall. Instead of industrious men and women working or pairs of lovers straining to please each other, small pops and explosions gave way to words of smoke that floated out into the room. FAGGOT, BITCH, LOSER. The words dissipated into clouds of bugs that spiraled into vapor, coming together again to make the next explosion of abuse. LAZY, STUPID, LONGHAIR. I stood and turned on the lights to find that the words had etched themselves into the walls. Standing in the center of the room I was suddenly unsure where I was. Perhaps I had wandered into the room, in the same position as mine on another floor. These looked like my windows but I couldn't remember decorating my walls with spray-painted insults. None of the stuff in this room looked like anything I owned. The rumpled clothes on the floor could have belonged to anyone.

I collapsed before I could figure out where I was, whose apartment I had wandered into, having forgotten that I had taken pills to do exactly that, but my mind had been racing so quickly that it couldn't be subdued. I lay there for a long time, a prisoner in my own body, listening to the red light over the intersection click on and off to the beat of my heart and my shallow breathing, watching Plasticine melt in my mind's eye like the images in a kaleidoscope until I fell into the darkness.

Six

I was out behind the More-4-You admiring the new piece by HOPE, this one a complex twisting of letters linked in impossible ways, when Russell showed up with the usual bulge in his waistband, this time a pocket flask he had stolen from his father. He opened it up and took a drink, then passed it to me.

"It's not even noon yet," I said. "And I have to work tonight if my boss doesn't fire me."

"It's noon somewhere," he said, "and you'll be fine by five. Smoke some weed or something and it'll give you the energy to get through it."

I took a small sip but held the flask up with my tongue sealing the hole to make my drink seem bigger than it was. When I handed it back to him, he turned south and waved for me to follow. We crossed Center on the tracks and continued along them. The water tower fell away, then the government center, and the last business in town, the A&W, and we were in the country. Looking straight ahead the tracks went on forever, disappearing as they converged on the horizon, a long arrow pointing to where I was headed: Minneapolis. The farther we got, the lighter I felt, and not only from the whiskey. I was surprised, after a long silence, to hear that Russell felt the same way.

"Sometimes I think about hitching the train out of here, I'd just take off and never look back," Russell said, each of us walking the rails as if they were tightropes, a long stick between us so we could use each other for balance. "I'd jump on and ride it south as far as I could take it—I bet this shit goes all the way to Texas."

"Don't you think it would stop in the Twin Cities first?"

"Even Murderopolis would be better than this shithole."

"I hope so."

Russell was pretty scrawny for a Holmer, which is to say we were the same size. So when I stumbled off my rail, pulling with me the stick between us, he fell off his and came crashing my way. We collided and he put his hand on my shoulder to steady himself but he didn't make another move like he had on the bridge. Though I was too embarrassed to talk about what had happened, I had to know if that night had been a fluke—whether it was me that he was after or if he would have rolled on top of anyone who pulled him out of that hole. As we made our way toward wherever he was taking me, I tried a couple more moves to land me in his arms, but it didn't happen. It was like he was two different people—he even started talking about girls.

"I fucked this girl," Russell said, climbing back onto his rail. "She was damn hot." He made gestures near his butt and chest to show me how hot she was.

"Yeah? What's her name?"

"Didn't even tell me," he said. "I met her at the fair after you ditched me. Took her over to the stables. Horses can really turn a girl on, probably from looking at their huge cocks."

This was supposed to be a joke but I didn't laugh. Was he trying to make me jealous? The stick twitched between us—Russell stumbled but regained his balance.

"What about you?"

"I've never kissed a girl."

"But you want to?"

I was quiet for a moment, thinking maybe he hoped I would say it was him I was after. I wanted to tell him this but the words wouldn't come. In the end I told him about Jenny, about the day at the More-4-You and our camping trip. It was true, after all, that I was drawn to both of them, similar as they were. Describing her as beautiful, smart, thin, and blond, it came to me then that the only differences between them were demeanor and gender. As I was finishing my story I turned to Russell and saw he was holding his free hand to his mouth to contain his laughter.

"You're here two weeks and you fall in love with the craziest girl in town?" he said. "That's classic."

I pushed out on the stick, sending Russell sprawling onto the rocks next to the tracks.

"Fuck, man, it's not my fault she's crazy," he said, standing up, brushing dirt from his pants. He got back up on the rail and took his end of the stick.

"Are you gonna tell me the story or not?" I asked.

"Not much of a story," he said. "I don't know the details beyond she got caught stealing when she used to live over that way."

He pointed off to his left, the wrong side of the tracks.

"It wasn't only shoplifting, I'm pretty sure I heard she stole a car or two as well. Like she's a kleptomaniac and she has been since she was a kid. She didn't look then like she does now, more a stick figure with a boy haircut and glasses, I mean real glasses—thick frames with lenses that gave her cow eyes. She looked like the most innocent girl in the world until one day the police came into the school and arrested her and she wasn't in class for the rest of the year. Weird thing is that when she came back, they moved her up a grade into my class. We'll be seniors next year. Someone told me she's a genius. I wouldn't know, I've never talked to her. Still looked all cow-eyed until a year or two ago. She's hot now, sure, but watch out."

I tried to imagine a younger Jenny in glasses on a shoplifting spree. It wasn't too difficult.

"I should go rob a gas station, maybe they'll put me in college."

"I don't think anyone will mistake you for a genius," I said. He laughed but we both knew it was true.

We walked on in silence, abandoning the stick and instead crunching the rocks alongside the tracks for a while before we heard the whistles behind us. Russell veered off the tracks to the right and I followed, stepping past him into the long grass at the edge of the trainway, but Russell stood a few feet from the rails, turning toward me to yell over the sounds of the train's approach.

"I'm gonna hitch it!"

The conductor sounded the whistle for a long beat as he passed and Russell held his ground. I didn't think he was going to do it but then he started jogging alongside the train until he caught its pace, reached out for the nearest car ladder, and pulled himself up. He hung off the side, looking back, and waved in a way that told me to come along. I stepped back onto the rocks and ran toward the train, pacing the nearest ladder but something went wrong. Instead of taking a rung and holding it for a few steps, I tried to jump and the momentum tossed me sideways, spinning me for a half circle before I landed on my back on the rocks, my head on a railroad tie. Looking up at the bottom of the train, I felt my hair being pulled as the wheels of a car passed by, a few strands that had landed across the rail. I rolled back toward the grass and looked up to see Russell running toward me but I stood, brushed myself off, and hitched the next ladder before he got back. Feet firmly planted on the bottom rung, I looked back to see Russell catch the rear ladder of the same boxcar and between us was one of the biggest HOPEs I had seen yet, blue and white, in bubble letters drawn so full they seemed about to explode.

The train picked up speed as we came out next to the highway, quickly catching and passing the southbound cars before we swerved off between two cornfields. We rode for a while, the train going so fast that I was afraid to jump off, but a few miles out it slowed again so I waved at Russell, then made my way down the ladder to dismount before it sped up. Hanging off the ladder, I saw why the train was slowing and swung my feet back onto the bottom rung as my train car eased onto the trestle. Twenty feet below, a river. The Spirit.

The trestle was two train cars in length and soon we were on the other side. We hung from the ladder and dropped into a run, slowing to a stop as the train passed. I stepped down the riverbank and dipped my hands in the water, splashed my face. Russell followed. When the train was gone I heard birdsong, insects buzzing like power tools in the trees. The river trickled by and a family of ducks, a mother and four fuzzy yellow ducklings, passed without a look in our direction. This quiet part of the forest was very peaceful so I sat down on an overturned tree, swinging my feet and watching the summer day unfold.

Although I had lived in the middle of nowhere all my life, I hadn't spent much time out in real nature. The closest I had gotten was a ravine that ran alongside our house in Grand Marais, a short valley with no wildlife, a rusted-out Volkswagen that must have taken a severe turn off the road, a number of old mattresses, and three sealed steel drums with no labels. All this in a stagnant pool that rose and fell with the rain. Even then I had enjoyed the privacy that nature allowed, and in that gorge with a long stick for a sword, I was the king while my mother and father determined the fate of my kingdom back at the house.

Russell was not new to the natural world and he soon stripped down to his boxer shorts and waded out into the river. After dropping underwater, he turned toward me and swung his arms like pinwheels, playful, splashing at me but not getting me wet.

"Are you coming?"

My boss called me into his office when I arrived for my shift at the Aurora. I had known this talk would come upon waking in my room and realizing that most of my confusion had been voices and shadows in my head. Delusions. Running out of drugs can be as bewildering and disorienting as having them.

I hadn't had too many words with Leon since he hired me. He had shown me how to use the dish machine and told me to do anything that anyone asked me to do and since then I had, until my last shift, of course. Aside from that, I knew he chewed short-cut tobacco from the lumps in his mouth and the paper cup that he carried with him around the restaurant, and he wore a dark curly mullet that he kept tied into a ponytail. On my walks around town I had seen him riding his motorcycle up and down Old Main, hair flying behind him as he passed.

The office was a dirty box of a room, an afterthought thrown together with plywood in the back corner of the restaurant, a low counter with two chairs, a couple of calculators, and the safe, protected by a flimsy door with a hefty lock. A small frosted window set high in the wall let filtered light into the room.

"So that other shithead told me you hid all the knives in the cooler and left him to clean up after himself."

I grunted, trying to hide my guilt.

"He said you're a drug addict and a fucking idiot."

I put my hand on the crook of my elbow and looked down at the table—neat stacks of bills and coins. He had been counting money for the cash register.

"I told him that he can't call my employees idiots and then I fired him."

Leon motioned for me to sit and he took the chair near the money. He pulled the band from his ponytail and ran his finger through his hair a few times. It was far longer than mine.

"You're having a rough patch here," he said, "I can see that. But I believe in you and I want to help you."

I must have looked confused. This wasn't how I had imagined being fired would go.

"Truth is," he said, tying his hair back up, "high or not, you're the best employee I've got. You're methodical and detail-oriented and you know how to sweep the floor. Best of all, you aren't running around here telling people how to live their lives. I can't stand the holier-than-thou attitude people have in this town. That other asshole can find a job anywhere. You need help and I want to give you another chance, but don't get me wrong, if you miss one more shift you'll be out of here too."

"That's fair," I said.

He turned toward the money. "Each day at the beginning of your shift," he continued, "you count out four hundred dollars in tens, fives, ones, and coins, and switch it out with the cash tray that's up there."

"But I'm the dishwasher."

"I hired a new dishwasher. Now you're my assistant. Part-time, of course. Seems you have trouble making it here three shifts a week already, but we have to work with what we got."

He put the money in a cash tray, flipped the clips down, and led me out into the restaurant. A rotund man sat alone at a table set for six with a plate of corned beef hash and eggs. I had seen him once or twice at the Arlington, hard to forget a man this large, but he wasn't part of the group of regulars, more a chatty loner. The waitress stood near him, smiling. She mentioned the weather.

"Has it really come to this? I come here every day and all you can say is how nice it is outside?"

"Tammy," Leon said as we passed, "could you roll some silverware?"

"Right away," she said and left the man with his afternoon breakfast.

"That guy talks to anyone who walks by and never stops," Leon said when we got to the cash register. "I sometimes make stuff up to get the waitresses away from him."

He put a key in a slot on the register and turned it, pushed a few buttons. The cash drawer opened and a long receipt printed. He made it very clear that an internal receipt kept record of the daily transactions as well—"Not that you would be stealing," he said, "but that's how I'll catch you if you are"—then he switched out the trays and ripped the receipt from the printer, folded it, and slid it in with the twenties.

"We make a lot of money from catering," he said and took an envelope from his pocket. "Three or four days a week there will be one of these in the office, maybe two, that you will need to ring up. Today we have five hundred." He pressed a few more keys and the drawer popped open again.

"Now we cook," he said and led me to the kitchen, where we put on white chef's jackets and tied our hair into ponytails before we pulled on poofy white hats.

Dinner service wasn't much of a rush, at no point were we preparing food for more than three tables at a time, so it was a good night to learn. Leon showed me how to make pork chops and hamburgers and, since we served breakfast all day, chocolate chip pancakes.

The service window looked out onto the entrance of the café and throughout the shift Leon would see people come in and step off the line to say hello or shake hands. He knew every person who walked through the door, though he avoided some by ducking to the side as they entered. Around seven o'clock someone I recognized walked in, the woman with half a head of long red hair from the laundromat, and Leon took off his apron and joined her. Something about her struck me as I watched them sit down at the same table by the window where Leon had interviewed me. Her face was so familiar, but I was certain I hadn't seen her since my first day in town. Fortunately, an order came in for a Cajun pita sandwich, a plate I didn't know how to make, so I walked out to take a closer look.

"They've been at each other's throats for days now," the woman said as I approached. "It's a good thing they aren't living under the same roof anymore, but something has got to be done."

They both went silent when I got to the table, the woman's blue eyes cutting to look me up and down but I still couldn't place her. She looked like someone—maybe she was related to one of the old guys I saw at breakfast at the Arlington—everyone in Holm looked more or less the same anyway. The feature that made her stand out was her hair, but this was also true of Leon and myself. I dropped my gaze to the two coffees and the white envelope on the table between them.

"My new assistant, Shane," Leon said, introducing me before pointing across the table. "Chelsea."

We shook hands and said our pleased to meet yous and Leon told me how to make the sandwich.

"Will you throw us on a couple of BLTs while you're back there?" Chelsea asked as I was about to leave.

"Bacon, lettuce, tomato, mayo on white toast with fries and a pickle," Leon said, though we had already gone over this one, then he picked up the envelope and handed it to me. "You want to ring this up as well? Catering for four hundred twenty."

Standing too close to the register, the drawer popped out into my stomach when it opened. I counted the twenty-one twenty-dollar bills and slid them in with the rest of the cash, then went back to work. Watching them from the kitchen while they ate, I saw that what they had was not a romantic relationship. Chelsea did reach out and put her hand on Leon's for a moment after the waitress cleared their plates, but then she was up and out the door without even a peck on the cheek.

After the restaurant closed for the evening, Leon let out the waitress and dishwasher and locked the door behind them so we could do some after-hours cleaning.

"Did you bring anything with you?" Leon asked. "A joint or something?"

I shook my head.

"I hate cleaning," he said. "Now would be a good time to smoke one, if you know what I mean."

He bent down near the deep fryer and opened the door. Threaded a spout onto the drain. He took a paper cone and mounted it into a five-gallon stockpot.

"I shouldn't have to tell you that you should never use a plastic bucket for this," he said. "But some people are fucking stupid."

He pulled the release and the hot brown oil ran out the spout and into the cone. Black fries and burnt shrimp surfed the waves. When it ran dry, he dipped a saucepan into the pot to fill it with oil, then poured it into the fryer to get the last of the blackened crumbs.

"Usually this will clean it enough," he said, "but once a month we boil it out with floor cleaner and water. Lucky for you, tonight's the night."

He handed me a towel. Each of us took a handle and we carried the stockpot out the back door to the grease bin. Back inside, Leon wiped the inside of the pot with paper towels, then filled it with water. While he did that I found the bucket of powdered floor cleaner and brought it to the cook's line.

"Put that down," Leon said. "That stuff is straight poison."

I set the bucket on the floor and helped him carry the pot back to the fryer. He took a box of gloves from atop the microwave and handed me a pair. He put some on himself and added three scoops of powder to the fryer.

I helped him lift the pot and pour the water into the fryer. He turned the temperature gauge to low and we went out to the cash register so Leon could show me again how to run the report. He pulled the cash tray and walked away, leaving the drawer open.

"Always leave the register open if it's empty," he said. "Some thieves are so dumb they can't tell there's nothing inside when it's closed."

We went back to the kitchen and the water was bubbling. Leon took a long brush with a wooden handle and dipped it in the water, scrubbing the greasy sides of the fryer while I counted the money on the cutting board. Aside from the day's catering charges, we made seven hundred eighty-eight dollars.

"More than half the money comes from catering?"

"Roughly," Leon said, still scrubbing away with his back to me.

"Where is all the food for that?"

"There's a warehouse around the way," Leon said. "I used to have a business partner who ran that end of the business for me but now his daughter and two sons have taken over. You met Chelsea tonight. I think you'd be pretty good at what we're doing over there too."

"Why do you think that?" I asked. "I just learned how to cook today."

"Just a feeling," he said. "But you don't need to worry about that now—we'll get you over there once you've gotten the hang of this job."

The next night Russell was passed out, sitting cross-legged between the dumpsters behind the Aurora with an empty liter of vodka on the ground in front of him. I found him at the end of my shift when I was taking out the trash and assumed he must have fallen asleep waiting for me. He didn't stir when I swung the last bag of garbage into the dumpster so I shook him awake.

"I hate you," he said, appearing to rouse a little. Then, standing up, he said: "I throw myself at you and then you tell me you love that dirty klepto. She stole you away from me too."

He stumbled two steps closer and punched me in the face. I fell into a heap on the ground, then rolled onto my back to find him swaying, staring down at me, eyes blank.

"I'm sorry," he said. "I'm sorry." He dropped to his knees, ran his fingers softly over where he had hit me, then leaned in to press his lips to my cheek. He kissed my neck and ears and moved down my body, his hands passing my chest, my stomach, my belt, reaching for what was stirring inside of me. When he got my pants open and found what he found, he must have assumed I wanted what he wanted. And though I couldn't then say it aloud, I did.

It was over in a few minutes, excited as I was, excited as we both were, our coupling in front of everyone and the whole world before rolling into the long grass behind the dumpsters. Then, light-headed and short of breath, I lifted Russell to his feet and carried him, arm under his shoulder, to a bench around the front of the restaurant where he could wait for me to finish up with the mopping.

"I'll be right here," he said, "wide awake."

But he was sleeping before I made it back inside. I brought him back to my place after I locked up, helped him stumble and stagger down Center and up the stairs and, after I gave him a glass of water, he lay down on my bed and fell asleep again. I slept lightly that night in the space next to him, tossing and turning while Russell lay silent and still long after the sun rose, long after I made my way to the bathroom for my morning shower.

That day, since I was with him when he woke up, was the first time I saw Russell sober, if you can consider a hangover of that magnitude sobriety. The first few things he tried to say came out as groans. I ran him a glass of water and found two headache pills in the bathroom. He swallowed them down and pulled his Twins hat down low over his eyes to block out the sunlight.

"Do you have a cat?" Russell asked me. "It tastes like a cat pissed in my mouth at some point last night. And who was that guy who kept hitting me in the head with that two-by-four?"

"You were passed out by a dumpster when I found you," I said. "I've seen cats over there from time to time."

Russell let out a laugh that was half groan.

"Get up," I told him. "Let me get you some breakfast."

I thought we might get a reaction walking into the Arlington, being two guys having just rolled out of the same bed, but the rednecks at the counter paid even less attention to me when I walked in with Russell. After all, they came to breakfast in pairs too. Looking around, I noticed for the first time the severe lack of women in the Arlington—aside from the waitresses it was all men, and I couldn't remember ever seeing a female customer.

"Oh, good, I can get french toast," Russell said. "That's the only thing I get when I go out to eat."

Seven

Henry Sibley State Park was built on the twisted hills that bank the Spirit River, tall leafy trees with grassy paths running south along the river for miles. I had somehow missed this place during my initial wanderings around Holm, mistakenly thinking that the only park in town was the thin patch of grass across from the library where Svenson had accosted me for the first time.

Mary led the way, past the pavilion and the sandbox, to a stone path that took us by a small brick building with a pay phone, then along the river through arches of leaning trees a hundred years old. We followed a trail of beer cans and cigarette butts from one clearing to the next, each with a picnic table, a fire pit, and a little dirt path that led down to the river.

We were a ways back when we stopped and sat around a table. J took out a bag of weed and some papers, Russell a small bottle of whiskey that he sipped and then passed. Mary's eyes shifted between J and Jenny, very obviously scanning for any subtle communication.

"Whhwwwooooo-eeeeeeeeee," J said after a long pull from the bottle. "Happy Fourth of July!"

We had no plan beyond going to see the fireworks at sundown and, given the size of the joint that J rolled, that was a good thing. J lit it and passed it to me and, after I passed it to Mary, my attention moved to the park around us. The whispering of the trees, the wind in the long grasses, the river flowing faster in the middle than at the edges, sun glinting off the little peaked waves. The water had risen since the night Russell had nearly fallen in at the double bridges, maybe five miles upstream from where we were. I got up and made my way to the riverbank, barely aware of the conversation continuing around me as a passing cloud blocked out the sun.

"Shane," Mary called, shaking me out of my trance. "Did you find your mom yet?"

"Nah," I said and tried to wander back into my thoughts.

A murmur went around the group and then we were all very stoned. Russell yawned. Mary put her head in her hands. A strong wind came up and shuffled the leaves over our silence. I turned back to the river and studied the opposite shore where another dirt trail led up into the woods, just like the one where I stood.

"Hey, Lucky," J called from the table. "Don't jump. It's not worth it."

The sun was high in the sky when we all walked back through the park, piled in the car, and headed out of town at J's request. Once we were on the road, he told us the plan: to drive around the country in the afternoon sun with the windows up and the heat on while we smoked another giant joint. I liked the idea but no one else did. Jenny said it was a waste, Russell was indifferent since he didn't smoke, and Mary was afraid we'd be pulled over.

"That's too fucking bad," J said, turning to Jenny and Russell for support. "Mary dragged us to the park and Shane wants to go to the fireworks. We should all get to choose one thing and this is mine."

Russell and Jenny agreed and soon we were in a cloud, thick and hot. Sitting on the middle seat in the back, I couldn't see out of any of the windows and there was no way to escape the heat. Leaning in close, I could see rivers of sweat at the temples of whomever appeared in the smoke—Jenny to my left or Russell to my right—or on J's hand when it popped out from between the front seats. Our wet fingers became a problem when sweat soaked through the paper, so much so that the cherry fell off and J was unable to relight the roach.

"I hope everyone is high," he said. "Now it's time for the payoff."

When Mary turned the car onto the next straightaway J told her to floor it, switched off the heat, and had us crank the windows down as quickly as possible. The wind was so cold and crisp compared to the heat that I couldn't keep my eyes open, the air suddenly so clean it felt like I had never breathed before. It drove into my eyes, pulling streams of tears down my cheeks. Giggles rose and fell all around, as if it tickled, as if it were funny. Even Russell was a bit giddy. When Mary dropped back down to regular speed and we settled back into our seats, I found Russell's arm around my shoulders and Jenny's hand on my leg, each of their heads lolling with the bumps in the road, eyes out opposite windows. J turned around and screamed for some reason, high and excited, then raised his finger and pointed at me.

"Look at him, Mary," J said, "look at him. Look at Lucky!"

She adjusted the rearview mirror and squinted into it.

"He's never been this happy."

At the time I couldn't remember when I had been happier so I smiled in stoned silence at J and Mary and settled in deeper in the backseat.

When Russell got his chance, he led us to a rope swing a couple miles south of Holm where everyone but me took turns sailing out over the river and dropping into the Spirit. I took off my shoes and rolled up my pants, watched from the riverbank, ankle-deep in the water. At first they swung and dropped straight in, but once they got a feel for it J and Russell started doing backflips and jackknife kicks, aiming their long splashes at the rest of us. They were taut stomachs and tensed arms fighting against the force of the swing but then, upon release, became weightless over the river, twisting and turning with an unexpected grace, like gymnasts, athletes. They tried to copy these poses and postures for a while and it turned into a game of HORSE with me, Jenny, and Mary as judges, assigning one letter of the word when Russell or J failed to imitate a jump properly.

The sun was low in the sky when J finally won with HOR over Russell's HORSE and Jenny's choice led us to the double bridges. Russell and I both sat up sharply as we arrived, as if waiting for someone to tell us that they knew what happened there. I could feel his paranoia, but we had nothing to worry about because Jenny quickly put us to work as her percussion section, seating us cross-legged among the gaping holes in the deck, clapping and slapping our knees in the specific order she prescribed, while she sang:

"While my love was risin', when I was young and gay, I wrote to the devil, to ask for a delay. But n'one tells the devil how sh'ought to take her debts, now I see the end, now my love it sets."

The clapping felt odd at first but once I fell into the rhythm it was easy. After she got us all going both singing and clapping, Jenny sat down and joined us. I closed my eyes and let myself go, became one with the rhythm, with the song, with my friends.

Only when a firecracker burst, tossed by someone at a nearby farm, were we shaken away from the song. We opened our eyes and found it was dusk, loaded into Mary's car, and hightailed it to the fairgrounds for the fireworks show.

———

The high spirits stuck with me throughout the next day until I came home from work to find Jenny lying on my bed, facedown. She startled when the door opened, sat up sleepy-eyed.

"I was looking for you, but I got tired," she said. "I hope you don't mind that I used your spare key." She rubbed at her eyes, not her usual self.

"No big deal," I said, taking a seat beside her on my bed. I told her I had been at work and she groaned in response.

"I need some air," she said, then stood, walked to the door, put her hand on the knob. "Come with?"

In spite of her mood, Jenny walked so quickly that I had trouble keeping up. We went west on Center, jaywalking between Cypress and Dogwood, and keeping on straight past Fern, but instead of leaving town Jenny veered onto a path that led under the bridge, to a long rocky incline down to the Spirit. We sat down at the top near the abutment and I read aloud the graffiti that had been sprayed with a sloppy hand on the beam nearest us.

"Beautiful day?"

Jenny turned to me with wet eyes, a tear rolled out, dripped off her chin, and then my arms were around her and she was crying into my neck, sobbing. My shirt grew damp with what came out of her. I ran my hand over her hair, a softness I had never felt, and breathed in the roses and violets that always followed her around. Her cries took a rhythm all their own and after a time it slowed, the hitching in her chest softened, and she pulled her head off my shoulder to speak.

"I'm never going to get out of this fucking town," she said. "All we do is sit around smoking weed, like we're waiting for something better to come along but what are we waiting for? Will we just get high all day every day until we die?"

She put her head back on my shoulder and we looked off down

the slope. The cement pillar that rose out of the water like a ruler was stained orange and, according to the tick marks painted on the south end, the water had once reached as high as twenty-five feet, though that day the current, weak and slow, washed up under the number ten. The traffic above grew heavy as the evening rush hour arrived, the sounds of engines giving way later to the far-off noises of children playing in the park. I didn't have an answer for Jenny's question so we chain-smoked and sat there together, my arm around her shoulders, as the evening light faded to nothing more than the rippled reflection of the moon on the river below.

In the darkness I stood and, taking Jenny's hand, pulled her to her feet, then led her back the way we had come. The streetlamps were on, the amber lights giving an air of mystery to the shuffling leaves of the trees. We took Fern south and walked toward the sheriff's office, turned right on Old Main, then headed toward the neon A&W sign hanging in the distance. The wind through the trees and a couple stray crickets were the only sounds to be heard. When we reached her house, Jenny stepped up on the curb and turned toward me, taking my hands in hers. We stood in a cone of light from the streetlamp above. That single step up made us the same height.

"I'm sorry I'm so sad," she said. "This hardly ever happens. Really."

I didn't know what to say so I squeezed her hands.

"Come on," she said and waved me toward the split-level house, dark and empty save for the blue flicker in the upstairs bay window.

Inside was a cigarette haze, and I understood why Jenny always covered herself with perfume. Up five carpeted steps and there she was, Jenny but twenty years older, awash in whatever was in the prescription bottles knocked over on the coffee table before her. *Jeopardy!* on the television, though I was unsure whether she could see it.

"Mom," Jenny said. "Mom. Ma! Mother!"

No response. Jenny stepped to the table and bent over her mother. "Have you gone to the bathroom?" She talked loud and slow but her mother didn't understand, instead leaned around her daughter so she could see the television. Jenny bent down and took her mother's hand, pulled her off the couch and, with an arm around her waist, walked her to the bathroom in a way that reminded me of how I helped Russell back to my place on the night we had met up behind the Aurora.

Alone and unsure what to do, I inspected the pictures on the walls. Russell was right: Jenny had been a cow-eyed tomboy and, aside from that, she wasn't much of a smiler. In each photo she wore a grimace that made it clear she wanted to be anywhere else. Jenny and her mother were in every frame, standing before lakes and mountains and rivers, but in no picture was her father. No aunts or uncles, cousins. In what I took to be the oldest photo, toddler Jenny was being held in the arms of her mother in front of Mount Rushmore. I had no idea who took these pictures. It seemed she had no family at all besides her mother.

A minute later Jenny was back, rustling through the mess on the table to take a look at each of the prescription bottles and, finding what she was looking for, shook two pills into her hand, tossed one back, and held the other out for me.

"What do you have to drink?" I asked as she gulped her pill down dry, no longer concerned with her fate of sitting around getting high all day.

"What is the Compromise of 1877?" Jenny asked the television, echoed afterwards by Alex Trebek, then waving a hand for me to follow her, she said, "Let's go check in the kitchen."

Jenny rattled in some cupboards as I ran some water from the sink and dipped my head into the stream. Pill swallowed, I turned to see her pouring whiskey over ice, putting the bottle back in the cabinet above the refrigerator. She handed me a glass. I heard the toilet flush and then Jenny's mother ambled by the doorway, made her way back to the couch.

"This is how she is now," Jenny said, leading me back to the living room. "She has always been a little depressed, but after the pet shop closed down she's been like this more and more." She sat down next to her mother and slid an arm around her neck. "Mother? Mom? Kristina? Are you in there?"

I sat in a chair to the side and watched Jenny destroy the competition on *Jeopardy!* Jenny's mother sat by, bleary-eyed and silent, and I watched her for a time, wondering what it must feel like to be that far gone, that far removed, but I would soon know myself.

"I'd do anything if she would get better," Jenny said at the commercial break. "Whatever it takes."

I don't remember leaving or walking home that night, I don't even remember the end of *Jeopardy!*, but I woke up in my bed the next morning groggy and tired, head ringing, Kristina's medicine having dropped me into a time warp.

I was still having trouble thinking that afternoon at work when I was counting the money at the beginning of my shift. My eyes faded in and out of focus and I couldn't contain my thoughts—I'd begin something in my mind but forget how it had begun by the time I reached the end. Scanning the room, my wandering eyes landed on a collection of photographs tacked up on the wall. Most of them were taken in the restaurant and Leon was in every picture. Some were with customers I had seen once or twice, one of him and a waitress I didn't recognize, another of him on the cook's line in his white jacket and hat, but the last photo was taken outside the restaurant. I took the picture off the wall to get a closer look and found a much younger Leon with his arm around some-one who appeared to be Sven Svenson, but older, both of them pointing up at what was then the new sign that read THE AURORA. I flipped it over to read *Grand Opening, 1990* in a script I had come to recognize as Leon's.

"Are you going to sit here on the clock looking at photos all night?" Leon asked me from the doorway. "You're supposed to be up front with the cash at four."

"I'm almost done," I said, then held the photo up for him to see. "Who's this?"

He took it from me and frowned.

"That's my old business partner," he said and sat down in the other chair. "The one that used to run the catering. We were army buddies."

I laughed.

"You were in the army?" I asked. "What did you look like with a buzz cut?"

"I was pretty funny-looking. We all were. But growing up around here there isn't much else to do. Neither of us were college material."

He looked down at the photo again.

"So you guys made it back from the war and opened this place?"

"We were in Vietnam, not the Gulf," he said, flipping the picture to see the caption. "Got back in seventy-one and this was taken in 1990. I bummed around getting high for a while, taking classes on the GI Bill, but that didn't turn out too well. Not much to do around here—factory work, farming, you know—but, in any case, I was cooking at the Arlington for a while, a long while, nearly fifteen years I guess. One day Sven came in and asked me if I had any money, if I wanted to pitch in and be his chef. And now, here I am."

At the word *chef*, the bell sounded from the kitchen. The waitress had an order.

"Where is he now?" I asked.

"Sad story there. Some drunk came down an entrance ramp the wrong way and took him out on his motorcycle a few years back. I mean, how do you even get on an entrance ramp the wrong way?"

He rubbed his thumb along the side of the photo, then handed it to me and I tacked it back up on the wall.

"Three kids left behind," he went on. "A lot in common with you actually. Mother went who-knows-where and the kids left to fend for themselves. I've tried to help them out. I do what I can. I see them from time to time. They help me out with the catering for extra cash."

"That is sad," I said and turned back to the money, now understanding why Chelsea had looked so familiar when I saw her: she was Sven's older sister.

"Shit, Shane, you got me all misty-eyed over here," Leon said. "Why don't you run up to the kitchen and cook? I'll bring that money up in a bit."

Once my training was over and I had the place to myself, Russell became a frequent visitor to the Aurora—he wouldn't go away. Those last weeks of June he was everywhere I went and he was always drunk. Most nights that I worked he showed up near the end of my shift, ordered a Coke, and sat in the back of the dining room mixing into his drink whatever booze he had found that day. Other nights, bottle in hand, speech slurring, he found me on my way home from hanging out with Jenny or Mary and J. When he got drunk enough he would pull me into some dark corner and try to kiss me, and I would let him. It wasn't anything we talked about, even at our breakfasts at the Arlington on the mornings after he ended up crashing at my place, in my bed, as if what happened in the dark when Russell was drunk didn't actually happen, but it seemed to me that something was growing between us. One day I even found myself able to put it into words.

"It was an accident that I stopped getting haircuts. My dad was too busy to bring me in and by the time we got around to it I decided that it was better long. My dad didn't care—he liked it too—but almost immediately the other people in Grand Marais began questioning me, though the word *questioning* makes it sound more polite than it was. My hair wasn't even to my shoulders when I first got pushed into a wall and called a faggot. Most people would have fought back or denied it, but I didn't know, I still don't know, how is anyone supposed to know who they are when they haven't had a chance to figure anything out for themselves? I feel like most people go along with the rest of the world, without asking whether or not it is right for them. I'm attracted to girls, but I'm also attracted to guys—I think that a lot of people are this way but are afraid to admit it."

Russell had stopped eating midbite, fork loaded with french toast halfway to his mouth. "Why are you telling me this?"

"That's why I'm living here and not with my uncle. My dad was fine with my hair, with everything else—he wanted me to be whoever I wanted to be—but my uncle, even before my dad died, was always asking what it meant, and when I tiptoed around it, he came out with it and asked me if I was gay."

"What did you say?"

"I said I wasn't sure. I told him I had never kissed a boy or a girl so I didn't know, but I'm pretty sure he took that to mean I was gay but didn't want to admit it."

"That's what it sounds like to me," Russell said, setting down his fork. It appeared that he had lost his appetite. "But, again, why are you telling me this?"

"Is this when you tell me you don't remember what happened last night or any of those other nights?"

Russell sat, silent, while I recounted the first night on the bridge, dropping his eyes from mine at the mention of the punch on the second night behind the Aurora, and finally slumping forward in his seat when he heard about the nights that followed. I didn't believe him at first, that he couldn't remember spending almost every night for two weeks in my bed, but maybe this was supposed to be a secret, our secret, so secret that I wasn't even supposed to tell him about it.

After I stopped talking he picked up his fork again, ate the rest of his breakfast, then got up and left without a word.

Eight

I hadn't considered Jenny's weight and split her off an equal dose. She receded into herself, pupils swallowing up the deep blue of her irises, body limp, eyes out the window. Breathing deeply but vacant, the wave had come for me but I wondered what it was for her.

When she came back around, I saw that getting high with Jenny was different than it was with J. Where the speed had made J quiet and more self-involved, it made Jenny talk without end, skipping from topic to topic sometimes without even a breath between, from snippets of songs to conspiracy theories to elaborate practical jokes. I sat on the floor, staring at the shifting shadows on the wall, while Jenny lay on my bed talking, her words materializing before me.

"We should write up a letter and sign it with Jim Morrison's name, then stuff it in a bottle and toss it in the Spirit," she said. "It would float until someone found it and then they would think he was still alive. Just to fuck with people, you know?"

I made a noise that could've been taken as a laugh, the familiar pressure of the drugs in my body holding back my words. I found my notebooks and gave one to Jenny and we went at them with pencils. Jenny doodled while she talked and I wrote about her doing that, transcribing as much as I could of what she said. The shadows shifted as the day rolled on.

"I've spent all this time angry," she said.

I didn't look up from my notebook.

"But I should be thankful to my father. I should be glad that he made me an aware and thoughtful person. And your mother has done the same by leaving you. You should thank her."

"What?"

"I know you know what I mean," she said. "I'll find her for you. I'll find her."

"I don't know," I said. "I've looked everywhere."

"It doesn't matter," she said. "Let's get out of here."

She launched off the bed, walked over to the window, peeked outside. Hours had passed. Night had fallen uneventfully.

"Come with?"

Down the creaky stairs and out on the sidewalk, we saw the streets were empty except for a couple cars parked in a circle down at the laundromat. We ran out across Center, cut around the bank and past Taco John's and behind the More-4-You. She led me over to the loading dock and kicked at a couple wooden shipping pallets before she grabbed one and struggled to get it out of the stack. I took the other end and we walked it out toward the train tracks, angling it between the trees, and dropped it next to a train car where we leaned it against the side like it was a ladder.

Jenny told me to wait and she walked off into the darkness, the crunching of the rocks beneath her feet echoing off the back of the strip mall so that each step sounded like two, then disappeared for a moment into a copse of trees on the far side of the yard. She came back with a large backpack, hauled it over by the train cars, dropped it onto the rocks, and took out a can of paint.

"Go keep lookout."

At the end of the string of cars, I saw a set of headlights pull up the hill where the tracks met Center, slow for the crossing, roll on, and then the night was quiet and peaceful, the clicking of the mixer ball and the slow fizz of the paint taking turns with the crickets, the stars out strong and bright above us.

The shadows fell into a silent stillness, so I turned back to Jenny and watched her climb up and down the slats to reach the different high points of her piece, dancing back and forth between them while she painted. After a few finishing touches, she stepped down and dug in her backpack, took out a flashlight, and lit up her work. It appeared to be two women facing each other, each reaching with one hand, HOPE spelled between them in a flowing cursive, but then when I saw that one of the ladies was wearing jeans and a flannel I knew she had painted a picture of us. The shiny metallic blue she had used for our eyes gave us both a haunting glare.

"Beautiful," I said, "just like all the others. I can't believe that you are HOPE. I've been checking out all your pieces since I got here."

I couldn't help myself, so high and so proud, I walked over and gave her the strongest hug I had ever given anyone.

"Of course it's you," I said. "Who else could it be?"

"I usually do this when I'm sad," she said into my neck.

I didn't say that I had seen hundreds of these tags since I had moved to town, didn't want to bring up how sad she was, how sad she had to be to have painted them all.

"But I'm happy today," she said. "Thanks, Shane, I really feel good."

Had I known what was coming, I might have poisoned Svenson when I had the chance. I could have sprinkled floor cleaner on his pancakes instead of powdered sugar.

He came into the Aurora one morning and I watched him through the service window as he waited for Leon near the host stand. He stood tall and straight, so much the son of a soldier that I was surprised I hadn't noticed it earlier. He called Leon sir and was very polite with the waitress.

It had been a slow morning at the restaurant so when their order came in I had nothing else to do. Leon got a BLT like he always did—I had never met anyone who ate as much bacon as Leon—and Svenson had two over-easy eggs with hash browns and a side of chocolate chip pancakes. Considering Svenson's plates, I saw that he and I were more alike than I wanted to admit. Svenson ate slowly and thoughtfully as Leon talked, pacing himself so that he and Leon would finish at the same time. He sat tall in his seat and responded to questions with a "yes sir" or a "no sir." He knew how to act in public but gave very few people the respect he gave Leon.

The waitress gave me orders for two more tables and, when I got a chance to check on Svenson and Leon again, I saw that their plates had been cleared and now Svenson was talking over the two cups of coffee between them while Leon nodded, his mullet waving back and forth over his shoulders. I wondered what Svenson would think of that long hair if Leon hadn't been his dad's best friend. Would he chase him down on his motorcycle and beat his ass? Would he at least call names after him?

They finished up and, as they stood, Svenson held his hand out to be shaken but Leon gave him a look of disbelief and spread his arms wide. Svenson resisted briefly but gave Leon the hug he wanted and then, scanning the restaurant to see who had seen it, he locked eyes with me through the window. I don't think he recognized me, as I stuffed all my hair up into my hat while I was cooking, but he was embarrassed. I grabbed an empty plate and set it in the service window and then turned away to make it seem like I hadn't been watching.

"This portion is a little light," Leon said, taking the plate in his hand as he passed by the window on his way to the back.

He walked onto the cook's line and I took the plate from him, put it back where it belonged.

"Against sound advice," Leon said, "it appears that the South will rise again. And also, they're all set over at the other location—no more caterers needed. They are getting rid of someone but he found someone else. I'm glad. I need you over here anyways."

Jenny and I got caught smoking right in front of the Arlington. On our way to my room Jenny had wanted to take one last hit for the stairs.

"To make it interesting," she said. "I hate climbing stairs, you know."

She was setting the flame to her foot-long pipe when lights popped, a siren sang, and the Holm County Sheriff car rolled up over the curb. Jenny threw the pipe to the ground.

"Illegal," the sheriff shouted through his window, pointing. He opened the door, stepped over to us, bent to pick up the pipe. "Care to explain this?"

Jenny rocked from foot to foot, stuttering, and the sheriff let her suffer.

"It's mine," I said. "I was smoking it when you pulled up so I threw it on the ground."

"Is that so, Shane Stephenson?" The sheriff looked me up and down. "You're a goddamn liar, but you're a stand-up guy taking the blame for your friend like that. Lord knows, Jennifer here needs a good friend, isn't that right, Ms. Freya? If more people were as loyal as all that we wouldn't need laws in the first place. And though I know that if I had shown up ten seconds later I'd've caught you with the pipe in your hands, that's not what happened, is it?"

"No, sir," I said.

"And polite too," the sheriff said. "Where'd you find this one, Jennifer? Now turn around and put your hands behind your back."

She did as he asked and he snapped handcuffs on her wrists.

"Really?" she said as she turned back toward us.

"You bet," the sheriff said. "Now I want you to tell me where you got these drugs."

"We were at a concert."

"Yeah right, everyone in this town gets their drugs at concerts. Not a single drug dealer for miles around."

"This was the other week—Shane was there. Some dude with dreadlocks fell asleep and I took it out of his pocket."

"You know that's bullshit." He pulled out his ticket book. "But I think you'll remember. Or maybe you'll find someone else for me. Who knows?"

The reds and blues of the sheriff's car washed over us for a time, then Jenny said something that shocked me.

"Maybe you should take me home and tell my mother."

The sheriff's face sunk but then he snapped into action. Without a word, he slipped the pipe into his back pocket, then took Jenny by the shoulders and spun her around. After fiddling with his keys for a moment the handcuffs were off and Jenny and I watched the sheriff pull his car down off the curb and back onto the road.

"What just happened?" I asked.

"I'll tell you what happened," she said, rubbing one wrist and then the other. "He took my pipe but he forgot to empty my pockets. You got any papers upstairs?"

I unlocked the door and let her in, followed her up the stairs, and we found my room awash in evening light. Jenny got right down to business at my desk as I looked for some rolling papers, then I took a seat on my bed after I gave them to her. Outside the window, the clouds to the west looked like neat rows of purple and pink muffins as they faded to gray.

"He's in love with my mother," Jenny said when she rose from the desk, "or he was at one point. I rode home in the back of his car once a week for a while and you can tell he's fucking moony. I wish they would get back together. Everything would be fine if he would come back."

I was no stranger to thoughts like these, and though I knew it couldn't be true, that whatever went on between the sheriff and Jenny's mother was far more complicated than what Jenny thought of it, I also knew there was no talking her out of it. There had been no talking me out of it when I had the same ideas about my parents.

Jenny sat on the windowsill, the sun setting behind her, flicked her lighter, then blew the smoke through the screen. When Jenny got high you could see her thinking—others, not so much. So many people stare off at nothing, thinking nothing—you could see the animal deadness in their eyes—but Jenny's mind never shut down. It must have been hell. I'd take a hit off a joint and float off into abstract thoughts about how clouds form or whatever, but she, well, you could tell she had something in there that she was trying to forget and it didn't seem to be working.

"I used to get in a lot of trouble," she said.

"No," I said with a smile. "That can't be true."

II

Nine

The signs said THE FIRST AMENDMENT IS THE BEST AMENDMENT (AFTER THE SECOND) and KEEP YOUR LAWS OFF MY FLAG. Holmers young and old parked their cars and trucks haphazardly in the abandoned lot of the now-closed Tweed's Discount, made their way to the makeshift barbecue pit for a free plate of chicken and ribs, and then wandered among the crowd licking their fingers and browsing the southern-themed merchandise for sale on folding tables or laid out on blankets on truck beds. It appeared to be a traditional community get-together, like a swap meet or a rummage sale, until Svenson arrived with a Confederate flag mounted in the bed of his truck, cutting through the crowd like the fin of a great shark. He climbed out to cheering and was handed a megaphone that he took with his bandaged hand, a thick wrapping of gauze around where Lucifer had shredded his wrist.

"What do we want?"

"To fly Dixie!"

"When do we want it?"

"Now!"

Some of those not already in western dress returned to their cars for cowboy hats or boots or fringed shirts. A tall boy with close-cut blond hair handed out Confederate flag pins. Music blasted from speakers in the back of a pickup truck, the singer claiming to have the biggest balls of them all. The whole scene was a strange reenactment of the field party—it was most of the same people. I was surprised that no one pulled out their guns for authenticity.

Svenson climbed into the bed of the truck mounted with speakers and turned down the music as a news van pulled up next to him and parked. Two men climbed out, one with a camera and the other a microphone.

"Now we all know why we're here," he said, pointing to his truck, the Confederate flag. "I was suspended from school for refusing to take down my flag. Our flag. I was told it was disrespectful. Offensive. But it's my flag." He paused for applause. "Our flag." More cheers, whistles, a *woo-hoo*. "Of course they don't like it—it isn't their flag, it's ours. It's the best flag. No better flag than this one."

Shouts now. A few more whistles. A *fuck yeah*.

"I was suspended from school and I couldn't catch up with the work that I missed, so it cost me my senior year and now I'll finish up next fall at the alternative school. Yes, I failed high school because of this suspension and *they* say *I'm* disrespectful. They said no one in this town agreed with me. I took my flag down because I thought they were right, but since then so many of you have gone out of your way to tell me how you felt that I put it back up. I had to do it. Now look at us. Look around. We are Holm. I just wish this news team would turn that camera your way so we could show the world all your beautiful faces, all this wonderful support."

The crowd was fifty or sixty people, I'd say. Not a majority of the town. Not even close. But they were excited, I have to give them that, and vocal. Skirmishes popped up here and there, horns and yelling, punches thrown. I was happy to see some opposition.

The ruckus went on until Svenson's truck started, over-revved, then burned rubber in place for a solid thirty seconds, shooting a jet of smoke out above the gathering. The crowd parted and he sped down the road, flag whipping behind him. The others pulled out of the lot, mostly pickups but also a few cars with flags hanging out the windows, until more than twenty vehicles were moving down the streets of Holm promoting the revival of Confederate values. I watched the parade snake out onto Old Main and turn north, the news crew following in the rear, and then I went back to the Arlington.

The sudden silence in my room was thick. As soon as I arrived I had to get away, had to get high. Spying my Nintendo in the corner of my room, I remembered finally that I was supposed to bring it to J, so I put it in a plastic bag and made my way outside. A block down Old Main I ran into Jenny on her way to Walmart.

"You're going to trade that for drugs?" she asked. "Are you even trying to find your mother anymore?"

I had been so successful in blocking my mother from my mind over the past few weeks that I had forgotten all about it. Embarrassed and guilty, I muttered something about how I had been working a lot and how my leads had dried up.

"Well, don't give up," she said softly, a murmur. "You don't want to end up like the fucking losers that live in this town."

"Are you okay?"

"Did you see those assholes with their stupid parade?" she said. "Where are we, Mississippi? Anyways, I've gotta get to the drugstore."

"I'll be at J's," I said, then watched her walk to the end of the block and turn down Center.

Heavy breathing and rhythmic creaking let me know that J and Mary were busy. Can't get a girl pregnant if she's already pregnant, J had said once or twice. Unsure what to do while I waited, I paced the hallway for a time before J's roommate, Rick, called me into his room.

The first time I met Rick, I thought he was one of the walking zombies that fed on speed and vitamins, which he indeed was, but he also owned the house where he and J lived. His short blond hair receded up his forehead and deep pockmarks pitted his cheeks. He sat in one of two chairs that faced the window, wearing only boxer shorts, his thin legs looking like someone had stretched old leather over a classroom skeleton. A single mattress with no sheets lay on the floor in the corner under a rumpled blanket. He motioned toward the other chair. As I sat, Mary moaned in the other room.

"Damn, they get straight to it, right?" he asked. "I swear they walked in there a few minutes ago." Then, when I didn't answer: "What's in the bag?"

"Something for J," I said.

On the floor before us were a number of what I took to be sculptures. Thick bases with thin stems that leaned one way or the other. Some were as small as baby squirrels while one was the size of an end table and had a small dip in it that Rick had been using as an ashtray. I picked one up and saw that it was the same hard, gray material as J's dog stick, the Indestructible.

Rick tipped his head back and flicked his lighter, bringing the flame to the end of a thin silver cylinder.

"It's not what you think," he said, holding out the makeshift pipe for me to take. "This is a real treat, not like that shitty sprack that's going around."

Turning the pipe over in my hands, I could see it was made out of the missing half of the television antenna. A white residue caked the steel wool Rick had stuffed down into the hollow of the cylinder. I wasn't sure what it was, but I figured it couldn't be worse than some of the other things I had been doing, so I brought the pipe to my mouth. The flame made it crackle as it warmed and then my lips went numb. My heart sped up and my vision faded, smoothing out my surroundings. I looked over at Rick to see that his hair appeared full and his pockmarks were gone, as if I was looking into the past. This new youthful glow made him look strangely like Russell.

"Now is when, if you were a girl, I'd let you have more if you, you know—"

Squeaks and creaks from the other room. Rick reached into the hole of his boxer shorts and pulled out his cock. Stroked it twice so it stood at attention.

"You're a little girlish," he said. "Girl enough for me."

I thanked him for the offer but declined, and then Rick put himself back in his pants and grew meditative.

"I have a girl of my own, a daughter," he said after a moment, possibly to himself. "And a wife. I'm gonna fix this place up and we'll all live here together again."

Another look around the room led me to wonder how he planned to bring a child into this mess. The broken glass on the floor, the bloody rags. I would have been disgusted if I wasn't so suddenly sad for him, a lonely skeleton abandoned by his family, now living in this empty room and smoking what I assumed to be crack. Maybe his daughter was somewhere looking for him like I had been looking for my mother.

I wanted more than anything for J and Mary to finish so I could trade J my Nintendo for more speed, but the creaking from the next room showed no signs of slowing. Six hours, J had told me this had lasted, but this was when both of them were high so Mary couldn't be expected to keep up now. I would have to wait, but not here. It was too much for me to take, Rick's skeletal appearance and his odd glances my way when Mary's moans came floating into the room, so I went out to the front yard, found the Indestructible, and tossed it to Lucy while Sissy sat and watched. They barked at me, I barked back. After I looked to be sure the grass was free of slimy surprises, we all sat down together under the willow tree and watched the people come and go at the Dairy Queen.

The sun moved across the blue expanse between the willow tree and the house across Ash and I found myself wanting more of whatever it was in Rick's antenna. The initial feelings had lasted no more than fifteen minutes, but the lingering aftereffect was a longing for more. I knew the cost, the image of Rick's cock pulled through his shorts was burned into my eyes, but as I lay there in the grass, I considered it. After all, I reasoned with myself, I had let Russell do what he wanted for free.

Both dogs were dozing with their heads in my lap when Sissy startled. She stood and walked as far as her chain allowed, growled toward the north. Lucy trotted out to join her. Jenny came walking up the road with a bag from the pharmacy at Walmart and plopped down onto the grass next to me, but the dogs had their eyes on something else.

The parade was heading our way. It had dwindled down to three pickups, a small sedan with its hatchback raised, flag waving behind it like a cape, and a news van taking up the rear. Svenson's truck still led, Svenson tapping his horn with no rhythm at the front of the line. As they approached, the dogs' growls grew furious. Jenny and I stood between Sissy and Lucy to watch the parade pass.

"Shouldn't those be Swedish flags!" I yelled. "You've never even been to the South!"

Svenson slowed his truck and stuck his head out the window. He shouted and waved his bandaged hand toward me and Jenny but I couldn't figure out what he was trying to say. The commotion continued for a moment, engines revved and horns sounded, then the parade moved on. I sat back down on the lawn. As the afternoon turned to evening the dogs calmed and so did Jenny and I.

"Swedish flags?" Jenny said. "You're funny."

"It just came out," I said, then picked up the Indestructible and threw it to Lucy but he brought it back to Jenny.

"What is this?" Jenny asked. "Where did you get this?"

"Why? What's the big deal?"

"Plastic products are made from pellets. You take your mold, fill it with pellets, warm everything up, scrape away the extra, let it cool, and there's your product. The waste gets pushed into the discard chute." She showed me what she thought was a ridge caused by a pipe angled at forty-five degrees, then twisted the sculpture to show me how it had been created. "This plastic drips and hardens like an icicle, a plasticicle. Whoever gave you this either worked at the plastics factory or knew someone who did. It's about time you came up with a clue."

"I'm no detective," I said. "We've been throwing this to the dog for weeks."

"What would you do without me?"

I must have lain long in the grass after Jenny left to take her mother's pills home, maybe napped a little, for even the twilight had faded into night as dark as the dogs' fur when I came to, the Indestructible still tight in my grip. I was happy for the clue but not looking forward to talking to Rick again, to testing my resolve when faced with another offer of whatever that was we had smoked earlier. Knowing it had to be done, I made my way back into the house but, instead of climbing the stairs, I veered into the kitchen and tried to tune something in on the television. The signal was weak due to the missing half of the antenna but I found the station from Minneapolis playing the ten o'clock news. A live feed of Svenson's truck, now parked again in the Tweed's parking lot. Svenson stood tall as the newscaster recounted the altera-

RAYMOND STROM

tions he had made to his truck to mount the flag. Then the camera cut
to Svenson, who hid his bandaged arm behind his back.

"How did people react to your parade today?"

"I'm not gonna lie," Svenson said. "We saw a lot of hate on the
streets. A couple of my boys got in fights. Others yelled at us as we
passed."

"Why would you say this needed to be done?" the newscaster asked.
"What is it you are fighting for?"

"I like to think of myself as a good ole boy," he said. "We need to
protect that. It's a part of our heritage, of all of our heritage, and we
don't want to lose it to political correctness. We're all good ole boys and
there's no problem with that."

His name appeared on the screen. *Sven Svenson: high school senior,
good ole boy.* He smiled at the camera.

Something about this final presentation of Svenson swept me into
a foul mood. I stood up and slapped the television, then paced back
and forth in the kitchen for a while. Upstairs I found J's room silent so
I knocked on the doorjamb. When I got no answer, I pulled the sheet
aside to find Mary alone, asleep on the bed, the thin blanket atop her
disheveled. Confused, I stepped back into the hall but found the bathroom empty. Had J left without me noticing? Walked past the kitchen
without looking to see who was watching the television? I stuck my
head back into Rick's room.

"I should let you . . ." he said, interrupted by his hyperventilation,
"suck it before I . . . tell you this . . . but it's all gone."

Maybe Rick wasn't so bad after all. I sat down. He reached into the
shadows around his ankles and found a cigarette pack, took out two
and gave me one. Rick continued to breathe deeply, so much so that I
had to ask him if he was okay.

He nodded and held up the pipe he had made from the television

128

antenna. "It's a good thing . . . I ran out because . . . I don't need . . . any more of this . . . shit right now . . . that's for sure."

"Where did you get this?" I asked, picking up a long plastic sculpture from the floor and holding it out to him.

"I . . . made . . . it," he said. "At . . . work."

"You worked at the plastics factory?"

"Used . . . to," he said. Eyes wide, he leaned forward with a tight grip on the arms of the chair, then his breath began to slow and he sank back into his seat. When he next spoke, his description of the process that led to the creation of the Indestructible was much more succinct than Jenny's: "That's what leaks out of the anus of the fabricator."

The guy at the plastics factory had said that all the workers on her shift had been drug addicts, a description that could be applied to Rick, so I told him my mother's name and I saw him smile for the first time.

"Good woman, your mother," he said.

Jorgenson was the name he told me. My mother had left town with a man named Frank Jorgenson. Gone to South Haven, Michigan, Frank's hometown.

"She was a kind person, your mother," he said again, "no matter what everybody else says. You know, I'll bet the baby's been born by now."

I was beginning to think Rick might be an all right guy, but I decided I should leave before the drugs wore off and he tried to talk me into going down on him again. I set the Nintendo on the floor.

"Did you see J leave?"

"No," Rick said. "He's gone? Now that you mention it, it's been quiet for a while."

"Can you make sure he gets this bag? I'm going to set it on the floor in his room. Will you tell him I put it there? I'll be back tomorrow after work to talk to him about it."

I was so excited about what Rick had told me that I got all the way home before I understood how useless the information was. A name and a town—what was I supposed to do, go there and find her? That hadn't worked too well here. What if she had moved on from that town already? My hopes came crashing down as quickly as they had skyrocketed. A heaviness came over me so I lay down and minutes later, by some miracle, I fell asleep.

The next day I made my way to J's house after my morning shift at the Aurora to find Rick sitting in one of his chairs in his boxer shorts, as if he hadn't moved since the last time I had seen him. He held a lightbulb in one hand and a lighter in the other, a straw hung from his mouth. The room was quiet except for birdsong coming through the window.

"Hey Rick," I said from the doorway to no answer. I stepped in. "Hey Rick," I said again, grabbed his shoulder and shook him.

He jumped. The lighter fell to the floor and the lightbulb exploded in his hand. He held up the broken pieces in his bloody palm. From the blood-stained rags discarded among the plastic figurines on the floor and a growing pile of broken glass along the wall, I assumed he was used to this sort of situation, but he sat there, stunned, staring at the thick flow of blood now running down his arm, dripping off his elbow.

Taking a bandanna from the small table between the chairs I tied a quick tourniquet around his wrist and blotted at the wound with the loose ends.

"I crushed it," he said in a calm whisper. "With my bare hand."

"You might need stitches, man," I said. "Or at least a bandage. Keep it elevated, above your heart."

He got up, tossing from his lap the broken bits of bulb, and left the room. I kicked a couple large shards over to the wall and took a seat in the other chair. Having slept, some of my good sense had returned, and though I was grateful that he had shared with me what he knew about my mother, I knew he wasn't a person with whose bodily fluids I wanted direct contact. A minute later Rick was back with a streamer of toilet paper wrapped around his hand, blood streaked across his chest, carrying a new lightbulb, a screwdriver, and a salt shaker. The straw still hung from his mouth.

"Sorry about that," I said. "I didn't mean to startle you."

"I didn't even feel it," he said, turning over in his hands what was possibly the last lightbulb in the house.

"Have you seen J?"

"Yeah, I saw him."

Rick held the lightbulb by the metal base, letting the glass end hang toward the floor. Gripping the screwdriver by the shank, he smacked the bottom contact with the handle until the coil and filament came loose inside.

"He was pissing and moaning in his room this morning, talking to himself," he continued. "I asked him what the fuck he was going on about and he said he had to go make up with Mary."

Rick shook the bulb until the filament and coil fell out, then uncapped the salt shaker and poured in half its contents. Thumb over the hole, he shook the bulb until the salt removed the thin layer of white powder that lined the inside, then reached over and dumped it all out the window.

"He sold me this shit and then he left," Rick said. "Said he'd be back with the car." He opened his hand to reveal one of J's folded envelopes. From that he took a pinch of powder and dropped it into the lightbulb. He offered it to me but I refused.

Rick brought his flame to the glass. The powder melted and he rotated the bulb to stretch the puddle into a long streak. Another few passes of the flame turned the liquid into gas and the chamber filled with a stringy white smoke that braided and twisted around itself. He dipped the straw into the hole and inhaled. At the peak of his breath he leaned back in his chair and held it in. He exhaled and his arms fell into his lap, the hot glass coming to rest on a pink hairless spot above his knee. His leg kicked, knocking the bulb from his hand to shatter on the floor, but Rick didn't notice—his eyes out the window at something far away.

"J's gonna suffer some shit if he keeps cutting with vitamins," Rick said when he came back around. He picked up a long shard of the lightbulb and pointed at two spots where the powder had burnt black and crusty instead of melting into the air. "Some people are pissed off. I'm one of them but not the only one."

"It's not his fault," I said. "He sells what he gets."

"This isn't the same shit you get. I can see it in your eyes."

He picked up the screwdriver, held it in his fist, then left to find another lightbulb. I went to wait outside, more to put a safe distance between me and the screwdriver in Rick's hand than anything else, and found J pulling up in the car as the door closed behind me. He got out and went to the dogs, slapping at Sissy's back with the force she liked, but didn't unchain her. Scratched under Lucy's chin, then made his way back to the car, waving at me to come along, leaving Lucy standing at attention next to his sister.

"Bitch won't let me take the dogs in the car anymore," J said as we pulled out onto Ash. "Said I'll never drive again if she finds one more hair."

Black T-shirts had been pulled over the backrests of the front seats and the floor was free of garbage. The floor mats had been straightened with care. In the backseat, the trails from the vacuum cleaner could still be seen in the faux plush.

"So this is how it's going to be then?" I asked. "You're the one who wants it more now?"

J didn't answer; instead he flicked on the radio, spun the knob through the stations back and forth, then, finding static and talk shows, gave up with a weak sigh. He turned the radio off and put his hand back on the steering wheel. He hadn't said, but we were heading to Svenson's brother's place again—outside my window the familiar sod farms, the loping power line, the occasional Pump 'N Munch.

"How's the Nintendo?" I asked when I remembered, hoping it would lighten his mood.

"What Nintendo?"

"You were busy with Mary when I first got to your place yesterday and when I came back inside later on you were gone so I left it on the floor in your bedroom and asked Rick to make sure you got it."

"You don't leave stuff with Rick," he said. "He'll sell anything. Where do you think all the doors went? If anything goes missing around my place you can be sure that Rick took it."

I apologized.

"You know he went in there and looked at my naked girlfriend too."

He shook his head in a way that made me think I had disappointed him as he pulled off the highway. A couple blocks later he parked and asked me for money. I gave him two fifties, then I lit my last cigarette and threw the empty pack out the window. I watched J walk away and turn the corner, leaving me alone with my smoke.

When a truck with a Confederate flag mounted in the back appeared at the end of the road, I locked the doors and rolled up the windows, crouched as far under the dash as I could. It was Svenson, of course, and he stared me down as he passed, bandaged arm out the window, pointing, as he slowed his truck to a near stop before revving his engine and spinning his tires. I turned and watched him go, staring in that direction long after his truck dropped out of sight, until a knocking on the window brought me back. J, returning with the drugs.

J's mood hadn't broken and he flew into a rage when he saw that, since the car was clean, there were no longer any old take-out spoons on the floor, ready to use. We drove to a Pump 'N Munch because J couldn't wait to get home for us to fix up and I was surprised to see that even the extra-large dose J mixed up in a bottle cap didn't bring a smile to his face. Although I hadn't known him for long, it wasn't like J to hold on like this and it worried me.

When we returned to J's house Lucifer was gone, and Sisyphus was lying in the grass at the end of her chain. J made his way over to the dog with a treat and I hung back by the door. I heard a sound that I assumed to be Sissy, but when I looked I saw J dropping to his knees, the beef jerky falling to the ground. J yelped like a dog again and I knew there was trouble. I ran to them to see that Sissy lay in a pool of her own blood, a jagged gash in her neck where she had bled out. I kneeled by the dog and put my hand on the wound but I felt no pulse, no heaving of breath in her body. Seeing that nothing could be done, I ran a couple long strokes down her back, bloodying my hand, then I stood and followed Sissy's chain to the willow tree. I had seen death before but not murder, and the bloody flap in Sissy's neck triggered in me feelings I didn't know I had. Even the drugs couldn't stop them. The world spun around me. I put my hand out to the trunk of the willow and puked.

"He used a knife or maybe a screwdriver," J guessed, now able to talk.

Between heaves, I told J that Rick had a screwdriver in his hand the last time I had talked to him, that he had been angry about the vitamins.

"Not so strange that he's nowhere to be seen now."

J rounded the house, then returned a moment later with a shovel in each hand, spearing one into the ground before going to work with the other. I wiped my mouth and hands on my shirt, then took the other shovel to join J in his labor. In silence we dug the hole, taking turns with the earth in an even rhythm of metal on dirt and stone.

When the hole was deep enough, J threw his shovel to the ground, then stripped off his flannel and threw it in the grass. His T-shirt was soaked through with sweat. Long purple and brown bruises ran up the insides of his arms. Clearly, he was using much more than I was. He unchained Sissy from her collar and rolled her into the hole. Picked up his shovel and stood at the head of the grave.

"This is all Mary's fault," J said, his attempt at a eulogy. "If it wasn't for her, we wouldn't have had to leave these two behind with that dog-killing crackhead."

"You really think Rick did this?"

J didn't answer, rather, he sunk his blade in the dirt and dropped the first shovelful over Sisyphus, then I joined him in the effort until her grave was a dirt mound in the middle of the front lawn. That done, we left the shovels sticking out of the ground and went inside to split and measure. After he gave me my share J worked on his knees over a mirror on the floor, hands shaking as he scooped the mixture of drugs and vitamins onto the little squares of paper, and I watched from the chair, an ignored notebook sitting in my lap. A single tear fell onto one pile, so he swept it into a spoon and prepared it as his next dose. This time I didn't get any—only when he pulled the needle out of his arm did he look my way.

"You don't want to be here when Rick gets back," he said. "I'm gonna fucking lose it."

I didn't want to be alone so I set out toward Jenny's, but halfway there I noticed a familiar truck trailing me so I veered off course. It was Svenson, and I knew he was after me when I made four rights around the same block and he was still there. I zigzagged through the streets back toward the Arlington and he fell off my trail a couple times but was quick to pick it up again, the last time screeching to a stop as I crossed Center. He lay on his horn as I stood there face-to-face with the grille of his truck, and then I ran down Cypress as fast as I could. Svenson floored it, took two rights without stopping, then he was coming down North First as I crossed. Behind me, he swung left and paced me at the speed I was running.

"Look at that pretty hair," he called.

I crossed another street onto a fenced-off block that was all grass, a spare field that belonged to the middle school. Halfway down the block I cut to the fence, swung myself over, and ran to the center of the field. Dropping his speed to a crawl, Svenson drove around the block, making lefts, Confederate flag billowing. Each time he made a left I turned with him, watching, waiting for him to stop his truck and get out, climb the fence so I could turn and run the opposite way. He circled the block once. Twice. He stopped at the corner, leaned out the window to let me know he was watching, then got moving again. Three times around the block. Four. Just when I thought it might go on forever, he jumped his truck up over the curb and crashed through the fence, barreling straight toward me.

Stunned, I did not run. Svenson fishtailed to a stop, tearing up the grass with his back wheels, then jumped from the cab. He didn't say anything, merely floated toward me with his fists before him, swung, and then I was on the ground. He dropped to his knees beside me and opened his hand. In his palm was a folding knife with an ivory handle. Sweat popped out on my forehead as I tried to struggle away from him but he held me down with one hand. When I gave up the fight, he swung a leg over me, straddling my chest with his knees on my shoulders.

"Are you nervous?" he asked, running his fingers through my hair almost lovingly with his left hand, the loose threads from the bandage tickling my neck. He sat there a moment with his hand on my head, and I thought he might lean forward and kiss me. He was beginning to remind me of Russell.

"I tried to go easy on his dogs," he said, opening the knife with a click. "But one got greedy and ate both steaks."

He took a thick lock of my hair and sawed at it with the knife until it came free. The blade wasn't sharp, but he made up for the dullness by pulling and tearing what wouldn't be cut. When the last strand snapped he put the point of the knife to my neck, my fear got the best of me and a patch of wet warmth spread in my pants.

"I had to use this on the other one," he said, sticking the point into the skin of my neck not quite hard enough to puncture. "It was easy and it was quick."

He stood up and snapped the knife shut.

"Your friend won't be so lucky," he said and stomped the heel of his boot down on my forehead. "If you see him before I do, tell him I did this to the dogs for the vitamins. My brother may have gone easy on him, but I'm in charge now."

He climbed up into his truck and slammed the door, my clump of hair still in his hand, then he drove a couple of circles around me, tearing rounded grooves into the grass with his wheels, before he left the way he came.

It took some time to get up before I made my way to the Arlington to shower and change my clothes. On my bed afterwards, wrapped in a towel, I wanted to climb under my blankets and never come out again, but I knew I had to go back to J's to tell him that it was Svenson who killed Sissy, not Rick.

When I got there I found Lucifer lying on the front lawn with his head on his paws and his eyes shut. I placed my hand on his collar, ran it down his back, rolled him over. No wound, no blood, only cold, dead dog. If I hadn't known, I would have assumed he died of grief over the death of his sister. Inside, the house was dark and quiet. No one answered when I called. In the kitchen, the refrigerator had been tipped over and the television thrown to the floor, the missing antenna no longer a problem now that the screen was cracked. I climbed the stairs to find that one of Rick's chairs had been tossed into the bathroom, breaking the mirror and the toilet bowl. Both bedrooms were destroyed. Holes in the walls. Windows shattered. The mattresses had been ripped open and the hay inside kicked all over the rooms. The floors were littered with beer cans, cigarette butts, shards of glass, needles, plastic figurines.

There was nothing to be done inside; J had broken everything in sight, but Lucy was outside lying dead on Sissy's grave. I went out front, picked up the same shovel I had used to help bury his sister, and dug another hole. As I was leaving, I found the Indestructible again, the plastic stick that would lead me to my mother, and placed it at the head of their shared grave—had all of this happened a day earlier, Rick would have taken off before I got the chance to ask him about my mother, and I never would have found her.

Ten

No one answered when I got to Jenny's house, though I could see the blue glow of the television in the front window. I tried the knob but the door was locked. I waited on the steps for a while as the sun went down and then made the slow walk home in twilight. The weight of the day hung heavy on my shoulders and even the envelope of speed in my pocket couldn't raise my spirits. I had been beaten and J's dogs were dead. J had disappeared and Mary, also nowhere to be found, had probably taken off with him. Back in my room, I hid the drugs in my desk, threw back six sleeping pills, and waited for the darkness to fall.

That night, I dreamt again that my legs didn't work but this time the town was empty. Not a single car or person or even a bird, just me, locked in place halfway between the Arlington and the More-4-You. I tried to move my legs and I could feel the effort rippling up and down my body but nothing happened. My mother, my father, J, Mary, Sissy and Lucy, Russell. All had left me and here I was, alone in the sun, unable to move, with no relief.

The next morning, standing in my underwear at the pay phone

outside my room, I called Jenny to be sure she wasn't gone too. When she answered I told her she had been right, that the Indestructible had been from the plastics factory, that Rick had worked there and known my mother.

"But what do I do with that?" I asked. "Get on the bus again? What if she's gone already?"

"We'll call information," she said. "You really don't know much about telephones, do you?"

We met up outside the Arlington and wandered for a while as I told Jenny about what Svenson had done, about the dogs and the chase, and we ended up in the cemetery. Most of the graves had humble markers, but a few were monstrosities. An angel the size of a full-grown woman mounted on a cement pedestal, an obelisk, and an aboveground crypt, large and square with a thick sheet of smooth black marble atop it. I slowed to read the names, to think about those who had passed through here mourning these dead. The older stones all had Swedish names. Karlsson, Söderberg, Ekström, Johansdottir. Of course, we walked past some Svensons, even a Svenson named Sven, 1949–1992, Leon's business partner and Sven's father.

I dropped what I was saying in the middle of the sentence, distracted by the image of those two, five years younger, dressed in black, sad and silent, watching a casket being lowered into the ground. Yet another thing Svenson and I had in common.

"I can't believe what he did to those dogs," Jenny said, drawing me out of my reverie. "J was a prick but Sissy and Lucy didn't deserve that. Did you call the sheriff?"

"No," I said. "What could he have done?"

She shot me a look that made me feel pretty stupid.

"Dog murder," she said, "destruction of property. Seems pretty clear to me."

"I guess drug dealers don't invite the police to their houses, even when they need them."

"Svenson's an animal," Jenny said. "He needs to be locked up."

We got on a brick path that led to the tall peaked church that stood at the entrance to the cemetery. We passed some Hansons and Forsbergs and we came to another large-scale grave, a double with a statue of a woman sitting in a chair, holding a book open but her eyes were looking over what she was reading at the empty chair above her husband's grave. The woman, Marta Mattson, had been born in 1883 and had died in 1920. The man, Johan, had been born in 1881 but, according to the gravestone, had not yet died. Or hadn't been buried next to his first wife but with his second.

"That's so sad," I said.

"It's all sad," Jenny said without stopping to look at what I saw. "It's a graveyard. What did you expect? Let's go to the park. There'll be plenty of time to hang out here when we're dead."

Jenny wanted to pick up some things on the way so we took the long way down Old Main and stopped at the dime store where the clerk eyed us as we entered, his leering suspicion appropriate.

"We need cowboys and Indians," she said, and the clerk pointed to the back of the store.

Jenny turned toward the wall of candy and I walked off between the aisles. After a minute I yelled to the clerk that I didn't see them.

"By the little green army men," the clerk called. "In the toy aisle. Not in crafts."

I walked into the toy aisle, looked right at them, and then yelled again that I still couldn't find them. The clerk came, pointed out the cellophane packages hanging in front of me, and walked me back to the cash register where Jenny was waiting.

Outside, we wove through the parking lot until Jenny found a car with her brand of cigarettes, then she led me through town, down the middle of the street past the library and the water tower, *Holm Sucks*, finally entering the park on a set of secret stairs at the dead end where South First met Fern. We came out of the woods near the main entrance of the park, shot past the pavilion and the playground, rounded the corner, and Jenny picked up the pay phone. It only took a minute. She dialed three digits and asked for the number and address of Frank Jorgenson in South Haven, Michigan. A moment later she said into the phone: "Sure, why don't you connect me now," and handed me the receiver before she dropped three quarters in the coin slot.

"Hello," the voice said. My mother. I knew from that first word. "Hello? Is anybody there?"

My heart pounded and my mouth dried up as if I had been approached by Svenson. In all this time thinking about my mother, I hadn't even thought of what I would say when I talked to her, so I hung up without saying a word.

"That was her, wasn't it?" Jenny asked. "I could tell by your face."

I nodded, then walked off toward the woods and Jenny was quick to follow. I wasn't sure what I was feeling but it felt good to be moving. We walked far enough so that no one could see us and found a picnic table overlooking a bend in the river where Jenny unloaded what she had stuffed into the waistband of her pants while I distracted the clerk at the dime store: a pair of scissors, a tube of airplane glue, two lighters, the bottle of sleep aid I had asked for, and five packages of Now and Laters.

Jenny lit a cigarette and told me to take off my shirts, instantly distracting me from my mother.

"What?"

"You're getting a haircut," she said. "I've been staring at that missing chunk all day."

I did as she asked and sat down at the table. She ran her fingers through my hair a few times, bringing goose bumps up all over my body, then picked up the scissors and trimmed at the ends to even it out with what Svenson had taken.

"When I first saw it I figured Russell did this to you."

I turned to look at her and the point of the scissors dug into my head near my ears.

"Hold still," she said. "These are brand-new—they'll pop your eyes right out if you aren't careful. Oh shit, you're bleeding a little but you'll be okay."

A woodpecker tapped at a nearby tree. The leaves went on whispering. The scissors snipped. A bird called and another called back. I asked Jenny what she thought they were saying.

"Who cares? They're fucking birds," she said and went on snipping, catching the hair trimmings as she cut and collecting them in a pile on the table. "Are you going to tell me what happened with Russell or not?"

"What about him?"

"You act like no one knows."

Pausing my haircut and turning my head toward her with a finger under my chin, Jenny told me that she had seen me and Russell go behind the More-4-You one night and, thinking we were going back there to get high, she had decided to sneak up on us. She had not been expecting to find us in each other's arms.

"I figured something like that from the beginning," she said. "With the way you act around girls and everything."

I wanted to tell her what I had told Russell at breakfast the day he left me, about my confusion, about how I felt most people weren't given the chance to explore this area of themselves but rather forced to choose something that wasn't really a choice, but I froze up. If anyone would have understood, it would have been Jenny, but something inside stopped me.

"It's not what you think," I said, a squeak. "Russell doesn't come around anymore."

"Oh, that's too bad," she said. "Any other guys you got your eye on?"

As her question died in my silence, she brushed away the stray clippings from my neck and shoulders and I stood to put my shirts back on. I turned to her and she looped my hair behind my ear with her finger.

"It's shorter than it was but it'll grow back."

The way she looked at me made me think she wanted me to run my finger behind her ear in the same way, move my hand to her neck, and pull her mouth to mine. Now would be the time, if ever, but as with Russell, I couldn't. We stood there staring at each other for a time, her head tilted with the confused look she gave me when I found we were standing a little too close together, my pulse pounding in my ears and my vision clouding around the edges as I waited for her to make the move but the moment passed. Jenny lit another cigarette and sat down at the table. I sat down to watch her as she glued my hair to the table in little tufts. She built bunkers out of Now and Laters, positioning cowboys and Indians here and there in mock battle, and atop the tallest she glued an Indian with his arm in the air, a call to battle.

"You said you don't have anything with you?" she asked. "Not even a joint?"

I shook my head.

"Well," she said, holding up the glue, "for now, there's always this."

She swept all the leftover packaging into the bag I had carried from the dime store, squeezed the last of the airplane glue over the garbage inside, then brought the bag to her mouth. She breathed deeply a few times, then lay her head down and watched the war scene she had created come alive.

"That's good and fine," she said when she came back around, "but it's not the same."

"I've got a stash at home if you want to get high," I said.

"But how long will that last?" she asked. "A day? Two? Do you know where J scored?"

"I guess," I said. "I'll see what I can do."

We went up to the Old Rail Terminal that afternoon and sat in the sun on two benches down the way from the More-4-You. I ran out into the lot when I saw Svenson's truck and it screeched to a halt.

"You wanna die, faggot?" Svenson called out his window.

I walked around to his door as my blood pressure rose. My heartbeat in my ears drowned out the words I spoke. He leaned out toward me and my eyes skipped past him to the rifle in the gun rack mounted in the rear of the cab.

"I . . . I know," I stuttered, staring now at the rifle. "I know you don't like me but I'm here on business. Are you still selling the shit you and your brother had out at the campgrounds that night?"

"The fuck is it to you?"

I waved Jenny over and when Svenson saw her, his face softened.

"Shit, she's with you?" he asked, leaning over to open the passenger door. "Ladies first."

Jenny didn't look too pleased but climbed in and I circled the truck, finding the barrel of the rifle in the gun rack pointing my way once I climbed in after her. As the door crashed shut I had a sudden vision of Svenson pulling up in his truck and giving Jenny the same talk he had given me when I came to town. Both of us thin with long hair, of course she was one of his targets, and these powders were what he was talking about the day we first met near the library, when he asked me if I liked to get rowdy.

Svenson kept on straight from where he picked us up, driving through the Tweed's parking lot still strewn with discarded protest signs and beer cans from his Confederate flag revival a few days earlier, and turning to the back lot behind the strip mall near the train tracks. A few cars were parked on the supplemental rails where I spied some fresh graffiti. A silhouette with an arm in the air reaching toward four balloons, the strings just out of reach, each connected to the letters, HOPE.

"I normally don't sell shit," Svenson said, jerking his truck to a stop, reaching under his seat for a crumpled cigarette pack that held a small bag of speed. "I have people do that for me, but look, I'll give you this bag here for a free taster, and you get whatever else you need from Russell. I got him working for me now that my brother and your buddy J have both left town."

When Svenson took his keys from the ignition and dug one into the bag of speed, I saw the twisted scars and stitch marks from his run-in with Lucifer. The passing weeks had closed the wounds but he would have a reminder of that day for the rest of his life.

Jenny turned to me as he held the snow-capped key out for her and I nodded. She leaned forward and sniffed. She exhaled through pursed lips like she was blowing out birthday candles, then lay back against her seat.

"God. Damn. It's been too long," she said, a whisper. The muscles in her jaw began to work, grinding her teeth.

"That's great," I said, "but no need to give this to us for free." I dug in my pockets and tried to give him what I had.

"No, no, no, I am not a drug dealer," Svenson said. "Keep your money for your boyfriend."

All the while Jenny sat between us, staring out the windshield, silent. When we were done, I opened the door. Svenson put his hand on Jenny's knee and she turned toward him.

"I'm always around to help a pretty lady," he said. "We'll let these faggots deal with each other but you and me, that can be different if you want it to be." She shook her head and slid down the bench where I helped her down. I shut the door, slapped twice on the outside, and then Svenson fired the engine.

"What a fucking creep," Jenny said as we watched him pull away.

Russell hung up the phone when I told him it was me but he showed up at the Aurora anyway, setting my heartbeat to double speed when I saw his sad face through the service window as he entered the restaurant. He did not want to be there, or maybe, I told myself, he wanted to be there very much. I met him near the cash register, then walked him back into the kitchen, led him into a corner where no one could see us, and wrapped my arms around him. He stood stiff and straight, resistant.

"So what do you want?" he asked, before I dropped my embrace.

I told him how much money I had and turned back to what I was cooking while he dug in his pocket. When I finished flipping my pancakes I saw the three gelatin capsules sitting on a piece of lettuce.

"That's sixty," he said.

I set down my spatula, wiped my hands on my apron, and reached into my pocket for the money.

"I didn't think you'd come," I said, handing him the bills, which he took and counted, stuffed them in his pocket.

"Yeah," he said. "I didn't want to, but business is business."

I walked around the corner to wash the money grime off my hands and when I returned he was gone.

I didn't think Russell would be a good drug dealer when Svenson first mentioned it, but every time I called he showed up on time with premeasured doses in little plastic capsules he had bought empty at

Walmart. We didn't talk much more than this on the handful of occasions that I bought from him for Jenny over those few weeks in July, but I did notice changes in him from time to time. One day, his hair was styled, not shaved at home with the buzzer. His clothes began to fit. Nice button-down shirts with the sleeves rolled up, tucked into jeans. And I knew he must be doing well when one night he pulled up to the restaurant in a car. Used but he owned it.

"That's what happens when you don't use what you're selling," Russell said when I brought it up. "Your buddy J was a fucking idiot the way he ran things. Vitamins. What an asshole."

And the biggest change was that he wasn't drunk either. After each of these times that I saw him, even though he treated me as if we had never met, something inside me ached. I missed him.

As if he had been waiting for us, Svenson pulled his truck right in front of me and Jenny as we left the Arlington, swung the passenger door open, and told us to get in. He pulled an aggressive U-turn, stopping traffic in the oncoming lane, then took Ash through town, up to the church and around the cemetery. When we got out into the country, Svenson took a gallon jug of red wine from under his seat and passed it to Jenny.

"Burgundy?" he said. Jenny took a big swallow and so did I, then we passed it back to Svenson, who capped it and set it in Jenny's lap without drinking.

"Y'all been up to the old jumping barn at the Andersen place?"

We both shook our heads and Svenson turned toward the road. The day was so hot we left the windows down, the wind a cyclone through the cab. Svenson reached out and ran his hand over Jenny's forehead, holding her hair in place.

"You've grown up, Jennifer Freya," Svenson said.

"It's too bad you haven't," she said, jerking toward my side of the truck.

"Don't say that, Jen. We're just getting started."

He took a left on a dirt road and then we reached that part of rural Minnesota where everything looks the same. Tree-lined roads dividing wide, flat fields. The occasional lake in the distance. The same single telephone line rising and falling. Only the numbers on the road signs varied but Svenson knew where we were going, bringing us onto a road marked as a dead end, two ruts with long grass sprouting from the middle. The meandering path through the woods led to an old barn that was once red, flanked by tractors, long unused, rusty, tangled in overgrowth. Three other pickup trucks were parked outside. My heartbeat rose into my ears. I took the jug from Jenny's lap and took another big drink.

Inside, standing near a mountain of loose hay, were three guys I recognized from town: a set of twins who had been the other two Klansmen at the field party that night, John and Mike, and another boy I knew until then only by face, also named Mike. They were very cordial. They offered me a tallboy and asked me where I was from, but my answers were steamrolled by one of the twins, who had once been caught shoplifting at Tweed's Discount.

"A fucking fifty-cent can of soda," he said, "and that asshole called the sheriff. I had to do twelve hours of community service for that. Four cents an hour that was. I'm glad that place went out of business."

"Did you do your service at the government center?" Mike the non-twin asked. "I vacuumed all the offices out there and once my service leader left me alone I cleaned out the pocket change from every desk I came across. Bought myself a nice bag of weed with that."

Jenny and Svenson were off a ways in the shadows of the barn talking in whispers. He put his hand on her shoulder and she leaned into him so he could whisper in her ear. She laughed then and lay her hand on his chest. Svenson pointed up toward the loft and a long ladder that led up there and after Jenny nodded and giggled they made their way together. My mind was racing—were they going to go up there together while the rest of us were still here? I noticed I was staring so I turned back to the others, where one of the twins asked non-twin Mike what he had done to earn community service and he told them it was possession.

"Of high concentrations of methamphetamine," he said, proud that the drugs he was caught with were pure. "None of that vitamin shit that was going around for a while."

"It's been super clean since Russell took over."

They talked awhile about the different dealers in town but they didn't mention Svenson, which I thought was odd. His friends didn't know that he and his brother were the ones supplying these people. The non-twin had known J, but there had been others, many others, and they all cut the quality down with fillers before they sold it. Baby laxative, ephedrine, B vitamins. Everyone but Russell, who was selling pills so strong that people around town were complaining of hallucinations.

"I thought he was mixing acid into it or something," John said. "But it turns out it's supposed to do that. One of the benefits of buying from someone who doesn't use what he sells."

Twin Mike shook his empty beer can and then kicked the cooler under me.

"Shane?" he said. "Another?"

I shook my can but it was still full. "No thanks."

"Will you grab me one?" he asked, shaking his own can again.

"You're sitting on the cooler."

I stood to get out of the way when a screaming came from where

Jenny and Svenson had gone. The four of us turned to see Jenny jump out of the loft with a running start, her legs pedaling like she was riding a bike, then she fell into the hay, dust and grain mushrooming into the air. A moment later Svenson stepped to the edge and fell backwards, no doubt an attempt to impress Jenny. His dust cloud poofed into the air, then he pawed his way toward Jenny as they descended the stack but she pushed him away, then they were back on the ground with us again, dusting themselves off.

"You got your kiss," Jenny said, "now take us back to town. Shane is sick of hanging out with these fucking losers."

Over the next few weeks, thoughts of the dogs crept up on me, left me rooted in place. I was as distracted and distant while sober as I had been on drugs before. I'd be right in the middle of showering or making a cheeseburger and suddenly I'd find that long stretches of time had passed, that the water had run cold or that my burger was burnt to charcoal. Like in my dreams, I was struck immobile, but from internal distraction rather than muscular failure. In my dreams I wanted to move, but in real life I'd forget that it was even a possibility. Most of July passed in this way. I found myself sleeping more than ever, twelve sometimes fourteen hours a night while during that same time I'm unsure whether Jenny slept at all. Even when I was awake I wasn't all there, sleepwalking back and forth to the Aurora, cooking on autopilot, forgetful. I more than once had to run back to work in the middle of the night to be sure I had locked the doors.

Jenny showed up at my apartment at odd hours, sometimes letting herself in with her spare key in the middle of the night. More than once I woke up to find her sitting on the edge of my bed, chopping powder on any hard surface she could find. I hadn't been able to bring myself to get high since the day Svenson killed Sissy and Lucy—I had even given Jenny my stash—but that didn't stop her from offering me some every time she brought it out. She was using more than I was bringing her from my meetings with Russell. I should've realized that Svenson was probably stalking her, plying her with a free sniff here and quarter gram there, but I was lost in my own fog most of the time so I didn't notice.

Day or night, Jenny would talk and talk and I would tune in from time to time, catching snippets. Often I found myself losing track of what she was saying and staring out the window at the fluffy white clouds that floated over Holm. Although she moved from topic to topic often without transition, one thing that came up again and again was her mother. She very much wanted her mother to be well, but thought for some reason that only the sheriff could fix the problem. Everything she did was an attempt to get the sheriff's attention: smoking weed on the street, painting graffiti, shoplifting. One day, fading back in from my ongoing depression, I asked her why it was so important that the sheriff and her mother get back together.

"I can't do this all by myself," Jenny said. "Not if I want to go to college or leave town or even get a job. I need someone to take care of her. If I could just get him to my house, to see how she's been since he left."

Then I gave her a plan that would cause everything to come crashing down.

"He's looking for a drug dealer," I said. "Why don't you turn in Svenson? Tell the sheriff to come over so you can tell him who gave you the weed that day. Call him from your house and tell him you have some information you want to share in person."

"Now that's interesting," she said, and this opened another flood of words under which I was soon lost. After a time I noticed she had gone quiet and looked up to find she was expecting an answer from me.

"What?"

"The problem with that is we've been buying from Russell," Jenny said after a thoughtful silence. "You still like him, don't you? We could turn him in and he'd probably give up Svenson."

"What?" I asked again, rubbing my eyes with my fists.

"Russell," she said. "Do you still like him?"

In spite of the way he treated me, how he had abandoned me, I did have feelings for Russell but I didn't want to tell her. I didn't want to tell anyone so I kept quiet, but Jenny knew what my silence meant.

"If only J were still around," she said. "I'd've turned on him in a heartbeat."

I was working the dinner shift a few nights later when the waitress said a guest was asking after me, so I walked out into the dining room to find the sheriff sitting before a plate of pork chops.

"How goes the search for your mother?"

"We found her," I said.

"That's great," he said. "You were pretty torn up about it that day." He picked up his knife and cut into his meat, took a bite.

"Is that all you wanted to ask me?"

"You ever think your buddy Jenny is an overachiever?" the sheriff asked.

"You could say that," I said, thinking of all the HOPE pieces that must have been traveling the country on the sides of trains. "Definitely, I'd say."

"She's going to get herself in trouble," he said. "Sven Svenson is a bad dude."

"She finally told you he was our drug dealer?"

"We got off the phone an hour ago," he said, then after a pause, "Jenny and I go way back."

"You mentioned that," I said.

"She was the cutest little girl," he said, forking a slice of pork and using it to scoop up some mashed potatoes. "Big thick cola-bottle lenses in her glasses, eyes ten times the size when you looked at her straight on. The first time I met her was going on eight years ago, when I got called to the Pump 'N Munch about a shoplifter. Of course, it was her. She was eight years old and, like I said, cute as a button, so I talked the manager into not pressing charges and took her home."

He took a bite and swallowed, then sipped his water.

"Great pork chops, by the way," he said.

"Thank you."

"So I took her home and met her mother, Kristina. We talked for a long time and I have to admit I fell in love with her, her mother I mean, not Jenny, before I left their house that day. I was done for, slain. I wanted to shout it from the rooftops but Kristina wanted to be more cautious. We met up when Jenny wasn't around, went on lunch dates but only when Jenny was at school. Her daughter was her number one priority and rightfully so, I thought, so I did what I could to help out. Mainly I talked local business owners out of pressing charges when Jenny got caught stealing, which happened a lot. This worked for a while, but I had no leverage when the principal of her elementary school called to tell me that she had seen Jenny get out of a car that she herself had driven to school that day. Clearly, she was having problems."

The bell dinged in the kitchen, the waitress letting me know I had an order. I left the sheriff with his dinner and after I checked the ticket I threw two hamburgers on the char-broiler and two buns to toast on the grill, then portioned out two orders of fries and dropped them in the deep fryer before I hustled back to the sheriff's table.

"She stole a car?" I asked. "She's just a kid and steals a car to get to school?"

"It was her mom's car," he said. "No big deal really. She was an excellent driver, even at ten. She still is, actually."

Jenny was right. He was delusional with love for Kristina.

"The principal pressed charges," he said, stopping for a bite. "Reckless endangerment. So I had to take her to the station but I made it into something good instead of punishing little Jennifer. We got them into a new house and Jenny got some psychological testing. Kristina got a small loan to open her store and these two nearly had it turned around. By the end, it was almost a good thing that it happened the way it did."

I got up and went to the kitchen. Flipped the burgers and rotated the buns, pulled the basket of fries from the fryer and shook away the extra oil. On my way back out to the dining room I noticed that my apron was covered in grease and tomato sauce so I took it off and tossed it on the cutting board near the broiler.

"And so for a time I was a silent partner in Jenny's life," he said when I sat back down. "We were together for a while, though she still never introduced me to Jenny as anything beyond the sheriff. Her store, Kristina's Pet World, was making money. The psychologists told us that Jenny was a kleptomaniac because she wasn't stimulated enough in school, she was too smart for her class and they had her skip sixth grade."

"She is very smart," I said.

"It all went well for a while but Kristina's mood changed when Walmart came to town, and then when her store closed things got tense," he said. "I couldn't make her happy anymore."

He took the last bit of pork, then pushed his plate away from him.

"But no matter my history with Kristina, I still care about Jenny and I want to see her succeed in life. I don't want her to get caught up with drugs and these idiots. I was only trying to scare her when I busted you guys that day. In any case, I've seen her driving her mom's car a few times, out by Svenson's place, and now that she's called me I know what she's up to."

The bell dinged again as if to punctuate my thought. Then a voice from the kitchen:

"Shane?"

"You need to arrest her if she's breaking the law," I said. "Even if that means you have to talk to her mother."

"I don't think that's the answer," he said. "She needs to get her shit together and she doesn't want an arrest record when she finally does."

"That sounds both generous and dangerous to me."

"Look, I can't watch her every move. You're a good friend. Be with her. Can I trust you to keep an eye on her? Help me out a little?"

"Shane?" the waitress called. "I see flames! Something's on fire!"

Before I could agree to the sheriff's request, I ran to the kitchen to find that my apron had caught fire so I pulled it onto the floor and stomped it out before the flames spread to the food. The new order called for a steak and two pork chops so I threw those on the grill before I put together the two burgers and fries from earlier. When I got back out to the dining room the sheriff was gone.

Jenny let herself into my room with my spare key before sunrise.

"I got you something," she said, then dug an envelope that had been folded in half out of the small purse she carried. "Two somethings," she said. "Round trip."

I opened the top flap to find bus tickets, the same company I had ridden with to come to Holm. South Haven, Michigan, listed in the destination box, transfer in Chicago. She had swung by the Pump 'N Munch where the bus stopped and bought them from the cashier. My eyes filled. In a week, I'd be meeting my mother again.

"I got you a return trip two days later, just in case," she said. "If she's batshit crazy, you'll want to get out of there as soon as you can—if she isn't, you can always change your ticket."

I blinked back the tears, climbed out of bed, and gave Jenny a hug that she wasn't expecting, pinning her arms down at the shoulders so she couldn't quite hug back.

"You're welcome," she said. "I helped you get your mother back, now you have to help me get mine."

"How do you plan to do that?" I asked.

She told me then how her call to the sheriff had gone. When she told him that she had some information, he had replied, "Everyone knows that Svenson is selling drugs, but no one has any proof. Have you bought anything from him? Could you set up a sale?" Of course, she had to say no to the first question, but she took the second as a call to action.

Eleven

I didn't see Jenny that weekend or for most of the next week. She didn't answer the phone when I called—neither did Kristina but that didn't surprise me—and no one answered the door when I stopped by. I thought I might not see her again before my trip to Michigan but then she called me at work on Wednesday.

"You need to come over here tonight," she said. Her voice was tight and forced in the way it got when she hadn't slept for a few days.

I got to her place around midnight and entered through the open garage door like she had asked. I climbed the carpeted stairs and turned a quick left to find her sitting on the edge of her bed, very high, inspecting a small plastic box that she held in her hands.

"Jenny," I whispered, startling her out of her trance.

She jumped up, slipped the object she held into a small purse that hung from her shoulder on a thin strap, then led me through her house in the dark, stopping me in the crease of shadow cast by the living room wall, and stepped into the light.

"Mom," she said. "It's drafty in here. Let me close these curtains."

No response. It sounded like *The Odd Couple* was playing on the television but I couldn't be sure. Jenny came back and pushed me toward the door I had come in, grabbed a set of keys from the hook on our way out.

This is when the sheriff wanted me to step in and stop her but it all moved so quickly that I had no control. Before I knew it, we were on the highway heading south. The road was empty. A sliver of moon hung in the sky. The clock on the dash read 12:34.

"When you told me to come over I wasn't expecting that we'd be stealing your mom's car," I said. "But this is nice."

"It is nice," Jenny said. She rolled her window down and her hair blew back behind her, the floral scent of her perfume trailing through the car.

We took a few turns, back roads off of back roads, to where houses became compounds camouflaged and otherwise hidden from sight. Jenny slowed to scan the brush on my side of the car, tall trees with long grasses and ferns growing below. She turned onto what I didn't think was a road, two wheel ruts running straight into the woods, like the path to Andersen's jumping barn. The going was bumpy but the trees had been trimmed back into a tunnel that opened onto a wide grass field with a house at the center. Jenny parked her mother's car among a number of other cars and trucks angled on the open lawn without any order. A single flood lamp on a tall pole shed orange light over the scene, casting long, eerie shadows from the vehicles and illuminating the face of a huge barn on the edge of the property. Parked beneath the light was Svenson's pickup—so this was where Jenny had been driving when the sheriff saw her on the road.

"This shouldn't take more than an hour," she said, leading me to the front of the house. "Come wait inside."

We stepped up onto the rickety wooden porch, steps bowing and creaking beneath my feet, then Jenny knocked. No one answered, but the door opened when she pushed and then we were in a dark living room with an old couch and two chairs set up around a coffee table. The walls were barren expanses of plaster and our footsteps echoed as we moved toward the slant of light that fell out of a doorway.

"Hello?" Jenny called.

"In here."

We walked through the dark living room and into the kitchen where a woman sat smoking at a table with a jug of wine and a coffee cup. She was facing away from us but I knew her by her hair—Chelsea, Svenson's sister. Dirty glasses and empty beer cans littered the counters and the windowsills, a banner hung across the kitchen wall: HAPPY 18TH BIRTHDAY!

"Is he around?" Jenny asked.

"Upstairs," Chelsea answered. "Did you bring this one for me?"

Jenny pointed to the table and I sat, then she walked across the kitchen, through the doorway that led to the staircase.

"Hello, Shane," Chelsea said. "Would you like some wine?"

I nodded and she rose to get another mug.

"So how goes the job?" she asked. "You like working with Leon?"

"It's good," I said. "And I do like Leon. He's a very generous guy."

I took the mug from her. She sat in the chair next to me and moved her hands to her hair, running her fingers over the bristles of the shaved side of her head before tying her long hair into a braid and tossing it over her shoulder. I sipped my wine and looked her over.

"You know what she's doing up there, right?" Chelsea asked. She made a circle with her thumb and fingers, held it up to her mouth, bobbed her head toward and away.

"No," I said.

"Ask her yourself when she comes back down," she said. "What else do you give your man on his birthday?"

Her man. Jenny's plan was working, but I'd never get used to that. I took down my mug of wine in one long drink.

"Where is everyone, Chelsea? There are at least five cars out there."

"They all left around eleven when Gramma got tired," she said. "Those vehicles are my brother's, he fixes them up. Five more out back. My other brother's got a couple around too, but he doesn't live here anymore."

An extended moment of silence passed as I thought about Svenson's grandmother. Had she seen him on the news with his flag? Was she proud of him? I guess even real members of the Ku Klux Klan had grandmothers that they invited to their birthday parties and helped up and down the stairs.

"I hate those cars. It's like a graveyard out there—he parks them wherever he wants. Fucking slob. Just like in the house. He does what he wants and expects me to clean up after him. I don't know why he has to buy every beat-down piece of shit he sees on the side of the road."

Chelsea squinted as she spoke, ground her teeth between sentences. She hadn't been awake as long as Jenny but she had taken some speed.

"I shouldn't talk like that about my brother," she said, before lighting a cigarette and blowing the smoke into the air above us. "He's a good guy. He does what he can to help me with my daughter. You should see him with her, really, I don't think you would believe it. And he doesn't have to do that—he could leave at any moment and live an easy breezy life by himself anywhere; his brother did it. Still, I wish he would listen once in a while."

She took down the rest of her mug of wine, then poured herself another full cup and stood.

"This pan here," she said, lifting a cast-iron pan off the stovetop and turning it to me so I could see the mess of grease and gristle inside. "This pan has been here for months. Sven made himself a steak sometime in April and this has been here ever since. I refuse to clean it because he dirtied it before I moved back in. I tell him that but you know what he says?"

"I have no idea," I said.

"He says it's women's work," she said. "That washing dishes is women's work. And it's true, I know. I've washed every dish that has been dirtied since I moved back in but I'll tell you one thing—I'm not going to wash this."

Chelsea took the handle of the pan in both hands and swung it like a tennis racket a few times before she lifted it up over her head and brought it down before her like she was chopping kindling.

"Someday I'd like to crack him over the head with it," she said without a smile. She set the pan back down and took her seat. "That'd teach him a lesson."

A sleepy-eyed child walked into the kitchen dragging a limp stuffed bear by the back leg. She was very much Chelsea's daughter, her face an exact replica—had her hair been dyed bright red and half shaved, she would've been a shrunken version.

"Mommy," the girl said, "why are you still up? It's late."

"I'm talking to my friend, dear," she said, standing up and walking toward the child, then picking her up. "Let's bring Paddington and you back to bed now."

"But I want to play Intenno," the girl said.

"We can play your Nintendo for a bit," Chelsea said. "But then you need to get some sleep."

"O-key," the girl said and dragged Paddington into the living room.

Chelsea stood and waved at me to follow them. The girl switched on a lamp and sat cross-legged on the floor before a television in the corner with Paddington's head in her lap. Chelsea's shoes clacked across the old wood, the odd echo bouncing back, and after pushing a few buttons near the television *Super Mario* came on the screen. Her daughter started up the game, dodging walking mushrooms and flying turtles, while I took a seat on the antique couch and Chelsea sat down next to me, a bit too close, her hand settling strongly on my knee.

"We weren't allowed on this furniture as kids," Chelsea said. "I never sat here. It was a room meant only to be shown, the kind of place where you would entertain, but Ma and Pa didn't ever have any guests."

"This is a nice couch," I said, squirming to get my knee out from under her, but my struggle only moved her hand farther up my leg.

The game was one I was familiar with, having owned it right up until I had planned to give it to J, right up until Rick stole it, so when GAME OVER appeared dead center on the screen I moved down to the floor and took the controller. Chelsea joined us, lifted her daughter into her lap, and echoed her excited ooohs and aaahs as I made my way through each level. They shuffled together near me as the girl grew restless and finally fell asleep with her tiny hand wrapped around Chelsea's pinky and ring fingers.

When I dodged the final dragon and beat the game, Chelsea carried her daughter off to bed so I shut off the TV and went back into the kitchen. The clock on the wall read 1:23. I tipped back my mug of wine and sat down at the table. When Chelsea returned, she lit a cigarette and then fiddled with her braid as she told me about her husband, how he had given her scabies—"Some crank whore gave him bugs and then he gave them to his girls"—and how she had left him for a while but now he was trying to get back with her, with their daughter.

The wine jug grew empty as the ashtray filled, our mouths reddened as the windows lightened. Just before sunrise, Chelsea pulled out what I thought was lipstick but then stuck the tube up her nose and snorted. Held the contraption out to me but I refused so she put it up her other nostril and went again.

"You're a shooter, eh? You've got that look."

"I've sort of been off it for a while now," I said.

"That's good," she said. "Stay off it if you can."

She lit another cigarette and asked me if I minded her asking personal questions. The first few weren't so bad. Where I was going, where I had been.

"Have you had roommates?"

"My dad, I guess."

"One thing about living with men though," she said and stood up, lurching now from the speed and the wine, "is that they never clean up after themselves."

She again staggered over to the stove and struggled to lift the cast-iron pan off the burner. Holding the greasy mess of fat and crispy meat chunks between us, I saw this time that someone had tapped cigarette ash into it and sunk the butt deep in the puddle of the white gelatinous goo.

"Do you know how many times I've asked Sven to wash this pan he dirtied going on four months ago?"

"Three?"

"Try thirteen," she said, "but then try again because it's closer to sixty. Every single day since I moved in I've asked him to clean up this mess, but he won't."

"Wow," I said.

"Wow is what he'll say when I crack him in the skull with this thing," she said, swinging the pan back and forth before her as she walked it back to the stove. She sat back down and lit a cigarette before realizing that she already had one going in the ashtray. Holding one in each hand she went back to her questions and I told her my plans to go to my mother's before coming back for school in September. After that she got up and moved her chair as close to mine as possible, then sat back down and scooted in so that our hips were touching. Hand on my knee, her line of questioning turned in the direction I knew it would.

"You mean to tell me you've never kissed a girl?" She leaned in closer. "Boys though, I'm sure, right?"

I didn't answer. She took my hand and placed it on her breast.

"So you've never done this before either? Squeeze it a little."

She arched her back and exhaled when I did it, then moved her hand to my neck, pulling my face toward hers, when footsteps creaked down the stairs and Jenny was back.

"Shane! I forgot you were here. Let's go!"

Jenny stepped into the kitchen and Svenson replaced her in the doorway, shirtless. His face, pallid and uncertain, overcome by tics and spasms, told me they had gone through a lot of speed in the hours they had spent upstairs.

"You forgot your purse, doll," Svenson said through clenched jaws, holding out the small bag.

Jenny spun and took the bag by the strap, tossing the contents onto the floor. Something made a plastic rattle as it bounced across the linoleum. Svenson watched Jenny chase after it but then his glance turned my way.

"What are you doing here?"

Jenny disappeared into the living room. I jumped out of Chelsea's embrace and ran out behind Jenny without answering Svenson.

"Nice to meet you again," Chelsea called after me.

The music came on loud when the car started, drowning out whatever Svenson was yelling from the porch as we pulled out. Jenny drove fast once we were out on the road, muttering under her breath, beating the dashboard with her right hand while she steered with her left, and I saw that she was wearing a glossy black ring around her middle finger.

"What is that?" I asked, leaning to point at her hand on the wheel.

"A glass ring," she said, "clearly. This though . . ."

Jenny fidgeted in her seat, pulled the tangled purse out from behind her, and popped into my hands a small plastic box wrapped in thin cardboard.

"This'll be Svenson's demise," she said.

Looking down at the disposable camera, I knew why I kept expecting Svenson's truck to appear behind us in the mirror.

"What time is it?"

"Six thirty," I said, reading from the clock on the dash. The sun now hung just above the horizon to the east.

"Oh shit, it's that late? I'm so stupid," she said. "So fucking stupid."

"You aren't stupid," I told her but she wasn't listening, rather talking to herself. Her face twitched as she wove the car through the early-morning traffic and I knew she was as far gone as Chelsea had been. When the speedometer hit ninety I put on my seat belt.

Back in town, Jenny pulled the car into the parking lot of the A&W, then told me to wait ten minutes before I went to her house. She was paranoid, so I did what she said without question and got out to the whistles of an oncoming train. The engine chugged out from behind the A&W and the cars picked up speed as the train made its way out of town. I stood in the middle of the empty parking lot, immobile like in my leaden-foot dreams, with an arm up to shield my eyes from the sun as I watched the graffiti pass by—one HOPE took up an entire train car and, painted in red and white stripes, the O a giant target with three arrows sticking out of the bull's-eye.

The front door was open so I rang the bell before I let myself in. The living room, flooded with morning light, was a disaster area. Newspapers and junk mail piled across the coffee table and, on top of that, overflowing ashtrays and prescription bottles. In the kitchen, dirty dishes piled up out of the sink, taking up most of the countertop. A second pile of newspapers and bills and junk mail on the kitchen table.

Jenny came around the corner from the bedrooms, meeting me at the top of the stairs, and told me to wait in her room.

"But don't look in—"

It was already too late. A quick glance to my left and I saw Kristina laid out on a sheet on the floor of her bedroom, staring at the ceiling above her, wet stains spread across the inner thighs of her pants. I stepped past into Jenny's room and sat on her bed.

"We have diapers," she said from the hallway, "but she looks so sad when you put one on her. I try to make it home in time so she doesn't have to wear them."

When Jenny finished and came to her room, she emptied her pockets onto her bed, a pack of cigarettes, a lighter, and three small baggies of speed. Next to all that she dropped the portable camera.

"I'm going to shower," she said. "I feel nasty."

Jenny hurried out of the room, so I took a cigarette from her pack and made my way to the patio to smoke. My second pass through the mess stoked my worry. Thoughts of Kristina floundering each day in this dirty house alone while her daughter chased her own good feelings made me wonder aloud to the waxing morning exactly what it was that we were doing. After I flicked my butt into Jenny's backyard, I went back to find the door to the bathroom open and Jenny, one towel wrapped around her wet hair, another around her body, standing before the mirror squeezing little patches of her face between her index fingers.

"I forgot you were here," she said, her face speckled with red spots, many dripping blood. When she smiled a red river formed in the line of her cheek, trailing down to the corner of her mouth. "I thought I was alone."

"You're doing too much, Jenny," I said. "Look at your face, look at this house. I'm worried about you and your mother."

She turned to me with a manic smile, blood dripping from the open wounds on her face, and nodded, but then turned back to the mirror, leaned in close and brought her two index fingers together near her widow's peak.

"Jenny," I said.

She jumped, startled, then with her arms in the air before her, she looked to the ceiling and yelled, "Why can't I stop picking my face?"

The photo lab at Walmart hadn't opened yet so Jenny sealed the portable camera into an envelope, wrote her phone number on the contact line, and dropped the package into the service box. It wasn't until we were crossing the tracks on our way back that I realized I would be gone before the photos were ready.

"That's fine," Jenny said. "I'll take them to the sheriff tomorrow. It'd be better if I get some sleep before I meet him anyways."

"You know the sheriff came to my work and told me to keep an eye on you," I said. "He'd seen you driving around and was worried about you and Svenson."

"Of course he did," Jenny said, "and I'll tell you what I told him. Svenson needs to be locked up. He's a racist and a dog-killing, drug-dealing rapist. Do you want to split hairs here? The sheriff told me to back off, but how can I do that now? You know how Svenson talks, what he calls people. If you know what he does but don't do anything about it, you become complicit—you become an inconsiderate, racist asshole of the same caliber. I couldn't care less about drugs, but that's all the sheriff is after. To me, if you don't contradict Svenson then you agree with him, then you fly the Confederate flag with him, wear the

KKK uniform with him, kill the dogs with him, call yourself a faggot with him. Silence in the face of Svenson makes you worse than Svenson himself."

I couldn't argue with that. Svenson may have done good for his sister and niece, but it didn't cancel out all the awful things he'd done. I'm sure that much of his tough-guy persona was posturing. He was neither a member of the Ku Klux Klan or the Confederacy, but the fact that he could slit a dog's throat with no remorse would be enough to convince the most forgiving of people that he was a monster.

"But more than that," Jenny said, "I need the sheriff and my mother to get back together. I can't take care of her and live my life. It's one or the other."

I was still a bit unclear how Jenny linked Svenson's downfall to her mother and the sheriff's reconciliation. It sounded to me a bit delusional—the type of idea that someone who hadn't slept for a few days might believe—but she spoke of it as a sure thing.

"I know he still loves her," she said. "When he sees her tomorrow, when he sees how she is now, he'll bring her to the hospital and I'll be free."

Jenny was quick to fix up when we got to my place. I let her into my room before I went to the bathroom and returned to find her sitting on the edge of my bed, lost in the changing patterns on the wall, needle still hanging from her arm.

"Look, Jenny," I said when she came back around, "you need to quit this shit. It's getting out of hand."

"This is the last of it," she said, shaking the three baggies she had gotten from Svenson. "After tomorrow I won't have anywhere to get it, but we only need one to give the sheriff with the pictures. You know what would help? If you did a little so there would be less for me."

I didn't want to do any speed—it had been three weeks—but I

didn't want her to end up with it so I chopped myself a long line and sucked it up my nose. That much less for Jenny. My regret was instant but short-lived. Soon I felt a smile breaking on my face and an optimism growing inside me. Svenson was going down.

"So how did you do it?"

"It was easy," she said. "He walked right into it when he gave me this."

She held her left hand out to me and I pulled it close to inspect the ring. Cold and smooth, it was made of glass—white speckles in a field of black—and it reminded me of the night of the camping trip Jenny and I had spent with Mary and J.

"What a dick!" she said. "I mean, who gives a girl a glass ring?"

"It's nice," I said, not sure why I was defending Svenson's choice of jewelry.

"I like it," she said. "I'd buy it myself, but what does it mean coming from him? Diamonds last forever, gold and silver are pretty solid, but glass? The first time you bang it, it breaks. That's some metaphor. How long is he planning on keeping me around?"

"How long are you planning to stay with him?"

"But what if it were serious?" she said. "Who is careful enough to wear a glass ring and not break it? I guess if anyone could do it, you could, but it'd be like carrying an egg around all day."

I took the ring off her finger and slid it onto the middle finger of my right hand—a perfect fit—then took it off and placed it back in her palm.

"So he gave me this, then I told him I wanted to get high. I waited for him to break it all out before I told him he stank and needed a wash. He left the door open as he showered and said the nastiest shit to me as I took pictures of his drugs, his safe, his desk. It's all there."

Jenny took the ring from her palm and slipped it back on her finger.

"You don't need to wear that here," I said.

"I should probably get used to it," she said. "Part of the game. I wouldn't want him to sneak up on me later today and catch me not wearing it."

"Well, I don't like it," I said.

"You're funny," she said, looking up at me with an odd smile.

"So he came out of the shower and didn't suspect a thing?"

"He's an idiot," she said. "I have a feeling he had something else on his mind."

I didn't want to know what she meant by that, didn't want to know how far Jenny went to preserve the illusion she described, so I turned to the window where the sun made its way toward high noon and the passing low clouds took turns darkening the day in shifts.

The notebooks came out and we each took a pen, scratching out doodles and nonsense as Jenny made her way through her constant medley of old songs and conspiracy theories but in a much better mood than usual, her thoughts for the first time I could remember turning to the future, the possibility of our reuniting in Minneapolis.

"Surely I'll get into the U of M," she said, "and my mom's broke so I'll get full financial aid and scholarships just like you."

Everything she said became a certainty and as she went on I listened, high and happy, her voice floating above us, calling out all her dreams now that Svenson was out of the way, now that the sheriff was sure to ride in and take her mother away. But as I began coming down, a nagging feeling developed. I wanted those pictures turned in before I left. I looked again at the new ring on Jenny's finger and felt we weren't safe. Not yet. We had to get those pictures to the sheriff.

"You're paranoid," Jenny said when I shared my worry.

"I could change my ticket," I said. "We could both sleep it off and turn it all in together. I have all month—I could go to Michigan at any time."

"I got this," she said. "Don't worry."

"It's hard for me not to worry about you, Jenny."

"You should worry about getting ready to see your mother," she said.

This was true. We had let the day get away from us, a frenetic blur of twitching and bodily tingles as the sun moved across the sky, throwing long shadows across my room. While I packed everything I owned except for the clothes I was wearing into my backpack, Jenny capped her needle and scraped the loose powder back into the baggie. We hardly put a dent in the pile of drugs and I was about to say something when she beat me to it.

"This," she said, holding the other bag of speed, "I do not need to take with me. I know it will end up in my nose or wherever, so can I leave it here?"

"Please do," I said, happy to hear this coming from Jenny.

She set the bag down on my desk and turned my way, eyes wide.

"What?" I said. "What is it?"

Jenny yanked my backpack from my hands, throwing it on the floor near the door, then moved into the space where it had been. She guided one of my hands to the small of her back, then took the other in both of hers, and running her thumbs over my knuckles, traced the bones beneath my skin.

"When we first met I made some assumptions about you," she said, "but lately I've been wondering if I was wrong."

"Such as?"

"You're so jealous about this ring thing," she said. "And were you and Chelsea kissing when I came downstairs?"

"She was about to kiss me," I said, "but no, we weren't."

"Good," she said, then she put her soft hands on my cheeks, and touched her lips to mine, once, twice, three times. The first, second, third, and only times I've kissed a girl. She pulled me down onto the bed and we lay there face-to-face, arms under and around each other, our bodies huddling together to get as close as possible. She touched her nose to my cheek and softly moved it up my face but, though it felt good to hold her close, there wasn't the same urgency as with Russell and this was clear to Jenny right away.

"No?" she asked. "Nothing?"

I shook my head. "S-s-sorry," I said.

"You are who you are, Shane," she said. "There's nothing wrong with that—no need to apologize for being yourself."

"It doesn't mean I don't love you," I said.

"If you still want to be around me and you don't want this," she said, "then that's true."

We didn't have much to say after that. Sitting side by side on the edge of my bed, Jenny's head on my shoulder, we stared at the wall together for a time as the afternoon sun gave way to evening. I tried to describe the people I had seen over the months I had spent staring, the work they did and the colosseum where they gathered, and then Jenny told me what she saw, a complexity of wires and cables on which all of the world's information was contained, ideas flashing along cables at the speed of light, a network that connected every single person on the planet.

"You see the past," she said. "And I see the future."

The sun had made its way west and the pinks and purples faded out of the sunset to tell us that the time had come. Jenny picked up a bottle of sleep aid and tapped six out onto my hand, the old remedy handed down by J. I took the pills and lay on my bed and Jenny sat on my desk chair, watched me as I fell asleep.

"Call me when you get back," she said in the last moments before I went out. "No, call me when you're there. Wait, you'll be busy, but I know how to find the number. I'll call you."

My eyes closed, the sleeping pills having shut off my body but not yet my mind, and Jenny shuffled around my room for a while. I felt her lips press against my forehead and then, after I heard the door click shut, I fell into a perfect, dark silence.

Twelve

I got up before daybreak, grabbed my backpack without even flipping on the lights, and made my way over to the Pump 'N Munch where my bus idled near the car wash. The sun rose over sod farms but I was back asleep before we hit Minneapolis and didn't wake up until we were deep into Wisconsin. We passed through Madison and, after hours of rolling plains, my mind too frazzled to think about anything but the scenery, came Chicago, where I met my transfer.

Raindrops tapped and clung to the windows as we rounded the south shore of Lake Michigan and then, after a few more hours on a highway that ran along the sandy sometimes rocky shoreline, a sign: SOUTH HAVEN. Lakeside mansions with long piers, lights green or red flashing at the end, then a sheet metal pyramid with smokestacks that reached the sky, the coal plant. Steam rose to meet the rain clouds. Beyond, the lake was red, a cloudy puddle of fresh water and clay. Even, light rains stirred the bottom. Along the shoreline white herons on long legs stalked prey among people, pasty white, stretched out on towels trying to catch what few rays were coming through the occasional showers.

The bus kneeled with a hydraulic *whoosh* and let me off at a Gas-N-Go on the main road. Friday afternoon traffic crawled in both directions. A phone book hung on a chain from a payphone near the door, so I looked up Frank Jorgenson and went inside to ask the attendant for directions. Then I wandered through the short stretch of downtown vacancies, most of the stores papered over and for sale like the downtown row in Holm. A bicycle shop, a bakery, live bait. All the other storefronts empty.

My heart pounded as I walked the streets of South Haven, nerves on edge as I prepared to see my mother for the first time in almost nine years. I still had no idea what I would say to her and when I tried to think of something I was distracted by the people of South Haven. A woman digging at a patch of dirt near her house, children playing touch football in a front yard. I wandered on, wondering why my mother would leave Grand Marais or Holm for a place like this, until I came to her street. The world blurred before me when I saw my mother's house. Three stories on a wide lawn with a porch along the front and a garage around the side, all beige with brown trim, it looked to me like a gingerbread house, and in a small heart-shaped garden on the front lawn, lilies and irises bloomed. Unsure if my misty eyes were from happiness, sadness, or some odd mix of both, I stepped up onto the porch and pressed the doorbell, my heart quaking in my chest. I hadn't been this nervous since the last time I had come knocking at her door.

The door opened a crack and a single brown eye peeked through.

"Hello?" she said.

"Hello, Mother."

The door swung open and there she was: my mother at thirty-four, twice my age. She had grown a bit thicker since I had last seen her, maybe from the baby, but aside from a few strands of gray, her hair still matched her eyes and she still had the same timid smile that I'd come to recognize as my own. She wore a navy-blue dress with red polka dots and her neck was wrapped three times with a string of what looked like pearls. On her way out the door—ten minutes later and I might have missed her.

"Shane! Hiiiiiiiiiiiiiiiiiiii." She said it with a nice high tone that dropped as it progressed, and I was nine years old again, knowing that my mother didn't want to see me. "What are you doing here?"

I pulled open the screen door and my mother stepped back, maintained a distance—she made no move to hug me; rather, she showed me to the living room. It had a high ceiling and big windows that looked out onto the front yard. A soft brown couch took up much of the room and a matching chair sat to the side. A framed print hung on the wall, a woman splayed out in a field of long grass looking toward the horizon where an old farmhouse and barn stood.

"Well, have a seat."

My mother sat on the chair, plucked a piece of lint from her dress, then crossed her arms and met my eyes in a way that didn't make me feel too welcome. I set down my backpack and flopped onto the couch as near to where I had come in as possible.

"So you live here with Frank?" I asked when I could no longer stand the silence.

"How do you know Frank?" she asked.

"I don't."

"Yeah, this is Frank's house," she said. "How did you even get here?"

"The bus."

"You know what I mean."

A flood of sadness welled up inside me until my throat grew closed and my nose ran. "Dad's dead," I choked out. I wiped my face on the sleeve of my flannel shirt and looked up to see that my mother was now looking out the window with great concentration. She stood and walked past me to get a closer look at whatever she saw. "I wanted to see you again before you were too."

Sinking deep into the couch, I told her back about my trip to find her using the Christmas card, how the money she had sent me all those years ago had gotten me this far, and how I had tracked her down while living in her old apartment in Holm. She listened to me but didn't look my way—of course, I had come unannounced so she may have had other things on her mind—and she didn't make a single movement when I broke down telling my story, merely waited for me to get through the checklist of things I had to say to her before she could go back to her life.

"You'll be staying here, I guess," she said when I finished. "Let me show you your room. Bring your bag."

I picked up my backpack and followed her through the dining room, past an old wooden table that seated six, and into the kitchen to the staircase. Three doors stood closed on the second floor but my mother only showed me the spare room, empty except for an old bed and a nightstand.

"Settle in," she said.

So this was it. Another dusty room in a small midwestern town. Stale, but at least there was light. I stepped to the window and between the peaked roofs of a couple houses and a few treetops I could make out Lake Michigan in the distance. A single sunbeam broke through the clouds to leave a trail of glitter on the water.

As I descended the stairs, I heard her pick up the phone. I froze in place and, a few clicks of the buttons later, she spoke.

"No, no, I don't know where he's going . . . couple days, he said . . . well, I'll bring him down there for now."

She hung up the phone and stood there a moment. The next step

I took made a loud creak and my mother spun with her hand on her heart.

"Oh my God, Shane," she gasped. "You scared the shit out of me."

She started laughing then, in the throaty way I remembered from my childhood, and I joined her it was so infectious. She leaned back against the counter and wiped her hand across her forehead as if the squeaky step had been a close call with death. Our laughter faded, but it eased me into feeling a little more at home. My mother picked up a pack of cigarettes, shook one out, and lit it with an unsteady match.

"I bought a restaurant, Shane," she said after a couple puffs built a wall of smoke between us. "I was struggling there for a while but I think this place is finally it. This weekend is the grand opening. We've been serving dinner for a few weeks already to work out the kinks, but here it comes. Tonight's the last practice night, tomorrow is the first official. It's nice that you've come—you can help out."

My expression betrayed me then. The smile dropped off my mother's face and she looked at the floor.

"I'm sorry, I don't know how to talk to you anymore, what to say. Is that something you'd want to do? If you came to see me, that's where I have to be."

"Well," I said, "let's see this place then."

"Great," she said and she was back on top. My mother stubbed out her cigarette, led me through the back door, and into the garage where a black jeep was parked. She pressed a button on her key ring that made the lights flash, the horn honk, and the doors unlock with a loud click. I climbed in and buckled my safety belt.

"Nice truck," I said. "Is it new?"

"It is," she said. "We had a little money left over from the restaurant loan."

She backed out onto the road and tiny raindrops speckled the windshield. We passed back the way I had come and, while I watched the scenery pass, my mother kept looking my way as she drove. When I turned to her she flicked on the windshield wipers and pointed.

"Look at that," she said.

"They work very well," I said and she smiled, looking back at the road.

The wipers kept a steady rhythm and as we pulled onto the lake road my eyes were drawn out over the reddish water to the small white-caps whipped up by the wind.

"Burrrr," my mother said, and when I didn't look her way she said it again. "Burrrrr, it's cold!"

"It is cold today," I said and when I met her eyes she shook her body in an exaggerated shiver.

The restaurant ran long and narrow along the lakeshore, with tall windows looking out at the water and a gravel parking lot out front. We parked among the few cars near the door and my mother left the keys in the ignition. Inside, a red-faced man with curly dark hair stood behind the bar talking to two women. He wore blue jeans and a shirt buttoned halfway up, chest hair sprouting. His hands were palm down on the bar, one in front of each woman. He said something I couldn't hear and slapped his hands down on the bar before he turned and came over to us. He leaned over and kissed my mother on the mouth.

"You must be Frank," I said.

The man set a tumbler in front of me and poured some brandy.

"Frank's long gone," my mother said.

The man nudged the glass toward me. My mother nodded her head and I picked up my drink.

"You can call me the Fisherman," the man said and lifted his hand to be shaken. I reached at an awkward angle. He gripped my fingers and shook them.

"What kind of handshake is that?"

My mother laughed. The Fisherman reached out and took a clump of my hair in his hand.

"What the fuck is this now?"

The Fisherman took a couple steps away, put his elbow on the bar, and then his face in his palm. "Jesus," he said. One of the ladies called him over and he turned to talk to her.

"He's the best thing that ever happened to me," my mother whispered.

I asked her about Frank but she didn't answer. Instead, she watched the Fisherman with eyes like slits, nothing that resembled trust. He talked to the ladies while he made two more drinks, brandy in tumblers, not the drinks in stemmed glasses like the ones in front of them. He put a cherry in one and a splash of water in the other. He said something and laughed into the air above him as he carried the drinks our way.

"Old Fashioned for the lady," he said, setting the drink with the cherry in front of my mother. "And a splash of lake water for the Fisherman." He raised his glass, my mother raised hers, then they both looked down at the tumbler before me. It would be a long weekend.

We drank. The Fisherman poured another round, made mine with ice and cola. This one would sit on the bar. The shot burned warm in my stomach and I felt lighter, giving me a much better feeling about what was happening.

"So this is your place?"

"We have one dinner that costs sixty dollars," she said. "We're going to be rich as soon as we pay off this credit card."

"Credit card?" I asked, looking away, my good feelings leaving as quickly as they had arrived. "I thought it was a loan."

Above three levels of liquor bottles hung giant cocktail glasses. My mother followed my gaze.

"Those are for family-sized margaritas," she said. "Should we get out of here?"

I nodded. I wanted to be as far from the Fisherman as possible but I wouldn't get my wish.

"We're going drinking, baby," my mother called to the Fisherman. "Get Susan to cover the bar."

Susan was a cousin I didn't know I had, my mother's brother's daughter, half a pair of twins. She walked behind the bar and set to washing glasses, loose blond hair bouncing on her shoulders with the motion of her hands in the sink. The Fisherman stood behind her, staring. One of the ladies asked for the check but he didn't even flinch.

"Get your jacket, baby," my mother shouted, startling him out of his trance. "We're leaving now."

The Fisherman didn't think to let me take the front seat so I climbed in back and tried to lean up into their conversation, only to be blocked by the Fisherman's arm, as he kept his hand on my mother's shoulder the entire drive. He told her about his day bartending and finished off his story by saying that all the women he had served in the bar that day were cows.

"I swear it, dear," he said. "Compared to you it was a real moo-fest in there today."

She laughed and swatted at his knee with her hand. The Fisherman knew how to talk to my mother.

The bar was called The Laughing Heron, a dark place where the tables and chairs were made from raw lumber. We were at a high table along the wall, my mother and the Fisherman were seated and I stood. The area between the tables and the bar was packed with men who had spent most of their lives laboring—painters, fishermen, a man who worked either in a coal mine or a foundry—and another group that appeared to have spent much time lifting heavy things. This was as good a time as any.

"So, I've come all this way to ask you to be a part of my life," I said. "I want to forgive you."

The Fisherman laughed. My mother furrowed her brow, then looked away.

"Forgive me for what?"

"For abandoning him, I believe," the Fisherman said.

"I know it's far," I said. "But we could meet up once in a while. I could take the bus again sometime. And soon I'll be living in Minneapolis in the dorms at the university. You could come visit on weekends. I'll get a job and put you up in a hotel."

"Weekends are going to be pretty busy at the restaurant," the Fisherman said, then under his breath: "College boy."

"What?"

"I should get more drinks," my mother said and made her way to the bar. The Fisherman and I looked at each other. He brushed my hair out of my eyes with a thick finger, then told me he had something he wanted to tell me later. My mother came back with a drink for the Fisherman and one for herself—I was still holding my first, unsipped, in my hand.

"You have a brother," my mother said, then dragged on her cigarette. "But you won't get to see him. Because of Frank."

"Your mother's a tornado, boy," the Fisherman said, "leaving broken homes and crying children all over the Midwest."

I shot a dirty look at the Fisherman, then asked my mother where Frank was again.

"He's probably getting it from behind right now," the Fisherman said and laughed. "Do you want me to tell this story for you?"

My mother looked down into her brandy and nodded.

"Well, your mother was at the restaurant and someone tossed melted butter all over her pants. She drove home quick, to find your stepdad bent over the kitchen table with a dick in his ass. I'll spare you the details, but your mother changed her clothes and went back to work."

"I knew something was up," my mother said. "He never cared when I gained weight. Said he would love me anyways."

"Maybe he loved you for who you are," I said.

"That guy only loves cock," the Fisherman said. "I'm going to piss."

He got up and his chair fell backwards. He looked down at it, then up at my mother before he walked off toward the bathroom. My mother stood and righted it for him.

"I'm not too lucky, Shane. First, there was your father, of course. Then Donald, who you met, the biker—damn, what a mistake he was. And now this business with Frank. It's not too easy for a woman, you know."

"You really fucked up when you left my father," I yelled, having lost what goodwill I had built up for my mother until then. "He was a rock." People at nearby tables turned toward us.

My mother looked into her drink for a moment, tapped at a floating ice cube with her finger. "He was a rock," she said, looking up from her glass. "You're right about that. But rocks are cold, Shane. People don't need rocks, they need warmth and love. I'm sorry, but when that's gone you shouldn't be tied to someone cold and unloving."

"That's what marriage is, Mother," I said. "A lifelong commitment. 'Til death do us part."

"This doesn't sound much like forgiveness," she said. "And you know nothing about it anyways. You're coming up on that time in your life when you're going to become something, Shane. You'll soon be who you are for the rest of your life. If you're going to be anything, don't be a rock."

"He's dead now so it doesn't matter either way, does it?" I asked. "But let me ask you one thing: Is that story about Frank true?"

The look in her eyes told me it was a lie but before she could answer, the man next to me swung his arm and knocked my drink out of my hand. Brandy and cola splashed on my mother and the man. The tumbler shattered, sending long shards of glass sliding across the floor.

"You better watch where you're going there, pretty boy," the man said. His sideburns continued down his jawline and up into a mustache. His chin was clean shaven.

My mother rose from her seat.

"What did you say to my son?" she yelled.

"I told your faggot son to watch what the fuck he was doing," the man snarled.

"We're going to leave," the Fisherman said from behind us, "but you better hope we don't meet again."

The man told us all to fuck off and turned back to the group he was with. The Fisherman sucked down his drink in one long pull, then my mother paid our tab and we left.

The Fisherman and I sat in the dining room after my mother had gone to bed. Six candle flame bulbs burned dimly in the chandelier overhead. A bottle of brandy and a bottle of cola sat on the table and some crooner played on a portable radio that followed the Fisherman around the house. He often sang along.

"Old Dino was my godfather," the Fisherman said. "Nicest guy you'll ever meet."

"Who?"

"Dino," he said, leaning toward me with a furrowed brow. "Dean Martin! The guy singing. Famous Dean Martin? Shit!"

"I thought this was Frank Sinatra," I said.

"Naw!" he yelled. "No, no, no, no, no! Sinatra is a pussy! He poked a hole in his eardrum to get out of the army. Old Dino never saw combat but at least he went where he was assigned."

I didn't care at all. I had no idea why I was still up, sitting with this man I hardly knew. I had taken a seat at the table upon our return from the bar, expecting that my mother would join us but, after the Fisherman and I poured drinks for ourselves, she had swept through the room claiming she was tired, then went to bed alone.

"Sinatra stayed behind to fuck everyone's wives."

"Well, that sounds familiar," I said.

A new song started up and the Fisherman garbled the words so badly I had no idea what he or Dean Martin were singing. At the second verse he pointed to the radio and smiled as Old Dino told us how he had been a rover, but now that was over.

"I once had sex with five women at the same time," the Fisherman told me as the song ended. "Five girls, one boy," he sang, mutilating the final lyric, "no grief, much joy."

Startled, I sipped my drink. I had been planning to let my drink sit untouched, but I reached for it every time the Fisherman made me uncomfortable.

"You could probably do that," he said and I sank into my seat, crossed my arms. "You could be a male escort. You've got the face, but you'd have to cut that fucking hair away from it."

Outside, the rain dripped from the eaves, tapped on the windows, and I tried to imagine anyplace other than where I was. I wondered if it was raining in Holm, if the sheriff had taken the evidence from Jenny and made a move on Svenson.

"I'd have to see your cock, of course. To be sure."

I sipped my drink and when I set it down my hands moved to the brandy and the cola, setting a bottle to each side of my drink, a wall of liquid between us.

"I love blondes," he said. "Blondes with Heavenly Bodies. That's the name of my club in Chicago. I'm part owner."

The Fisherman stood and walked into the kitchen. Opened the freezer.

"Blondes get me into trouble with your mother," he called from the kitchen. "There are a couple at your mom's restaurant that I'd like to fuck. Your cousin Susan, for one. Her sister I haven't met yet, but I'm sure I'd do her too—they are twins, after all. She probably looks just like her."

I heard the rattle of an ice tray being emptied into a bowl and then water from the tap. Refilling the tray. The Fisherman may have been a drunk but he was a man with priorities. He came back with the ice and finished his drink. He took one cube and filled the rest of his glass with brandy. I took three and added cola. He raised his and downed half the glass in one pull.

"I'm a bad man," the Fisherman said. "Do you know why they call me the Fisherman? 'Cause I throw people in the lake."

I sipped my drink and absentmindedly shook my head.

"You don't believe me?" he asked, chair screeching across the floor as he stood up. He looked hurt by my betrayal. "I'm actually on the run right now, staying here while things cool down. My club's going through a bankruptcy. I stopped at this bar on my way out of town, met this woman, and walked into this."

"My mother knows about this?" I asked. "You remember that you're talking about my mother, right?"

But he wasn't talking to me anymore. Maybe he was recounting his life to himself, stacking up his feats of manhood, justifying his presence to the world. The song on the radio changed and he sat back down, singing along to snippets of Old Dino; sometimes he knew the words, sometimes he didn't. His bravado reminded me of Russell's stories about girls from the days before our night together behind the Aurora and, horrified, I came to understand one thing I had inherited from my mother: her taste in men.

"People in Chicago know that if you're giving someone cement shoes I'm the man to call."

His eyes cut at me with the same hungry look he had set on my cousin earlier. I picked up my glass but didn't drink, held it for a moment, then set it back on the table. The phone in the kitchen rang but the Fisherman didn't notice.

"Five women at the same time and they paid me to do it. You could make a thousand dollars a weekend and all you would be doing is fucking women."

"I don't think I could do that," I said but he didn't answer. He leaned back into his chair and his head lolled on his neck, his eyes fluttered, and his mouth popped open just enough for his tongue to slip out. When his unseeing eyes stared off at the wall beyond me for a moment I thought he had passed out sitting up, but then he shivered back to consciousness and smiled so wide I could see that one of his frontmost molars was missing.

"What did you say?"

"I said I don't think I could do that."

I reached for my drink and the Fisherman came out of his chair, wrapped his hand around my bicep, dug his fingernails into the soft skin on the inside of my arm. He pulled me out of my seat and pushed me backwards until I was against the wall. His strength made me weak and I folded into his arms.

"Show me your cock," he said through clenched teeth. His brandy breath tickled my ear and sent goose bumps up all over my body.

My free hand went to my belt and he let go of the other. I undid my pants and closed my eyes. When I opened them, the Fisherman was

now in my chair, brandy in his hand, staring. The phone was still ringing in the kitchen.

"You couldn't even please one woman with that little thing," he said
and laughed. "And look! Your little guy is standing up! Your mom was
right—you are a faggot. Just like Frank."

It took me a moment to understand that he was mocking me. I
looked down at myself, now fully aroused, then pulled up my pants,
walked past the Fisherman into the kitchen, and picked up the receiver.

"Hey Jim," a woman's voice asked. "Have you put her to bed yet?"

"What?"

"Jim?" The voice grew flustered. "Come over here and fuck me
right now."

I cut the connection and dialed Jenny's number. It rang ten times
with no answer. It was late—maybe she was sleeping. When I hung up,
my mother was behind me, eyes heavy with sleep, creases on her face
from her pillow.

"Who was that?"

"It was nothing," I said. "Wrong number, then I tried to call my
friend."

"A friend in Minnesota? Long distance?"

"Yeah, no one answered."

"You could've asked."

"Whatever," I said. "I'm going to bed."

My mother made her way to the dining room but, before I could hear
what she said to the Fisherman, I climbed the stairs. The guest room was
quiet and cold, rain tapping at the window, so I got under the blankets
and shivered until I warmed the bed with my body. I was on the edge of
sleep when the phone rang again. A crash came from the kitchen and my
mother started yelling. The Fisherman's voice grew just as loud. I thought
for a moment that I should go break them up but then it was morning.

My sleep a mere second of restless darkness, I stumbled downstairs to find the Fisherman was still awake, still drinking, the same Dean Martin songs playing on the portable radio. He smiled at me over his liquid breakfast. Red eyes and messy hair but otherwise unfazed.

"I told your mother you showed me your cock last night," he said. "We had a good laugh about it when I drove her to the restaurant this morning." He lifted his glass, toasting me, and then drained it.

I walked past him to go to the bathroom.

"And you need a fucking haircut," he said, holding a twenty-dollar bill in the air. "Your mother gave me this for your barber."

On the way to the barber shop, the Fisherman stopped at the bar on the ground floor of the big white hotel that overlooked the lake. He ordered me a Bloody Mary and for himself, of course, brandy and water. He drank in silence until he was halfway done with his second drink. My first sat sweating before us.

"You need to start taking care of yourself," he said. "You're all mousy and queer-looking. You need to look sharp. Get a haircut every two weeks. I mean short hair, not any of this hippy bullshit. Clip your fingernails and use a file. That's important. No woman wants to be all clawed up on the inside."

The bartender was sorry to interrupt but wondered if the Fisherman had paged someone. He said yes and ordered another drink.

"Probably the barber," he said. "Told him to call when a spot opened up."

"You paged a barber?" I asked but the Fisherman didn't answer. He finished his drink and went off to the phone.

The bartender came back with the drink and set it down. Then he picked up the empty, looked over at the Fisherman and back at me.

"Your old man always drink three of these before noon?"

"It's likely," I said. Then, in a moment of genius that I haven't matched since, I told him he wasn't my old man, rather that I was a prostitute from Chicago and we had a room upstairs. The bartender stepped away when the Fisherman returned, tapped the other bartender on the shoulder, and they both looked our way for a while.

"You gotta go to where the pussy is," he said. "Go dancing. Trim your pubic hair, for God's sake, and get a suntan."

The Fisherman tossed his drink back in one big swallow. He set the twenty my mother had given him for my haircut on the bar and we left. Outside was gray, raining again. The Fisherman drove two blocks and pointed. Said he would be back to pick me up in twenty-five minutes.

I ran through the rain to the door. A bell jangled when I entered and a woman with blond hair and bangs asked if she could help me.

"Someone called and said there was an opening," I told her.

"I'm the only one here," she said, "and I haven't called anyone. No matter, there's no one waiting."

She put me in the chair and faced me toward the mirror so I could watch my hair fall in long swaths to the floor. The change was immediate and, as she made her way around me from one side to the other, I could see side-by-side how my long hair had made me look like a girl. It didn't help me understand why it had led some people to the edge of their wits, but I could see the cause for confusion in a way that I hadn't before. I had always been me, as far as I could tell, the change in my hair so subtle from day to day that I had grown into my own vision of myself over the years it took to get that long.

When she was done, I appeared to be a respectable young man. My hair shorn close on the sides but still long on top, a cowlick in front kept my bangs out of my eyes. I bent down, took some of the cuttings in my hand, and thought of my father. Now I looked very much like him. He had been the one who allowed me to keep my long hair in spite of my uncle and everyone else in Grand Marais, telling me all along that I was my own person, that it didn't matter what anyone thought. It was a defining aspect of my personality and I had expected having short hair to cause some deep change to my very being, but I felt no different. With or without my hair, I would still be as much of a man as I always was, the man my father encouraged me to be.

I paid for my haircut with the last of my cash, left five bucks as a tip and pocketed three quarters, then waited in a seat near the window, watching the rain. Two hours after he dropped me off, the Fisherman pulled up and laid on the horn, didn't let up until I was in the car. I didn't ask where he'd been, but I imagined it had something to do with the woman who had called for Jim.

My mother made a little squeal when she saw me, ruffling my new haircut.

"So handsome, just like someone else we know," she said and looked around, but the Fisherman was already standing at the bar, lake water on his mind. Then, pressing a folded banknote into my hand, she got to the point: "I want you to help out tonight. If anyone asks you for anything, do it. I have a lobster in the back for your dinner."

Another hundred-dollar bill. I stuffed the money in my pocket and left her at the host stand where she and my cousin planned out the seating chart for that night's reservations. In the dining room, the busboys draped white linen over the bare tables, then laid out the flatware and the waitresses followed with cloth napkins and metal carafes of hot water to polish the wineglasses and silver. Fresh roses had been cut and a small vase had been prepared for each table with a single stem and baby's breath. For the finishing touch, I lit candles in tiny gold-flecked cups and placed them just far enough from the flowers that the petals didn't wilt.

It was the nicest restaurant I had ever seen but I had a sneaking feeling that even if it did live up to its looks, my mother would grow bored with it and move on to the next thing that caught her wandering eye. My father, me, Donald, Holm, Frank, her other child, the restaurant, the Fisherman. My mother wasn't hospitable; she knew nothing of hospitality. I knew she didn't care about any of the people who would visit her place that night—she was looking out for herself and there wasn't anything wrong with that. I decided I'd do best to follow her lead, and with that thought I was free. An incredible lightness came over me. It was done. I had found my mother and taken it as far as it could go, and soon I would be back in Holm with Jenny again for the last few weeks of summer, then off to the rest of my life.

The people were few at first but by seven o'clock the restaurant was full and the rain had stopped, a warm evening sun angling in on the dinner guests through the lakeside windows. I followed the Fisherman around the dining room and watched him stare at my cousin. He had no purpose or function at the restaurant and, as if to prove this, he ordered dinner at seven thirty when the dining room was still full. He had a tall glass of lake water and the sixty-dollar entrée that my mother had been so proud of the previous day: lobster tail, crab legs, and filet mignon. Halfway through his meal he got up to find Susan, asked her if she would melt some more butter and bring him another drink. She brought the butter and when she set it down the Fisherman grabbed her wrist and pulled her close. He licked her face from chin to ear, then pushed her away and told her she forgot his fucking brandy before he picked up his silverware and went back to his meal.

At sunset, while clearing plates from a table near the window I was distracted by a heron stalking through the shallow water near the shore, hunting. As I watched, the bird stopped in the glittery trail of sunlight on the water, poised on one leg, and struck before it stalked off down the beach, a crayfish hanging from its beak by the claw. The crayfish struggled, swinging from its trapped arm, clapping at the bird's neck with the other claw until its wrist was severed, when it fell to the sand incomplete. The bird waddled after it to take another stab but came up with an empty beak before it flapped its wings and lifted itself into the air.

After the dinner business was finished, I asked my mother to bring me to her house so I could rest before my bus ride home. I told her I wasn't hungry but she sat me down at a table by the window with a glass of beer and stomped off toward the kitchen, then came back with the biggest lobster I had seen all night.

"It's a three pounder," she said and pulled out the chair opposite me to sit down. Uncomfortable, she shifted in her seat, folded her hands, smiled up at me. "Is there anything else you need here?"

I thought for a moment that maybe I had been wrong about my mother, but when I told her I had everything I wanted she stood and walked off. Thinking she was planning to return, I set down my fork and watched her weave through the men milling near the bar and around the bartender, take a glass, and fill it like the Fisherman had—ice, brandy, cherry—then, bringing the straw to her lips, she turned and leaned against the bar, eyes on the television mounted in a corner I couldn't see. I waited for a while, watching her watch television, but when she went for a second drink I turned back to my meal.

I had never eaten lobster before and, though I had seen people eating it all night, I wasn't sure how to use the cracker, didn't know how to get the meat out of the claws. I struggled with a claw for a while but then moved on to my potatoes and corn on the cob, forked out the tail and got that down. I sipped my beer and looked out at the lake, now dark, but I could see the lights of a passing tanker and a sailboat anchored out in the distance. In the reflection I saw the Fisherman approaching and tried to ignore him, hoping he would leave me alone, but he walked right up to my table and ripped the claw I had been working on right off my lobster.

"What, do you not know how to do this?" he asked, then snapped the claw in half with his hands and slurped the meat out of the shell before he picked up my cup of butter and took a sip. He looked down at me and shook his head before he tossed the empty claw back on my plate and turned toward the bar.

In bed that night, my thoughts about the Fisherman became images that haunted my dreams. Having his way with my mother, my cousin Susan and her twin, and Jenny. Then all four at once, making eyes at me to be the fifth, reaching out, taking me by the shoulder, shaking me.

"Be a fucking man," he said, rattling me with each word, but that scene fell away and I opened my eyes to see that it wasn't the Fisherman's hands on my shoulders but my mother's.

"Wake up, Shane," she said, eyes closed, still asleep herself. "It's time to leave."

My mother dropped me off at the Gas-N-Go without getting out of the jeep, rolling down the window to thank me for helping out at the restaurant before spinning the wheel and heading back to the Fisherman. No mention of another meeting and then she was as gone as she had always been, the only thing remaining was the hundred-dollar bill in my pocket. I made my way into the Gas-N-Go, bought two shitty donuts, and told the cashier she could keep the change. Ninety-eight dollars plus coins. I didn't want anything to do with it. Stood outside and ground the nasty pastries in my mouth, swallowed them down while I waited for the bus, alone, in the dark. Soon all of this, my mother, the Fisherman, and South Haven itself, would be behind me forever.

When the bus pulled into the station in Chicago, I had an hour before my connection and just enough change to call Jenny's house from the pay phone. No answer. This worried me. She hadn't called my mother's house like she said she would, hadn't answered when I called, and now she still wasn't around. My paranoia from my last day in Holm returned and I was certain that Svenson had figured us out and gotten his hands on her. I did what I could to squash those thoughts, but soon I was back on the phone, growing more and more worried until it was picked up on the nineteenth ring.

"Jenny?" I asked. Silence. "Jenny?" Only breathing on the line. Something was wrong—Kristina had answered the phone. She had made her way from where she was to the kitchen, in her drugged-out state, hoping it was Jenny. This was not a good sign.

"Kristina?" I asked. "Answer! Are you okay? Do you know where Jenny is?"

More deep breathing and then a dead line. My three quarters fell into the phone, leaving me with nothing, and I wished then that I hadn't been so hasty with my mother's money.

I made my way onto the bus when it was time and, in spite of my worries or maybe because of them, I passed out and moved right into a dream. Jenny's house stood before me, so close yet impossibly far as I stood immobile in the street, watching Jenny approach on foot. I called her name but she didn't hear me, couldn't see me. Oblivious, she stepped up onto the curb, focused on her front door until the sound of a pump action drew her attention up the street. We both turned to see the barrel of a rifle sticking out the open window of a pickup truck, like in a cartoon or an old movie, holding her as its target. The door swung open with a screech and a young man stepped out, not taking his sights off Jenny. Although his silhouette could have been any boy in town—cowboy hat, T-shirt, jeans, and boots—neither of us needed light to know who was after her.

"Don't even think about it," he said, though she hadn't. "You get your ass in the truck."

She stood her ground for a moment and a swell of wind came over them, shuffling the leaves of the nearby trees.

"But my mother," she said, not pleading but rather calm, "you know she needs my help."

"You should have thought about that before you tried to cross me."

"I didn't cross you," she said. "You've been running on that shit for days. We both have. Let's go inside and get some sleep. I'll hold you 'til you're tired. You aren't thinking straight."

"I'll be the judge of that," he said and motioned with his gun that she get moving.

As she stepped across her lawn, she looked to her neighbors' windows, all dark. Defeated, her shoulders slumped and she made the last slow steps to the open passenger door. After she climbed in, Svenson circled the front of the truck, sights still trained on her, opened his door, and stuck the barrel of the rifle deep into her stomach before he got behind the wheel. After his door screeched shut he threw the truck in gear and peeled out into the street where I stood, lead-footed, unable to jump out of the way as he ran me down. I raised my hands before my face to block the light, then bolted upright in my bus seat, the lights of the tall buildings of downtown Minneapolis flickering on in the growing twilight. An hour to go and we couldn't get back fast enough.

Thirteen

Only three days had passed but Holm was different, even the smell. Walking down Center, the burning plastic, the hot steel of the metal works shop, and whatever those other factories produced all made their way to my nose for the first time. Sour and spoiled, the humid air hung around me and hurried my steps. By the time I reached the train crossing I was running.

"Jenny!" I called as I turned north on the tracks toward where I knew she painted trains but I received no response so I called again. "Jenny!"

Flicking my lighter near each boxcar, I looked for any new HOPEs but found none. Dejected, I made my way toward the Arlington but saw from half a block away that my light wasn't on. I had hoped that she was hiding out at my place, maybe she had even called my mother's house to find me gone. The lights being out wasn't proof that she wasn't in there, however, so I climbed the rickety stairs to the third floor and knocked while I fumbled with my keys. No one answered, so I opened the door to find a mess that I wasn't expecting, the bed unmade and garbage strewn across the floor, but no sign of Jenny. I flipped off the lights and shut the door again.

"Where is she?" I asked the empty hallway.

After I dug into my backpack to find I had no change, I picked up the pay phone and dialed 0. When the operator answered I told her I'd like to make a collect call and gave her Jenny's number.

"Your party is not answering," the operator said, having cut off the call after the tenth ring. "Is there anything else I can do for you?"

I gave her my mother's number and she picked up on the second ring.

"Jim?" my mother asked before the operator could even go into the spiel about the collect call. She sounded panicked. Once the operator got her to accept the charges she asked me a question I didn't expect: "Have you heard from Jim?"

"No," I said, "why would I know where he is?"

"I don't know, Shane," she said, defeated. "I don't know what to do anymore." I couldn't help but feel sorry for her, knowing that he was off with some woman in town—my mother facing now what she had put my father through all those years earlier—but I wasn't going to let that distract me now.

"Has anyone called for me?"

"For you? Why would anyone call *my* house for *you*?"

The little goodwill I felt for my mother left me then.

"Is that a no?"

"Of course it is," she said. "How can you call me at a time like this and ask that?"

"He's cheating on you, Mother," I said, "and you deserve it."

I slammed the receiver into the cradle, then stood there for a moment, staring at the phone, amazed at what I had done, but was startled out of it when the phone rang. Assuming it was my mother calling back,

I turned and ran down the stairs and out into the street, my backpack bouncing hard behind me as I descended. Only when I was halfway to her house did I realize that the callback could have been Jenny.

I came upon Jenny's house to find the garage open, the car gone, and the door into the house ajar. Someone had left in a hurry. Pulling the garage door closed from the inside, I switched off the light and stepped into the house to hear a newscaster pass it to the weatherman on the television at top volume.

Every light in the house was burning and mosquitos, having entered through the same door I had, swarmed around the fixtures. Finding a bottle shattered in the kitchen, brown liquid pooling in the low parts of the uneven floor, I smelled a touch of whiskey mingling in the air with cigarette smoke and, moving into the living room it all came together with the stink of days-old shit: Kristina, lying on the couch with her hand to her mouth, dead to the world, liquor and pill bottles on the table before her.

"Kristina?"

I shook her shoulder and her hand fell away limp, but when she moved it back to cover her nose, I knew she was still alive. Looking her over, I saw the stains causing the smell, a sludgy wetness moving from her jeans to the couch cushions, and had to choke back down what tried to come out of me.

Unsure what to do, I went into the kitchen and paced for a moment. On the counter was an overflowing ashtray next to a pile of dirty dishes that extended into the sink. I rinsed out a glass, took it to the living room to pour myself a drink, and then stepped out onto the deck. The whiskey was warm and rough and once I got it down my mind slowed a bit. Jenny had been gone for a while and, though I knew she was often late and came home to her mother's accidents, she wouldn't leave Kristina alone for this long on purpose. These were bad signs. I needed to call the sheriff.

I found the phone receiver hanging at the end of its spiral cord, no dial tone, but it chirped back to life after a few taps on the hook and I dialed the police station. While it rang, I saw that an answering machine lay in a jumble at my feet—Kristina having ripped it out of the wall at some point, I assumed—so I plugged it back in and turned it on, just in case Jenny was trying to call from wherever she was. When Claire answered at the station, she patched me through to the sheriff in his car and I tried to tell him what I knew but it all came out at once.

"Stop, Shane," he said. "Slow down."

"Jenny's gone," I said. "The car is missing."

He said he'd come within an hour and hung up. I had plenty to keep my mind busy while I waited. First I had to take care of Jenny's mother.

I took the top sheet from Kristina's bed and spread it on the floor next to the couch, rolled her down. Although I could see the direct line between mother and daughter, the youthful glow in Jenny was fading in Kristina. Her face had begun to grow hollow, her cheeks sunken, her hair thin. Her lips were dry and cracked and the skin of her hands too. Drugs, whiskey, loneliness. She was Jenny's future, if Jenny was lucky enough to have one.

I started with a sponge and some towels to clean the vomit out of her hair before I moved to the mess in her pants. It took a moment to overcome my embarrassment when I saw what the job entailed, the creases that needed to be wiped clean, but I got her changed and carried her to bed, so light she felt like no more than a cat in my arms. She lay back in her clean pajamas and stretched against her pillows, yawned, and then sunk back deep to wherever she came from.

After I poured another quick sip of whiskey, I slapped a few mosquitos, then started in the kitchen with the broken bottle on the floor, soaking up the liquor with a towel before I swept up the broken glass. It hit me while I was doing the dishes. Jenny was gone. I knew it was Svenson, he had to have done it. I had seen up close what he had done with the dogs. Poison, a knife through the neck. These thoughts disappeared into the work, the cleaning, the dishwashing, but would resurface. I was clear-headed when I made my way to the garage to find bug spray, which I sprayed at the clouds of mosquitos and then watched them fall out of the air, but later, as I pulled the corduroy covers off the couch cushions, I understood that maybe this life had grown to be too much for Jenny. I had only been here an hour and I could see that Kristina needed full-time supervision, someone to wipe her ass and keep her away from the whiskey.

I took Kristina's soiled clothes out into the backyard, laid them out on the cement beneath the deck, and sprayed them with the garden hose, a preliminary rinse before I put them in the washing machine. I tried to breathe deeply, remain calm.

Back inside, I collected all the prescription bottles in a garbage bag and stuffed it under the sink. The other trash filled two bags: junk mail, cigarette butts, newspapers. Important-looking mail, those envelopes stamped with FORECLOSURE NOTICE, FINAL NOTICE, or PAST DUE, I stacked on the counter by the answering machine. I found the vacuum cleaner in the hall closet and, after closing Kristina's door so the sound wouldn't reach her, I took solace in raking the threads of the carpet this way and that.

When the sheriff arrived I met him in the front yard and told him how the house looked when I got there, then I told him about our trip to Svenson's and Jenny's plan. He shook his head while he listened to how I had not done anything he had asked me to do.

"No, I haven't seen her," he said when I finished. "Maybe she knew she was in trouble so she took the car and drove as far as she could make it."

That was the best possible situation, but we both knew this wasn't the case.

"She would never leave Kristina like this," I said.

"If this is true," the sheriff said, "if he went after her, then I want you to stay the hell away from him. Don't you go confronting him now."

The sheriff told me he was going to ask the neighbors if they had seen anything and walked off toward the house next door, so I went inside and finished vacuuming. Once I tied up the cord and wheeled it back into the closet, the place looked somewhat presentable. Unsure what else to do, I sat down on the couch and was met with the racing thoughts that my cleaning had displaced, images of Jenny twisted and beaten, stabbed through the neck. The wound deep into Sissy's neck superimposed on Jenny, lying in a grassy ditch. I turned the volume on the television back up to where Kristina had it when I arrived but it was no help.

The sheriff rang the doorbell when he returned to tell me that the neighbors hadn't seen anything.

"I'll go talk to Svenson about her," he said, "to see if he cracks, but without that evidence we don't have probable cause. At this point it's your word against his. We have a young woman with a history of running away who appears to have run away. I can't go search his place because you tell me you think he did it."

I invited him in and he climbed the stairs to the living room, gave a quizzical look toward the couch.

"What happened to the cushions?"

"You don't want to know," I said.

We sat down and went on with the missing persons report. Unlike with my mother, Jenny was still a minor so her disappearance was cause for immediate investigation. I didn't know the make of the car but the sheriff did, he knew the license plate number and Jenny's middle name and birthday. I would have had a lot of trouble filing this report with any other police officer. He also knew the information for next of kin. He used a few acronyms I didn't understand, ATL and APB, and told me that every police officer within fifty miles would be on the look-out for her once he called the report into Claire. He was on the phone for a minute and it was done.

"How is she? Kristina, I mean."

"The usual," I said. "Drugged out. She's got an entire pharmacy up here. She's sleeping now and I'll bet she has no idea Jenny is missing."

"Drugged out?" he asked. "What do you mean?"

I went to the kitchen and came back with the bag of prescription bottles, held it open for him. He reached in and came out with three bottles, held them to the light to inspect the labels.

"Jesus," he said. "I'm going to have a talk with this doctor."

He dug through the bag for a while, took two bottles out, and set them on the coffee table before cinching the bag and tying it shut with a knot.

"Do you think you could stick around here for a while?" the sheriff asked. "Watch over the place, take care of Kristina? I could give you a ride down to the Arlington quick if you need to pick anything up."

"Everything I own is already here," I said.

"You can tell her in the morning that if she wants these drugs back she can call me."

I was surprised that Jenny had been right, that a single visit from the sheriff would drum up his affection. He hadn't even seen Kristina yet but was working to help her.

———

The sheriff was gone no more than twenty minutes before I felt the crush of emotions heading my way so I took another sip of whiskey and picked up the telephone. When the car pulled up a few minutes later, I hid the bottle under my shirt and ran across the front yard, keys jingling in my pocket. I opened the door and sat down, pulled the bottle from where it was hidden, and set it on the floor.

"Nice haircut," Russell said and put the car in gear. I ran my fingers through my hair, having forgotten about my trip to the barber. It felt like a lifetime ago, my mother and the Fisherman.

He turned the first corner and I reached over to put my hand on his knee, sliding it up his leg until it hit metal, smooth and cool. A flask on the seat between his legs.

"I thought you quit drinking," I said.

"I did," he said, "but then I decided to quit quittin'."

I moved the flask to my right hand, returned my left to his knee, then tipped it back and drank until it was gone. I wanted to drown the parts of me that were calling out for Jenny, to retreat into the darkness of whiskey and Russell, with the hope that the sheriff would have it all figured out when I returned.

"Thirsty?" he asked.

"I brought more," I said. "Don't worry."

Russell turned left onto Old Main and a strange noise filled the car. At first I thought something was wrong with the engine, or maybe the sheriff had caught us speeding, but when Russell pulled onto the shoulder and turned toward me it became clear that it grew from deep inside my chest, a siren of sadness I didn't know I was sounding, didn't know I was capable of making, and was not able to control. Not knowing what else to do he put his arms around me, his hand on the back of my head to muffle my wails with his body. The car shook with my convulsions. I bit Russell's shoulder until I felt it give and then the pressure behind my eyes began to fade in waves. I wiped my nose with the sleeves of my flannel shirt and we settled back into our seats.

"What's wrong?" Russell asked.

"Everything."

"Beginning with?"

"Jenny's missing."

"Where'd she go?"

"If I knew that, she wouldn't be missing," I said, wishing I hadn't, but Russell could tell I was upset and let it go.

"Where do you think she is?"

"I think Svenson did something to her."

"To Jenny? I doubt it. Unless you mean he put her on a pedestal. Dude is dopey in love with her."

We cruised the dark streets of Holm as I told him the story, beginning with the sheriff busting us smoking, through our plans to take Svenson down, and ending with my arrival to find the car missing.

"What were you guys thinking?" he asked as we pulled up to an apartment building on Cypress.

"You can't stop Jenny when she has her mind set on something," I said.

As we got out of the car his pager went off. He looked down at his waistband and clicked on the light, then he took a key off his key ring and told me he was in 3A before he got back in his car, turned wide, and took off.

Russell's place was a single room with a stove and a sink along one wall. The smell of fresh paint hung in the air and my footsteps made a loud echo that reminded me of Svenson's living room. Aside from a mattress in the corner near the window, a single suitcase lay flopped open in the middle of the room, all of Russell's belongings spilling across the floor. I stepped to the window and saw the water tower in the distance, a silhouette a touch darker than the night sky, and seeing that the sill was wide enough, I perched there and watched the occasional car pass by on Center while I sipped from the bottle.

Russell walked in twenty minutes later and I kept my eyes pointed at the window, watching his reflection as he approached, then stood when he came up behind me so that we were both looking outside.

"I missed you," Russell said, wrapping his arms around me and putting his chin on my shoulder. This was the first time he had acknowledged with words our shadowy moments together. It was simple, but I knew that it went against everything he believed to admit that to me. In the window I could see that my haircut made us look alike. Little blond twins. Whereas I had looked like Jenny before I went to my mother's, I had come back looking like Russell. I turned toward him and he buried his face in my neck.

"I missed you too," I said and we sat down on the edge of his mattress.

We passed the bottle back and forth while he told me of the latest falling out with his parents, disowned like he had predicted earlier in the summer, and how he had ended up moving in here a few days earlier.

"I slept in my car for a while," he said, now fully drunk. "I was pretty mad at the time, but it doesn't seem like such a big deal now. I'll get by."

"You'll be fine," I said, then leaned in and kissed him. "We'll be fine."

He stood up and pulled from one pocket a huge wad of cash and a plastic baggie full of capsules from the other, then stood there for a moment, looking around the room. The windowsill, the unsheeted and uncovered mattress, the empty floor.

"I need some furniture," he said, and laughed.

"You can put that stuff right here," I said, holding out my hand.

"You want one of these?"

I didn't want speed specifically but I needed something, some good feeling, comfort. Russell took a single capsule from the bag and placed it in my hand, then stuffed the rest into the corner of his suitcase. He had no surface, no mirror, so I wiped off the windowsill and prepared it there, breaking it up into eight thin lines. I asked Russell for a dollar, then rolled it up and took down a line, then stood and held the makeshift straw out to Russell as the tingly well-being washed over my drunken sadness.

"I don't know," he said, but it only took a subtle nudge, a moving of the bill a little closer to him, and then with a quick sniff both of our sad moods vanished and we grew chatty. Russell paced between the window and the door, suddenly aware of why his business was booming, and I watched him from the bed as he tried to describe how he felt.

"It's like you realize you've never done anything wrong," he said, arms spread wide, eyes toward the ceiling, "like all the guilt and shame is lifted away and you can be yourself without judgment."

We snorted again and passed the bottle and then it was my turn to pace while I told him about my trip to Michigan, about my mother and the Fisherman, the long ride home, and what had been waiting for me.

"You shouldn't have come back," Russell said.

"I have nowhere else to go. I didn't want to stay there."

"You could have gone straight to Minneapolis," he said. "I'm the one who has nowhere to go. I barely make enough money to pay for this place and my car. I'll never get out of this shithole town."

"You'll be fine," I said, running my fingers through his hair, calming him to silence. "We'll be fine."

We lay there for a time, staring into each other's eyes until Russell could no longer hold back. He heaved his lips toward me, lurched his chest, but I held him down and the struggle became a dance, rhythmic convulsions of desire. When I finally dropped my hold it felt good to give in, to give myself to him. We rolled off the bed, onto the floor, around the room, in a speed-fueled storm until Russell took his mouth off mine. The moon shone a white rectangle on the floor next to where we lay in the dark.

"I shouldn't have gone and left her here alone," I said. "Visiting my mother was a giant waste of time anyways."

"Look, she saved you," he said, eyes wide in the moonlight, earnest. "If you had been in town I'm not so sure we'd be here talking about it now. I mean, if you're right about what happened."

After a few more lines and shots, the pins and needles passed over my body in waves and I reached again for Russell, tore his clothes from his body, and tried to make every inch of my body touch every inch of his.

"I hope you won't have any trouble remembering this tomorrow," I said.

Then it was morning and Russell lay in the bed so peaceful and quiet as I found and put on my clothes that I didn't wake him, but I couldn't help pressing my lips to his and running my fingers through his hair before I left.

Kristina was awake when I got back, frying an egg in the kitchen, a hand to her eyes to block the morning sun that streamed through the little window above the sink. I was surprised when she spoke.

"Thank you for cleaning up, Shane," she whispered, having no problem identifying me in spite of her constant condition or my new haircut. "Can I have my pills?"

"I don't think that's a good idea," I said. "There's something we need to talk about."

She took her egg to the table and, hand shaking, stabbed at it with her fork. She kept her eyes on her food as I told the story of how I found her, but crumpled her napkin and held her fist to her head, eyes closed, when I moved on to how I had cleaned her up. I thought it was her reaction to what I was saying, embarrassment, or the possibility of her daughter never returning. What she said next made clear her only concern.

"The pills," she said. "You can't take away someone's medication."

I stepped into the living room to grab the two bottles that the sheriff had left behind and set them before her. She read the labels, looked up at me with a scowl, then threw the bottles at the sliding door, each of them clunking against the glass with a hollow drum sound before falling to the floor.

"Where are the others?"

"The sheriff said you could call him if you want the other bottles," I told her.

"Sheriff Braun?" she asked. "When did he say that?"

"Last night," I said. "I called him when I got here."

She muttered something, then stood and brought her plate to the sink, throwing it in with a clatter. Breakfast done, she stretched out on her tiptoes to reach the cabinet above the refrigerator, took out another bottle of whiskey, and when she stumbled taking it down, I saw how the other bottle had broken but she saved this one. With a shaky hand, she took a glass from the drying rack near the sink, poured it half full of whiskey and ran some water from the tap to fill the rest, then she walked into the living room. The television came on and I heard Bob Barker asking his viewers to be sure to have their pets spayed or neutered.

I went to the sliding door and picked up the prescription bottles, Lithium and Ferralet, and put them on the table. I had no idea what these were, but I assumed the sheriff had taken all the good stuff, those pills Jenny and I had taken that night and any other narcotics, leaving the pills she needed but now refused to take. To follow his line of thinking, I went to the cabinet above the fridge, took down the three remaining bottles as quietly as I could, and poured all the liquor down the sink.

I had to wonder how Kristina lived like this, how she made it to the liquor store, the grocery store, and anywhere else and what money she used when she got there. I had no idea how she paid for anything: the house, the bills, the car. My father had been gone at work for most of every day to pay for a house much smaller than this one. Maybe alimony or child support, welfare or disability, maybe Social Security. The stack of past due bills on the counter caught my eye again, but I'd wait for the sheriff to discuss that. Instead, I spun the caps off the two prescription bottles, shook a pill out of each one, then walked into the living room and held them out for Kristina. She leaned around me so she could see the television but held her hand out, so I dropped the pills into her palm and took a seat on the couch so I could make sure she took them. A long moment passed but she washed them down with her whiskey and water.

Kristina's restlessness became impossible to ignore an hour later, when I looked up from the closing credits of *The Bold and the Beautiful.* Until then she had been quiet and still, as subdued as the other times I had been around her. Her symptoms were subtle at first. She reached across her chest to massage the muscles in her shoulder, moving on to sore points down her arms, and after a while she began rocking back and forth in her seat while she kneaded her thighs. Beads of sweat popped at her temples and she couldn't get enough air. After a few huge yawns, she bent over at the waist with stomach cramps, her hair soaked, plastered to her head.

"Kristina," I said, stepping over to her and putting my hand on her cold, sweaty forehead. "Are you okay?"

She looked up at me with wide, watery eyes, her irises a thin ring of blue around her growing pupils. I held my hand there until Kristina doubled over and puked egg and whiskey all over my feet. I had forgotten that running out of drugs could be so much worse than having them.

"Should we go to the bathroom?" I asked and, receiving a violent nod in return, wove my arm under her shoulders and lifted her so we could walk down the hall together, setting her on her knees before the toilet.

"Please shut the door," she said, but it didn't keep the sounds of her heaves contained.

I called the sheriff and then, after changing my pants and socks, I went to work cleaning up the vomit. It was a quick job compared to the overhaul of the previous night and I was back on the couch watching the next soap opera when the sheriff arrived. He walked right past me when I opened the door, followed my pointing finger to the bathroom and knocked.

"Kristina, baby," he said. "It's Joel. Can I come in?"

I didn't hear her answer, but he went in and closed the door and within a minute the water was running in the bath. The sheriff stuck his head out and asked me to pack a few changes of clothes into an overnight bag while they finished up. When they came out, Kristina was in the sheriff's arms, wearing a bathrobe. She held tight to the sheriff's shoulder, wild eyes darting to the shadows.

Outside, once we succeeded in getting Kristina into the car, the sheriff took a key ring from his pocket, removed a key, and gave it to me.

"Looks like you're the man of the house now."

I was grateful I had a job to distract me from the madness. That first day after the sheriff took Kristina away I lost myself in cracking eggs for pancake batter, in slamming potatoes through the french fry maker, in dicing onions for the huge pots of soup we made. Cooking was something I could control, a science of a sort in which my experiments always turned out more or less the same. My plates were worthy of photographs. Egg platters that could be featured in menus. The cross-hatched grill marks on my pork chops were impeccable. Aside from the orders that trickled in one at a time, something was always dirty enough to be cleaned at the Aurora. The deep fryer and grill were on metal stands that I pulled out from the wall so I could scrub the floors, sweep away the odd chicken chunk or french fry that went flying during service. I took a rag into the cooler to soak up the puddles of condensation that collected in the corners. It was a fine balancing act, keeping my attention on these necessary yet trivial tasks while the sheriff sought out what had happened to Jenny.

One afternoon a few days after my return, a familiar figure in a tiny blue hatchback pulled into the Aurora and I ran off the line into the dining room to see him pass the wide window there and into our back lot. Leaving what I was cooking to burn, I cut back through the kitchen, the dish room, and the break room, and rounding the last corner I heard the screen door slam shut as Leon made his way outside. Peeking around the cooler, I saw Svenson climbing out of the little car as Leon approached. They shook hands and Svenson called Leon sir before he pulled an envelope from his back pocket and pressed it into Leon's hand. The sight of the catering money sent my mind into a frenzy. Suddenly, I understood why Leon would prefer to have a sometimes truant stoner working for him rather than the previous cook, who had gone to him about my drug use. I snuck closer to the screen door to see if what they said would confirm my suspicions but I couldn't quite hear. I wanted more than anything to run out and confront Svenson—he couldn't kill me with Leon around, could he? When they shook hands again I turned and ran back to the kitchen to throw a couple more chicken breasts on the grill to replace the ones that were now charred black.

Leon walked up from the office a few minutes later with the envelope in his hand, made his way to the cash register to key in the catering totals, then left through the front door without a word to anyone. Not that this surprised me; I was working the closing shift and he often took off for hours at a time when I was in charge, but my new suspicions about him and Svenson led me to wonder if I knew him at all.

That was when I began pacing. I lost hours up and down Jenny's hallway, back and forth in the living room, out on the back deck. I stared hard into the thin forest that lined the edge of the property. Tall and narrow firs obstructed my view of the neighbor's house and beyond that, Old Main and the A&W on the other side, behind which the train tracks ran. The train whistle was the only thing that could draw me out of my thoughts. If I wasn't already out there when I heard the signal— two long, one short, one long—I'd make my way to the deck, descend the stairs, and cross through the neighbor's yard to the A&W where I could watch the HOPEs pass by.

I slept every night at Jenny's, made it my home. Russell came by when he could and I launched myself at him, tearing off his clothes, losing myself in his arms, but I was most grateful for the nights when he would show up tired, lie next to me on the couch, and fall asleep while we watched *The Odd Couple* or *The Jeffersons*, his breath on my neck, a tossed-over leg keeping me weighted down, grounded.

Although I could've gone into Jenny's room at any time, I didn't. I had, of course, checked to make sure she wasn't in there, but beyond that I left her room alone. I told myself each passing day that she had run away—that Svenson had nothing to do with it—that she would be back.

But then, on my seventh day back in Holm, I knew something was wrong. Standing at the crossing as the morning train made its way south, I noticed the HOPEs were disappearing; rather, they were already gone. Jenny had known this would happen when she made them, you can't expect graffiti to last, but their absence caught my eye: new patches of brown paint covered most of each train car and fresh identification numbers had been stenciled in where Jenny's pieces had hidden them. On the afternoon train I would find it was the same, not a single HOPE remained. The cars were free of all graffiti.

Fourteen

Cars and pickup trucks lined the county road for a quarter-mile, so Russell pulled right up to the gathering and let me out. He had been planning to join me, to park the car and return, but his pager buzzed as I opened the door.

"I can come back," he said. "It shouldn't take long."

"No problem," I said. "I can find my own way to town."

We stood there looking at each other for a second before I leaned back into the car and pressed my lips to his. He smiled when I drew away, a departure from the last time I had tried to bring our shadowy relationship into the light of day, then honked his horn twice as he drove off.

I watched his car round the bend, then stepped into the huddle of volunteers, a mass of red-and-black plaid and denim rolled up over leather boots, to see the sheriff standing before the crowd, a small light strapped to his head and a bottle of water in each hand as he addressed the group of about fifty, some of whom I recognized from the Arlington and the Aurora and even a couple from the field party and the Confederate flag revival. The sheriff was haggard, the bags under his eyes suggesting he hadn't caught more than a brief nap for a while, and his voice was weak, going hoarse. He turned one way and then the other as he explained proper procedure for searching, giving tips on how not to miss anything, then pointed out as an example the chain of men in chest waders and orange safety vests, arms linked, slowly crossing the river as one.

"A young couple found the car here," he called to the crowd. "It had been here for days, long enough for the bell and the light that signaled that the door was open to kill the battery. No sign of Jenny, not even her fingerprints—the car has been wiped clean, the door handles, the rearview mirror, the keys. No sign of her mother, the car's owner, either. Very suspicious. A smarter person would have worn gloves and let the old prints remain. All I can say is that I hope we don't find her here, because then there is still a chance that she's okay. Certainly, she has been the victim of foul play."

This last statement hit me like a fist to the chest, taking my wind and filling my eyes with tears. The sheer number of people had raised my hopes for a moment but now I understood that these people were expecting to find her dead body. This was a search for a corpse in the woods, not for Jenny. I turned away from the crowd as the sheriff answered some questions from the volunteers and took in the afternoon while I blinked back my sadness. The sun hung over the western bank of the river and a few wispy clouds spanned the sky, long white brushstrokes on the blue canvas.

The search parties organized and dispersed, five groups of nine sent in different directions. I walked arm in arm through the woods with the others in my group, only dropping our linked elbows to maneuver around trees. We didn't speak, our boots and shoes shuffling through the brush the only sound aside from the occasional shout of surprise as one of us tripped over a hidden branch or sunk in a sinkhole. A pair of squirrels followed us for a time, one brown and one black, leaping from branch to branch and watching us from the canopy as we inched through the forest.

There was one moment of excitement when someone at the end of our chain stumbled over a pile of bones, but it turned out to be an old deer carcass, long ago picked clean by the scavengers of the woods. We stood around the animal for a moment, each of us taking in the sharp ribs that reached toward the sky like saplings, then we kept on in the same direction until the volunteer leader called time. We moved one length of our line away from the river to cover new ground on our return.

Back at the meeting site, the other search parties came back empty-handed as well. I went down to the riverbank to watch the crew still pacing the river to the south but aside from a few car tires and mattress frames they hadn't had any luck either. I stood there a long while battling what I thought was the strongest feeling of déjà vu I'd ever had before I looked up and saw the rope swing. This was the place Mary had driven us to at Russell's request on the Fourth of July.

The sky was darkening by the time we finished a second sweep of the woods, pulling up nothing. I found the sheriff standing out on the road, thanking people for their help as they made their way to their cars.

"You know Svenson did this," I said. "What are we doing out here?"

"I went out to check on that," the sheriff said. "And the funny thing is that both Sven and his sister say they last saw her with you."

"Yeah?" I said, my heart suddenly pounding in my chest. "Of course they did. I told you that too, that we were out there on his birthday."

"I don't know what to think, Shane. I have no evidence one way or the other. It's your word against his and his sister's."

"I can't help but notice that neither of them was here today."

"It is unsettling that he didn't show up to help search for his girlfriend, if that's what she was, but that doesn't mean he did it," the sheriff responded, eyes on the road, dragging a foot back and forth across the gravel. "Just because I have no proof doesn't mean I don't think he did it. I've already told you he's dangerous. There's nothing I can do, Shane. Not without a photo or an eyewitness account."

"What exactly are you looking for?"

"Now, I'm not trying to send you after him. Don't think that," the sheriff said. "Do you need a lift, by the way? I need to pick up some stuff for Kristina."

I told him I'd take a ride, then went back down to the edge of the water while I waited for him to see the rest of the volunteers off. The crew that had been working the river was still going, now fitted with headlamps like the one I had seen on the sheriff, shining their beams in semicircles around them as they stepped.

I had a long list of messages that I was keeping in a notebook by the phone, mostly creditors and collection agencies looking for Kristina, so I hit play on the machine and picked up my pencil while the sheriff gathered Kristina's clothes and whatever else she had requested. The first was another call from Bonded Accounts, the most common caller on my list, but the second was from Walmart.

"Hello," the voice of an older woman said, "this is a courtesy call from the photo lab. An order was placed using this phone number ten days ago. Please pick your photographs up at your earliest convenience. Thank you."

Five minutes later we were on the road again, a basket of Kristina's stuff riding like a prisoner in the backseat of the sheriff's car while I further detailed the night Jenny and I had out at Svenson's.

"I'm not sure why this is the first I'm hearing about these pictures," the sheriff said as he made the right onto Center from Old Main. I looked again up at my window on the third floor of the Arlington, still dark.

"I told you we had taken pictures," I said. "I assumed she had picked them up."

The car hadn't yet come to a stop when I got out and ran. Through the sliding doors, past the greeter, down the wide empty aisles to the photo lab. Out of breath, I told the attendant Jenny's phone number.

"I see you got our message," she said, pushing the paperbound stack across the counter. "That'll be four ninety-nine."

I took a bill from my pocket and she gave me the photos. I flipped past the first few because they were blurry, then past the next few that were too dark, then to the end and when I reached that last photo my heart sank and I went back to the first. Odd squares of light stood out against dark borders. The brightness of a lamp drowning the rest of the photo in midnight shadows. I could make out a cluttered desk or table, but couldn't tell what made up the clutter. One single picture had a sharp image, even a hint of detail, and it was Jenny's face with the camera before it, reflected back from a mirror lying flat, a long white line of powder across the glass.

"No flash," said the sheriff from behind me.

I turned and handed him the stack of photos, crestfallen.

"Look, Shane," he said. "This is bad enough. Promise me you won't do this again, that you'll leave it to the adults."

That night I tossed and turned so violently that I woke up on the floor before sunrise, soaked in sweat. After I untangled the thin blanket from my legs, I stood and made my way to the front window and saw a pair of deer standing so still beneath the oak in the front yard that I thought for a moment they were perhaps decoys placed in the night. They must have sensed my movements and froze in place, muscles taut, ready to flee, lips inches above the acorns on which they had been feasting. The female raised her head to scan for danger, and after deciding I was no threat, she dropped her head again to the grass. Although both deer were spindly thin, the male had thick antlers with five points on one side and three on the other. I watched them until a car rounded the corner, sending them bounding off in sharp zigzags to the thin forest behind the house.

Then, with nothing outside to see but the wind shuffling the trees, I sat back down and put my head in my hands but couldn't sit still. Pacing Jenny's house in the dark, I relived the night we had gone out to Svenson's in my mind—all the moments I could've stepped in. The first, of course, was the car. My body made noises as the story played through my mind, grunts and moans as if the pain was physical, sighs of regret. When I sat back down on the couch, the clock on the VCR read 4:19. I was due at the Aurora at six for my morning shift so I took a long shower and walked over as the sun rose, trying to keep the pair of deer in my mind, but it was no use—my entire life circled around Jenny. As long as I was in Holm, Jenny would be on my mind.

After all, I was surrounded. The first customer to come in that morning was Chelsea, her red hair tied into a knot, dancing atop her head as she made her way to a booth a few feet from the service window, her daughter sleepwalking beside her. The waitress brought her a coffee and a menu as she lay her daughter out on the bench seat, and Leon joined her after a minute. She was upset and I could hear some of what she said from the kitchen.

"I can't leave her out there with him," she said. "He's been awake for a week, carting that rifle around the house like he's Yosemite Sam."

"Who?"

"I'm sorry," she said. "I've been watching too many cartoons. He's losing it is what I meant, and I don't feel safe there anymore."

"He's your brother," Leon said. "You need to help him."

"He needs to be put in his place," Chelsea said, an echo of what she had said the night I had spent with her.

Their order came in—egg breakfast and toast for Chelsea and a BLT, of course, for Leon—so I sprinkled some hash browns on the griddle and popped some bread into the toaster. When the food was finished a couple minutes later, I dropped my apron on the cutting board and walked off the line with a plate in each hand, both of them turning toward me as I approached.

"Where did you come from?" Chelsea asked as I set the eggs before her. "I had the law out to my place asking about you and Jenny."

"I have some questions for your brother myself," I said, setting down Leon's BLT.

"I would stay away from him if I were you," she said. "He is not your friend."

"I'm looking for his girlfriend, so I won't need to talk to him if you tell me what he did to her."

"Last we saw Jenny, she was with you," Chelsea said. "Sven was looking for you two for days."

"Why did he stop looking? I've been back a week now and he hasn't said shit to me."

"He's got eyes on you, don't worry about that."

"And where's his truck? Why's he driving around in that little hatchback?"

"It's in the shop," Leon said sharply. "The passenger door is broken. Will you please go back to the kitchen and let us have our breakfast?"

"You shouldn't stay around here," Chelsea said, one last warning. "Don't you have somewhere to be? Some other town? Some other life?"

Chelsea stayed for most of the breakfast rush and they carried on the rest of their conversation in whispers so no matter how hard I tried to listen I couldn't hear a thing over the sizzling bacon and popping eggs. I assumed they were talking about Svenson—how could they not be? Leon looked my way more than once while I was staring, causing me to snap back from the window as if something was burning.

When Chelsea left, Leon walked through the kitchen to the office, then came back up on the line in a chef's jacket and hat.

"You need to get out of here," he said. "You don't have time to wait for your check."

"But," I said, stopping my sentence at the finger he held up to me. He took three one-hundred-dollar bills from his jacket pocket and set them on the cutting board.

"Go to Minneapolis," he said. "Today. While you still can."

"I can't stay here any longer."

Russell, though he knew I was supposed to work until four, had dropped by Kristina's just after noon, mere moments after I arrived. Had I not been so upset I might have thought it suspicious but, given my mood and that Russell had tackled me in the entryway when I opened the door, this escaped me. We lay together on the carpeted stairs that led to the living room, my shirt still on, Russell's jeans hanging from one ankle.

"You're going to give up now?" he asked. "But you're so close."

"Close?" I said. "I've never been further from anything in my life. I know he did it but I can't get anyone to believe me."

"People believe you," Russell said. "The sheriff believes you, I believe you. It's that you have no proof."

I stood up and climbed down the stairs, stepping into my jeans and pulling them up, then cinched my belt. Russell spun in place so that he was sitting up and began tugging at his clothes as well.

"But maybe you need to find some."

"What?"

"Some proof."

"But it's you," I said. "You're the only proof."

"What?"

"That's why Jenny did what she did. She wanted to turn you in but didn't. Because of me."

He looked at me then the same way Jenny would when I put my hand on her leg or stood too close to her. Head tilted, eyes squinted, confused.

"You did that for me?"

"She did," I said. "I never told her anything, but she knew."

"Of course she did."

I stepped into my shoes, then climbed the stairs past Russell. In the living room, I stopped and stood, unsure what to do. I wanted more than anything to put all this behind me as soon as I could.

"Where are you going to go?"

"I've always been on my way to the same place," I said. "There was never any chance of me staying here."

"So after he killed those dogs and chased your friends out of town, after he beat your ass and did who knows what with Jenny, you're going to leave?"

"That's right," I said, pressure building behind my eyes, mucus climbing into my throat. "I don't know why I even came to Holm anymore."

The train whistle sounded in the distance as if answering a question I hadn't asked. I wouldn't have to wait another minute. Taking my backpack from the floor, I tore around the living room for my belongings.

"What are you doing?" Russell asked, now dressed, standing at the top of the stairs with his fists at his waist.

I didn't answer. Instead I zipped the last of my stuff into my backpack and let myself out the sliding glass door to the deck, then ran down the steps and into the woods with Russell behind me. The train was already rumbling past the A&W on the other side of Old Main, so I stepped up my pace as I cut through the neighbor's yard and I was about to run across the street when I was pulled strongly from behind, suddenly finding myself on my ass on the rocky shoulder. A quick moment later, cars came from both directions zooming through where I would've been had Russell not yanked me to the ground.

"What the fuck are you trying to do?" Russell screamed, but the train was still passing so I leapt to my feet and ran across the road, through the A&W parking lot, and alongside the rear ladder of the caboose before it picked up enough speed to leave me. In one last stretch, the tips of my fingers just missed the bottom rung and I tumbled into the grasses that grew in the gravel along the rails.

Russell caught up to me then, reached down to take my hand, and pulled me to my feet. Then, moving his hands to my hips he pulled me closer, pressed his lips softly to mine.

"I can tell you one thing that wouldn't have happened if you hadn't come to town."

Tears welled in my eyes, casting a watery sheen over the A&W and the passing cars. I shook away from Russell and tossed my backpack into the parking lot.

"Look, Shane," Russell said, walking around me so I could see him.

"I don't care if you go to Minneapolis. I have a car, so here or there doesn't matter to me, but you can't leave this behind you."

I took three running steps and kicked my backpack, then tried to turn away from Russell.

"Would Jenny have left?" Russell asked, taking me by the shoulders and shaking me.

"I'm tired," I said, then sat down cross-legged and put my head in my hands.

"We need to know what happened to that truck," he said. "If we find it, we find Jenny."

"Okay."

I lifted my head from my hands to find him in front of me. He dropped to his knees and wiped the tears from my cheeks with his sleeves.

"If she's not out there," Russell said, "if we don't find her today, I'll drive you to Minneapolis tonight myself."

Cicadas called for mates with a power line hum and the engine idled in accompaniment. We were stopped on the county road near the path to Svenson's place, my door open, one leg in the car, one leg out.

"Hide over there when you get back," Russell said, pointing at a thick patch of bushes and ferns a ways off the road. "But don't come running out when you hear a car because it might be him. I'll honk twice."

After I eased the door shut, Russell turned down the tire ruts to Svenson's house and I followed on foot, rustling the brush and kicking up grasshoppers, hoping he could keep Svenson distracted in the house talking business while I snooped around outside.

The automotive graveyard came into view first and beyond that the big red barn. Long grasses grew up along sedans with doors ajar, rusty hatchbacks, and more than one station wagon. Off in the distance were a couple pickups and an old van with no windows. These hadn't been moved all year and I imagined Svenson, or more likely Chelsea, had passed as close as possible to the old cars with the riding lawn mower over the summer, leaving shoots as tall as corn in places. The house came into view as I rounded the bend and, before it, the three cars parked by the front porch: the tiny hatchback Svenson had been driving, Russell's car, and Chelsea's red sedan. Russell had made it inside.

The house stood on high land and the rest of the clearing sloped away. I circled the perimeter, a foot or two into the foliage, looking up at the property. The oldest part of the house must've been built a hundred years earlier, the old front porch and antique living room where I had hung out with Chelsea and her daughter, but a couple newer additions, asymmetrical and sided in vinyl, doubled its size. These remodelings had no unity of theme or style; no one had bothered to line up the windows, which hung in a random pattern on the side of the house like spots on a dog. I saw two quick flashes in an upper window, Svenson and Russell coming to a landing, then turning to the next flight of stairs, and a splash of red in a window below, Chelsea in the kitchen at the sink. A thin wisp of smoke rose from the chimney, though I wasn't sure why, as the day was hot and humid.

Scanning the field, I saw Svenson's truck wasn't among those parked in the long grasses—of course he wouldn't leave it out for anyone to find—so I jumped out of the woods and, trying to stay low, ran to a long station wagon with wood paneling along the side. Crouching behind it, I peeked through the passenger window to be sure no one had come outside, then ran to the barn. Through the crack between the doors I could see something the shape of a vehicle inside, but when I tried to pull the door it wouldn't budge. It had fallen off its upper hinge, the corner sunk deep in the sod. I lifted it off the ground and swung it open a foot on the low hinge, so rusty and dry I was sure the screech it made could be heard in the house. After I snuck sideways through the narrow opening, I peeked back through the boards to see if anyone had come to check on the noise, but the front porch was empty.

The afternoon sun slanted in beams through the cracks between the old boards, leaving stripes of light across the tarpaulin that had been draped over the truck. I stepped to the corner and pulled the tarp, scattering dust motes in the air, and then I saw a shadow in the passenger seat, head leaning against the window, a stray sunbeam illuminating a mess of blond hair so that it looked like a halo.

I could have turned back then, snuck back into the woods then out onto the road. Even if it turned out not to be Jenny I knew it was someone, some dead body that Svenson was storing in his truck, but I had to see for myself. I tried the door but it was locked, or maybe it was broken as Leon had said, so I walked around and tried the driver's side. The raw animal rot had a floral hint, roses and violets, and I knew it was her. I pulled my T-shirt over my nose and climbed in, the dome light illuminating the bullet hole in Jenny's stomach, the sticky bloody mess that had leaked all over her seat.

Svenson wasn't calculating, he was a blunt instrument. The empty gun rack behind us proved he'd had no plan when he killed Jenny, no plan beyond shutting her up immediately, in the most painful way possible. He had shot her in his truck with the gun everyone knew he owned, then drove her here where he left her paralyzed, bleeding, in pain. She had suffered for hours as the life drained out of her, maybe days, her body freezing into this final pose. I took her cold left hand in my right, then looked up to see her eyes open, staring.

"Jenny!" I said and jumped back in my seat, dropping her hand, but she was still dead. I reached over and lay my palm on her forehead, shut her eyes with a downward swipe before I took her hand again.

I sat there for a long while, staring dumbly out the windshield at the weathered beams of the barn, until I felt what I first thought was a cold stone between our clasped hands. It was the ring Jenny had claimed was so fragile, intact, having survived the assault that had taken her life, now serving only as a marker, a tag, proof of Svenson's ownership. I tried to pull it off but the ring caught on her knuckle, swollen thicker in death than it had been in life, and I struggled with it for a bit. Finally, I took her hand and put her finger in my mouth, then massaged my saliva into her dry skin and under the ring until it popped off, straightening Jenny's twisted finger with a crack. The still-wet ring slid easily onto my middle finger, then I put my hands on the steering wheel.

Had the keys been hanging from the ignition I could have backed up through the door and driven to Holm with Jenny's dead body as my passenger but, like the rifle, they were missing. The plan was to get back to the road and wait for Russell there, so I got out, leaving the door ajar so it made no noise, then reset the tarp in place—I didn't want to tip Svenson off, then show up later with the sheriff to find that he had moved the truck. After sneaking back outside, I tried to close the barn door but it was heavy. Kneeling to get a good lifting grip, I took the bottom rail with my right hand and held my left high, then pushed the door toward its hinge.

The wood flew to splinters before I heard the bullet that shattered the door. The world went topsy-turvy as I stumbled back toward the station wagon with my hand in the air, two fingers hanging off the side in a way I knew wasn't right, but in my sudden confusion couldn't say why. The wound was so clean before the blood came, so sharp, I thought maybe I could prop the fingers into place and my hand would grow back together, but then the opening sputtered like a tap long unused.

One vessel shot a thin stream with my heartbeat, I felt it in pulses there, in my head, in an odd syncopation all over my body. Two more shots whizzed by me before I dropped into a crouch, scurried toward the station wagon, and put my back to the rear passenger door of the car. I shook my flannel shirt off my right side, pulled it up my left arm, and, aligning the wounds, wrapped up my hand. I held the wrap against my chest while I took off my belt with my right hand, made a loop, and cinched it around my wrist. An imperfect bandage and tourniquet but it would have to do.

A soft wind rustled the trees that bordered the property before the window shattered above me, dropping jagged cubes of safety glass in my hair. I crawled a few steps over to the back end of the station wagon and peeked around to see Svenson with his elbows perched on the abandoned car nearest the house, rifle pointed at the barn. He tried to keep his eye trained on his aim but the drugs were getting in the way. He squinted, then shook his head and tried to line up his shot again. The bullet that hit my hand was meant for my head and on a better day I wouldn't have been so lucky.

I found a rock near a wheel of the station wagon and threw it at the barn. It fell to the ground before it reached but bounced and thunked against the wood. Peeking around the car again, I saw that Svenson came off his mount toward the sound. As he moved past the station wagon I crept in a circle to keep the car between us. He walked from car to car, checking each blind spot where I could've been lurking, and finding the area clear he stepped around the barn. Figuring he would loop the barn looking for me, I made a break for the house, passing a dead hatchback and a pickup truck, but I ran out of energy when I reached the car Svenson had been using for a bunker. My flannel was soaked in spite of my tourniquet, so I again cinched the belt tight, then dove into the open back door and lay across the seat, holding my wound above my heart.

Svenson now out of sight behind the barn, first Russell then Chelsea stepped out onto the porch and, when he thought it was clear, Russell ran for his car, jumped in, and turned on the ignition. He whipped backward and stopped at the point of his turn, one taillight exploding in a spray of glass as he spun the steering wheel, then, finding his gear, the tires tore up the loose gravel and the car sped down the wheel ruts back to the road as bullets found the trees along the path. The screen door slammed shut on the porch as Chelsea ran back inside.

"I know you're in one of these cars, Stephenson."

Rusty hinges shrieked open and closed as he made his way from vehicle to vehicle looking for me.

"I'm gonna find you," he called, now very close.

Windows shattered as his rage grew. Though all I could see was the front door of his house, I heard him busting the glass of the different cars with the butt of his rifle when he found them empty. He taunted me while he searched the grounds.

"Your faggot boyfriend may have gotten away for now but I'll find him. He won't get far."

Another window went to pieces.

"He set you up, you know," Svenson called. "Your boyfriend did."

A car horn sounded twice in the distance, the signal.

"We knew you were in the barn. This was his idea. That's why he brought you out here."

More glass shattered, followed by a single drawn-out note from the road—Russell laying on the horn. He must have realized then that I hadn't gotten away.

"I was going to pick you off from my bedroom window but he said we should wait so you could find her first before I killed you."

Crash.

"What were you doing in there so long anyways?"

My eyes began to pulsate on beat with my heart, the pressure of the blood behind my eyes making images in my vision. Like back in my room at the Arlington, the patterns and people I once saw on my wall now moved across the ceiling of the car, the seats, the house. Was that shadow on the porch in my mind, or was it Chelsea?

"There's only one car left!"

Then Svenson stood over me as he always had, blocking out the world and the sky.

"So I did hit you before," he said, kicking my leg. "I should let you bleed out like I did that snitch friend of yours, but that wouldn't be satisfying."

He brought the butt of the rifle to his shoulder and leveled the barrel at my face. His eyes, following the bead of the rifle sight, looked right into mine as he pulled the trigger but there was only a click.

"Was that ten shots already?" Svenson said to himself and laughed. He set the butt of the rifle down by his feet, leaning the barrel against his leg as he reached to his back pocket for more ammunition. "Just a bit more suspense—"

The sound that interrupted him was a wet crunch followed by the subtle drone of a tuning fork, like nothing I had ever heard, then Svenson dropped to his knees, eyes rolling back in their sockets before he fell forward onto me, head lolling on my lap, spasms roiling his body. Where he had been standing Chelsea now stood with the cast-iron pan in her hand and a shocked look on her face. My belly grew warm from the blood pouring from Svenson's head and then the world went dark.

Fifteen

I woke up paralyzed, my left arm and both legs locked in place with restraints. Scanning through the buttons on the armrest, I pushed the yellow one with my free hand and my vision blurred. My arm grew heavy and my aim inaccurate, so I slapped a few times at the control panel hoping to hit the call button, and soon after a nurse pushed a steel cart into the room.

"I hear you, darling," she said, "I'm on my way."

Whatever the yellow button released into my blood had made my tongue thick and dry, my head heavy. I tried to answer but instead I fell into my pillow, floated above my bed, and the nurse was there too, billowing. She rolled my head her way to shine a light in my eyes.

"I see you in there," she said. "Welcome back. I'm going to check your bandage now."

On my way toward darkness again, eyes closing, my head came to rest with a clear view of my hand, bound at the wrist, wrapped with a wad of white tissue so that only my thumb and two fingers poked through.

"Got yourself into quite a mess here," she said, unwinding the gauze and setting each piece on the cart as it came loose, until I could see that half my palm was missing and the spot where my hand now dropped off toward my wrist had taken on the texture of bubble gum, as if someone had tried to stop the bleeding with a wad of Big League Chew.

"It's swollen and gooey for now," the nurse said, "but it will get better. Don't be alarmed."

I had no worries, not with those drugs dripping into my arm—I was about as far from alarmed as could be. I had a strange yet persistent feeling that I was watching a movie and in it everything would turn out okay.

"This will help," she said and tapped the morphine button again, dropping me into darkness.

Late that night my fingers returned made of fire. Even the yellow button couldn't stop it, didn't even faze me. The pain brought a sharp edge to consciousness, a clarity I had never felt before. A new nurse, sleepy-eyed and slow, came with a syringe and stuck the needle into the back of my hand.

"Your nerves think the fingers are still there," she told me as the coolness expanded to the tips of my remaining fingers and the screams in my mind quieted. "They keep sending messages and then activate your pain receptors when they don't receive a response."

She stood for a moment to be sure I went numb, then I settled back into my bed. The pain didn't return but neither did sleep and, though I hit the yellow button a couple of times, I sat there awake, shifting back and forth, unable to get comfortable. I was unsure what day it was, how long I had been asleep, and there was no way to find out. I heard a steady ticking that I knew was a clock, but I couldn't find it no matter where I looked. Maybe my morphine drip was on a timer—that would explain why the button was no longer working. Restless, I tossed my blanket to the floor and saw that my restraints were mere buckles on leather straps so I went at them with my good hand until I was free. I swung my legs out onto the floor, my bare feet on the cold tile, and my fluid cart followed me on wheels as I made my way into the hallway.

Outside the door of the room across the hall, a security guard sat slumped in a plastic chair, arms crossed, snoring. Svenson lay on the bed inside, a thick white tube jammed down his throat, his head shaved, and a long zigzag of stitches across the top of his skull. I wheeled my cart past the guard and leaned in close to find that the youth had fled from his face, his cheeks loose and jowly like an old man's.

"Sven?" I said, expecting no response, but his eyes bolted open and I jumped backward, my cart jangling in the shuffle. I gave him a wide berth but when I saw he wasn't moving I leaned in close again to see that his eyes were unfocused, sightless. I picked up one of his arms by the wrist and watched it drop, dead weight. He wouldn't have struggled had I held a pillow over his face, but I was no killer and he was no longer a threat, so I wheeled my cart back to my bed and lay down.

At sunrise, a woman in blue scrubs sat me down at the table by the window and pulled the remaining fingers on my left hand back one at a time, middle, index, thumb, working to maintain elasticity. She had set up two mirrors so I could see my hand from other angles—an old trick to get the brain and the nerves to realize that an amputated part of the body is really gone.

"You'll get on without those you are missing," she said. "It'll be painful but you'll get over it."

Outside the window an old oak tree had dropped a long, leafless branch onto the gentle grassy slope that led down to Fern Street. A black squirrel lived in the oak and that first morning I watched him tap at this twisted stick with his paw while we stretched my fingers. The angle of the slope and the corkscrew shape of the branch made it roll back down the hill every time the squirrel pushed it up, and each time it came rolling the squirrel jumped a foot, flipping backwards and sideways into the air to dodge the stick and hide for a time in plain sight before returning for another push. One strong push sent the stick rolling a little farther, and when the squirrel landed on top of it, the pair rolled down the slope like lovers. At the bottom, the squirrel wiggled out from under the stick and gave it another go but this time, stuck in a groove on flatter land, the squirrel's partner was unresponsive. The squirrel tapped a few more times but without the same response he turned his head and went on his way, though he did return a few minutes later to try it once more.

I longed for Russell in those first few days in the hospital, but he never came. The hours passed as I lay in bed, listening to the odd ticking mark rhythm against the melodies of the machines keeping Svenson alive and reliving the moments that led the two of us to the hospital. The mystery that remained was whether or not Russell had set me up like Svenson claimed. Svenson would have loved to shoot me in the head and throw me into that truck with Jenny, I had no issue with that, but remembering the blaring horn that afternoon, our signal, I had to believe Russell had done what he could for me—at the very worst he'd been playing both sides—running off alone only when everything fell apart. I couldn't blame him for not making his way back to check on me. No one had been counting on Chelsea's rage and the cast-iron pan.

When the stretching was through, the therapist did nerve tests with safety pins, dragging the point along my wound. She explained the surgical procedure: the operating doctor had taken the skin from my discarded ring finger, sliced it lengthwise and peeled it away, then used it for a patch to cover the gap made by the amputation—my skin had set, so now we were waiting for the nerves to begin working.

"When do you think that'll happen?" I asked.

"Maybe never," she said. "We have a long treatment plan ahead, so get ready to be here a lot."

I told her then that I'd be moving to Minneapolis at the end of the month, then struggled to remember the name of the dorm that had been listed on my college papers.

"The university hospital is the best in the state," she said. "I don't think you have anything to worry about."

She dragged the pin across the back of my good hand for comparison and I turned back to the window, wondering how long Russell had waited out by the road. Of course we hadn't talked about it, hadn't made a plan beyond meeting up there—had no plan at all for if it turned out badly—so I'll never know what he was thinking. Our inability to plan beyond the immediate had been a main feature of our time together. I knew he couldn't help it. He and I had been raised to think that something was wrong with people like us and the less we said the better, the less of a chance anyone else might catch on. My hope was that he would be able to open up, wherever it was that he finally found himself.

When my physical therapy ended, I wheeled my cart over to Svenson's room, past the again sleeping guard, and watched the television that they left on to stimulate Svenson's brain. The remote by his bed could switch the set on and off but I couldn't change the volume, stuck on loud, or the channel, stuck on the news. The big story that week was Timothy McVeigh's formal sentencing and his final comments before the judge handed down the order. The commentary went on and on, talking head after talking head, until they finally released his statement, a quotation attributed to Louis Brandeis. I stood and wheeled my cart as close to the television as possible to hear.

"Our government is the potent, the omnipresent teacher," read by someone else, played over a chalk sketch of him standing up in court wearing a fresh buzz cut, a cream-colored jail uniform. "For good or for ill, it teaches the whole people by its example."

Particularly true here, I thought, looking over at Svenson. Too bad he didn't get to see it, but I took comfort in the idea that, soon enough, he'd get a sentencing of his own.

The sheriff came by with flowers and sweet treats. We nibbled cookies as he told me of Kristina's progress, still tired all the time but sober now. She hadn't taken the news of Jenny's death well. The sheriff had to hold her down in her treatment center bedroom when he told her, until she cried herself to sleep, and since then she had been in a somber and silent mood. She was to be released from the treatment facility the day after I would leave the hospital.

"You know," he said, pointing at the cart next to me, "if you don't want to end up where she is, you might want to take that out of your arm."

"It's the only thing that can stop this phantom pain," I said. "It's like the air where my fingers were itches and pulsates. It was worse before, but it's getting better."

"Well, I don't like it," he said.

I took a shortbread and ate it in one bite, then asked the question I had been saving since he arrived.

"Have you seen Russell around?"

"The other phantom pain?" the sheriff teased. "We had an APB on his license plate, found his car a block away from the Amtrak station in Saint Paul with a bullet from Svenson's rifle lodged in the back."

"So he got away?"

"You could say that," the sheriff said. "He's running from something but he hasn't done anything worth my time. We wanted to talk to him at first but now I'm just glad he isn't in here with you. Or in the morgue."

Every security guard posted outside Svenson's room was always sleeping so I was happier when anyone else was on the wing, even a nurse checking Svenson's catheter or a janitor stopping by with the broom. Late at night when no one else was around, I worried about Svenson waking up, ripping the tubes from his face and arms, then making his way to my bed to finish the job that his sister had interrupted. My dreams took us outside the hospital, to the More-4-You parking lot, where I was happy to see that my legs had come unglued, the worst part of my recurring nightmare finally over. I could walk when I had to, and when Svenson came after me in his truck, I could run. Each of these dreams roused my fear that he would someday wake up, but I would find out that this could not happen.

One morning, a screaming in the hallway pulled me out of sleep. "Untle Sven, Untle Sven, wake up!"

I opened my eyes to see the little girl I had met out at Svenson's house, Chelsea's daughter. Wearing a bright yellow sundress, with her hair pulled back into two braids, she danced around the hallway and made her wake-up request into a song, shaking her hips from side to side and pointing at the ground with her fingers.

"Hey Untle Sven, wake up. Hey Untle Sven, wake up now. Hey Untle Sven, wake up. Hey Untle Sven, wake up—YOU COW!"

An older man scurried into view and picked the girl up, told her to be quiet. I was startled to see who it was.

"Rick?"

The man turned to me with the girl in his arms. He was still the same skeleton with rough leather skin pulled tight, topped with thin blond hair and a face full of pockmarks, but no hint of recognition in his eyes. My hospital gown and new haircut were the perfect disguise.

"I'm sorry," he said. "Did you say something?"

"No, no," I said. "I thought I recognized you."

"No problem."

Rick turned around and took the girl to Svenson's room. I climbed out of bed to follow and lingered in the hallway. As they neared the bed Rick picked up Svenson's hand and gave it to the girl, who held it in both of hers. Svenson's eyes opened to slits and he turned his head toward them. Eavesdropping from my room, I had heard the doctors discussing his injuries—it was hard to tell if he knew what was going on around him, but he wasn't dead or dying and he didn't need the machines to keep him breathing anymore.

"Untle SVEN!" the girl yelled. "WAKE UP! Daddy! Make Untle Sven wake UP!"

Footsteps clicked down the hallway and when I saw Chelsea's long red hair swing around the corner my heart sped up to a drumroll. I spread my arms wide as I walked toward her and she did the same, so that we came together in a tight hug. I didn't know what to say, how to thank her, but she would soon let me know.

More footsteps broke our embrace, then Leon came down the hall with a doctor and three other men in suits, chatting in whispers on their way to Svenson's room, failing to notice me and Chelsea. I thought she would join the group but she turned back after we watched them pass.

"This is going to be very hard on Jennifer," she said.

"Jennifer?"

"My daughter. Once she understands what's happened to her uncle, she'll be crushed."

As if this was her cue, Jennifer came running into the hallway with Rick behind her but he grabbed her by the armpits and hauled her back into the room.

"Rick's her father?"

She nodded and the little drama of their family came into full view. Chelsea, clueless and young and not yet aware of the family business, had taken Rick up on an offer similar to the one he had made me on the day of Svenson's Confederate flag revival and ended up with more than she had expected: little Jennifer. Rick must have kept on his same reckless course, leading them to the laundromat on the day of my arrival to wash the scabies out of all their clothes.

"And he's back in your life now?" I asked.

"Since the accident," she said, "yes. He isn't living with us yet but he's her father. It doesn't feel right to keep her away from him. Not now."

We stood there for a moment and Leon's words floated down the hallway as he discussed vital signs and rehabilitation plans with the suited men and the doctor.

"The Aurora is all we have now," Chelsea said. "My mother and brother both gone who knows where, my father dead, and Sven now like this. I know you think he was a monster but, no matter what I've said before, he was our protector, he did what he had to do to keep our family together. If the Aurora gets shut down, me and little Jennifer will lose everything."

Her daughter ran out into the hallway again but this time Rick didn't catch her. She came over to us and wrapped her arms around her mother's leg.

"I know you," she said. "You're good at Intenno." Then she laughed and hid her face behind her hands, peeking through her fingers. Suddenly, I understood that the Nintendo I had played with her that night was my own, stolen by Rick and given to his daughter.

"Hello, Jennifer," I said.

"Hey, Chelsea," Leon called, sticking his head out the door, then when he saw me: "What are you doing here?"

I held up my hand, wound toward him.

"I tried to warn you," Leon said, then waved Chelsea over as he turned back to the group.

Chelsea dropped a kiss, warm and wet, on my cheek, then left to join the group in Svenson's room. I took two steps nearer the doorway and listened as they all turned toward Sven. The doctor looked into his eyes and ears and did reflex tests before one of the suited men asked him a series of questions.

"Can this individual hear?"

"Possibly."

"Can this individual see?"

"No."

"Is this individual fit for trial? And if so, would he be able to participate in his own defense?"

"No. And no."

"The prosecution of this case is hereby suspended," another of the suited men piped up, "however, the indictment stands and, if this individual again becomes competent to understand the charges against him, he will see his day in court."

"I wouldn't count on that," the doctor said.

The suited men left the room and I was enraged but held my tongue as the doctor discussed with Leon and Chelsea how Svenson would be released to their care, a convalescent's room in the farmhouse where he had grown up, free from prison. I could only hope that somewhere inside that shut-down body he was still awake and aware of what he had done, living out in complete isolation the life sentence he deserved.

My first night out of the hospital, I lay in the dark on Kristina's couch, sleepless, when the sheriff came up the stairs with a plastic bag. He whispered my name.

"I'm awake," I said, then sat up and switched on the lamp.

"I forgot to give you this," he said and tossed the bag. "It's the clothes you were wearing that day and whatever else you had when we found you. Might want to open it in the kitchen."

There was a lot of blood. Being the tourniquet and the bandage, my flannel shirt had soaked up most of it, but the rest of my clothes would have been ruined even if the emergency workers hadn't cut them off me with jagged vertical slashes. The three hundred-dollar bills I had gotten from Leon were still in my pants as well as the keys to both my place and Kristina's, and beneath all that, alone in the corner of the sack, was the glass ring. Though I did keep the keys and the money, the ring was the most important object among everything I owned. Jenny had said that if anyone could care for a glass ring it was me, so I threw my clothes in the garbage and slid Jenny's ring on the finger nearest my injury, then made my way back to the couch in the dark and drifted away.

We didn't get much done that next day while we waited for Kristina's discharge time, but we did box up Jenny's room, as well as all the pictures of her that hung around the house, so Kristina wouldn't have to be reminded of her right away. The bulky safety glove that I wore slowed me down. The main protection was a curved piece of plastic that I strapped in over the missing fingers, to protect the wound from being banged or otherwise injured, but the wider, heavier hand caused it to happen more often. I was ready to quit long before the sheriff said it was time.

I waited on the front steps for the sheriff to return with Kristina but the look she gave me when they pulled up made me wish I hadn't. The sheriff parked the car, then walked around to open the passenger door and help Kristina out. She moved slowly, even with the sheriff's help, and didn't look at me again as they made their way inside so the sheriff could lay Kristina on her bed, where she would spend the rest of the evening. Late that first night she was back, in a moment that gave me flashbacks of my mother and the Fisherman, I heard Kristina and the sheriff arguing in her bedroom while I tried to sleep on the couch.

"There wasn't any problem until he came around," Kristina shouted.

"For the last time," the sheriff yelled, "he was the one who figured it all out!"

Kristina thought Jenny's death was my fault and that was fine. If that gave her the strength to get through her days, then she could think that. Not that I'm blameless, of course. I could have done more to keep Jenny safe. We all could have—me, Kristina, the sheriff—but I felt that we had done right by Jenny in getting Svenson off the streets and, though I wasn't sure that Leon's continuing business was a good thing, Chelsea and I had at least finished what Jenny had started.

I couldn't stay at Jenny's funeral, couldn't watch them lower her into the ground, so I left my seat next to Kristina and the sheriff and wandered off through the cemetery, back past the obelisk and the aboveground crypt and, finally, Marta Mattson, the lonely reader whose husband never returned to spend his death beside her. She stood out as a silhouette before a beautiful late-summer day—fluffy white clouds lazed about in the sky and the scent of freshly mown grass hung in the air. I stuck my hand in my pocket and came out with the key to my place at the Arlington and figured I might as well go return it.

"Sorry to hear about your friend," the super said when he answered the door. "She was a real beauty. Even in the newspaper you could see it. It's too sad to think about. No one deserves to be treated like that, especially a woman so young."

I nodded, blinking back the tears I had been fighting all day.

"I've come to give you back your key," I said and held it out for him to take.

"I gave you a spare if I remember correctly," he said.

My spare.

"I don't have it."

"Are you sure it isn't up there?"

The only chance was that Jenny had given it back to me on that last speed-fueled day but I couldn't quite remember everything that had happened. It had been my first time getting high since the day Sissy and Lucy died and much of the day had gotten away from me. The only memories I had were Jenny's beautiful but bleeding face, talking at warp speed as she smiled at me from my bed and, of course, our three kisses.

"Pretty sure."

"Pretty sure is not certain," he said. "If you'd run up there and check again, it'd mean the world to me. These knees can't climb three floors like they used to—it would take me half an hour to get to your room and back. If it isn't up there, I'll have to ask you to go make a copy. As you might imagine, a trip to the hardware store is much shorter for you than it is for me."

He told me I could knock on his door when I was ready, then I climbed the stairs. The dusty smell, the creaky staircase that turned back on itself. The wind whipped the curtains in my room, I had left the window open in my hurry to leave for Michigan, and the breeze had blown the loose circulars and other papers onto the floor. Then, turning to my desk, I saw the last bag of speed, the one Jenny had asked me to keep, and my spare key sitting atop the notebook Jenny had been using on that last day we spent together.

Here is your key—I knew I would use it to come back for this once you were gone so I left it here. I don't want to end up like my mother. I'll get the key back from you when I see you. She had drawn an arrow from the word *this* to the bag of speed.

I picked up the drugs and took them to the hallway, into the bathroom, and dumped the last of it into the toilet. Once it flushed and the tank refilled, I threw the empty bag in and flushed again, making sure it was all gone before I returned to my room, restless. I paced back and forth for a moment, picking up the loose trash on the floor, and when there was nothing left to be done I sat on my bed and finally cried.

My whole body shuddered as grief passed through me. As in Russell's car, sounds came out of me that I didn't know I could make. The sadness I had been holding back since my father had died came out in a fit of convulsions. A great pressure hung in my muscles, as if my entire body was working to force something out, and instead of fighting against it I let it go, I let the convulsions take over. I rode the will of my muscles until they calmed on their own and I came out hyperventilating, shaking, sitting up on the edge of the bed to face my staring wall, now alive with the same old shadows. The people were all known to me: my father, my uncle, Mary, J squatting near Sisyphus and Lucifer, my mother and the Fisherman, Russell, and finally Jenny, blue eyes glowing out of the darkness, out of the shadow that had hung over me all this time.

My eyes dropped from the wall to my eight fingers splayed out before me, one of them ringed with the night sky. Nothing to do but move on.

———

The sheriff drove, I sat in the middle, and Kristina, asleep but belted in, bobbed her head with the motion of the moving van. We stopped at the light on the corner of Center and Old Main and, looking out Kristina's window, I could see right into the Arlington where Karen stood before an older couple, smiling, taking their order, still there when we turned left. The old streets passed by, all the alphabetical trees, and soon we were on the bridge, where I took a glance in the sheriff's rearview mirror to see Holm for the last time.

"You can't wait to get out of here and forget all this, can you?" the sheriff asked.

"Can you blame me?" I asked, holding up my wounded hand.

We had spent the week after Jenny's funeral packing up Kristina's stuff, cleaning, painting, and that morning placed the FOR SALE sign out front as we left. Kristina hadn't helped much. Most of the time she sat on the front steps smoking cigarettes while the sheriff and I did the heavy lifting. She hadn't been too present since her return, but to wake up one morning to find you had lost two years of your life, your daughter, and your house would lead most people to deep introspection.

The sheriff turned left on the first county road out of town and pointed out a row of long temporary structures nestled under some trees and beyond that a large brick building in the midst of construction.

"There's Holm Community College," he said, "PBU, some people call it now, Pole Barn University, but it looks like the new building will be nice. Are you sure you want to move away? There's plenty of room at my place for the three of us."

This wasn't the first time he had hinted at this. I laughed as if it was a joke, again, but he was afraid of what would happen once I left. To be alone with Kristina was something to fear, these new crushing losses on top of the others that had already sent her spiraling out of control. Plus the thousands of dollars of Kristina's debt the sheriff took on by taking her into his home. Her house had been foreclosed on and she had huge credit card balances but, in spite of all this and how cold and angry she had been since her return, he was very much in love with her.

The sheriff's house was two turns down the road from the college, a split-level sided in vinyl with a three-car garage that sat on an acre of grass lined with tall pines. He pulled the truck in backwards down the long drive and we both climbed out his side since Kristina didn't stir when I shook her. While we were clearing a spot for her stuff in the garage, she climbed out of the cab and walked across the front lawn, stopped in the middle to lie on her back in the grass and stare at the sky. The sheriff and I watched with interest as she did this, but in the end he waved his hand at her as if to say *She'll be fine there*, and we began walking boxes down the silver ramp.

It was difficult for me to understand why Kristina hadn't moved in with the sheriff earlier, when Jenny was still alive, but such clarity only comes when looking back on things. Life isn't easy while it's happening and sometimes people can't figure out how to say what they need so they choose to walk away. Then, instead of doing what we know is right, we let them go. I knew the sheriff and Kristina wanted to talk about this about as much as I wanted to talk about my mother, so I kept my mouth shut and stacked the boxes higher on my dolly, trying to get done faster. By the time the sun stood high in the sky, we had cleared the truck and Kristina was still in the grass. The sheriff slid the ramp back up into the truck and closed the door, then looked around at his place, now complete by means of Kristina's presence.

"Well, I guess this is it for you," he said, "next stop Minneapolis."

He walked over to Kristina and sat down beside her. He said a few things, smiled, and then waved me over. We each got an arm under one of her shoulders and lifted, then carried her to the front door. The sheriff took over when we reached the threshold and Kristina jerked her arm away from me before she disappeared without saying good-bye. When the sheriff returned, he led me to his patrol car and let me in the passenger side.

"So," the sheriff asked after he climbed in the driver's seat, "is there anything else I should know about before you leave town?"

I thought of little Jennifer a few miles away, dancing around her house in a sundress, pointing with her tiny fingers, playing Intenno, and Chelsea tending to her brother in his vegetative state while she made drug deals in her kitchen, piling up the catering money for Leon.

"No," I said, "that's all I got. Jenny might have known more but if she did, she didn't tell me."

"Well, let me ask you one more question then," he said, pulling the car onto the highway. "How fast do you think this thing can go?"

When I said a hundred he flipped on the sirens and lights and showed me I was right, all the way to the county line.

Acknowledgments

Thanks to:

My teachers—Kay Pekel, Johan Christopherson, Kate Lynn Hibbard, Robert Gremore, Carolyn Whitson, Michele Wallace, H. Aram Veeser, Mikhal Dekel, Salar Abdoh, David Greetham, Emily Raboteau, J. Fred Reynolds, Geraldine Murphy, Linsey Abrams, Michael Klein, Fiona Maazel, Laurie Stone, Gordon Lish—and all my fellow students.

Another of my teachers, Mark Mirsky, my first real writing coach and an early champion of my work, who published two of my stories in his magazine, *Fiction*.

The City College of New York, especially the Division of Humanities and the Arts and the Department of English, and PSC-CUNY, who provided a grant so that I could study at The Center for Fiction.

Sue Deen, Carlton Deen, Abby Abernathy, Larry McMurtry, and the city of Archer City, Texas.

Laura Isaacman and Randy Rosenthal, who published a story of mine in their magazine, *Tweed's*.

Acknowledgments

Adam Eaglin, who found my story in *Tweed's* and encouraged me through three years of drafts before it all came together.

Ira Silverberg, who helped me find this book's final form.

HOPE4, who is still out there somewhere, working nights and painting trains.

About the Author

Raymond Strom was born in Hibbing, Minnesota. He moved often as a child, living in small towns across Minnesota, North Dakota, South Dakota, Montana, and Wisconsin before attending college in the Twin Cities. He received his MFA from the City College of New York, where he now works as an academic advisor. His writing has appeared in *Fiction* and *Tweed's*. *Northern Lights* is his first novel.